Toby Alone

Timothée de Fombelle

translated by Sarah Ardizzone
illustrated by François Place

CANDLEWICK PRESS

For Elisha,
for her mother

Text and illustrations copyright © 2006 by Gallimard Jeunesse
English translation copyright © 2008 by Sarah Ardizzone

First U.S. paperback edition 2010

Library of Congress Cataloging-in-Publication Data is available.

Library of Congress Catalog Number 2008928922

ISBN 978-0-7636-4181-8 (hardcover)
ISBN 978-0-7636-4815-2 (paperback)

09 10 11 12 13 14 MVP 10 9 8 7 6 5 4 3 2 1

Printed in York, PA, U.S.A.

This book was typeset in Adobe Caslon and Tree Boxelder.
The illustrations were done in pen and ink.

Candlewick Press
99 Dover Street
Somerville, Massachusetts 02144

visit us at www.candlewick.com

The Tree

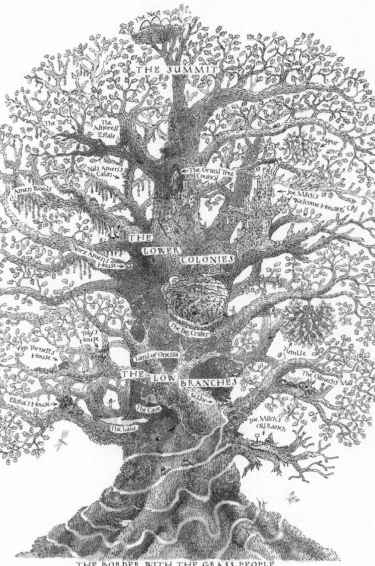

THE BORDER WITH THE GRASS PEOPLE

Contents

The Angels' view:
Perhaps the tips of trees
Are roots that drink the skies

Rainer Maria Rilke

PART

ONE

1
Tracked Down

Toby was just one and a half millimeters tall, not exactly big for a boy of his age. Only his toes were sticking out of the hole in the bark where he was hiding.

Looking up through the enormous russet-colored leaves to the starry sky above, Toby felt there had never been a night as dark and shiny as this one. *When there's no moon, the stars dance more brightly. Even if there is a sky in Heaven,* he told himself, *it couldn't possibly be as deep or as magical as this.*

Toby began to calm down. Lying with his head resting on the moss, he could feel his hair was wet with cold tears. He was tucked inside a hole in the black bark. His leg was injured, he had cuts on both shoulders, and his hair was matted with blood. His hands were stinging from being ripped by thorns, but the rest of his tiny body was numb with pain and exhaustion.

His life had ended a few hours earlier, so what was he still doing here? That's what people used to ask him, when he poked his nose in everywhere: "Still here, Toby?" Today, he kept whispering it to himself: "Still here?"

But he was definitely alive, and his misery was even vaster than the sky. He was staring at the sky in the same way he used to cling to his parents' hands in a crowd. *If I close my eyes,* he thought, *I'll die.* But his eyes stayed wide open, behind two lakes of muddy tears.

Then he heard them. And in a flash the fear was back. There were four of them: three adults and a teenager. The teenager was holding a torch to light their way.

"He can't be far. I'm sure he's not far."

"He must be caught. He has to pay too. Like his parents."

The eyes of the third man shone yellow in the night. He spat, then said, "We'll get him, you'll see, and we'll make him pay."

More than anything, Toby wanted to wake up from this nightmare; he wanted to run over to his parents' bed, and cry and cry. . . . He would have given anything to go through to their bright kitchen together, still in his pajamas, where they'd make him a hot honey drink with cookies and say, "It's over now, Toby sweetheart. It's all right."

Instead, Toby was trembling at the bottom of a hole, trying to tuck in his sticky-out toes. Toby was only thirteen, but he was being hunted by the whole Tree, by his own people, and what he could hear was much worse than the cold, scary night.

What he could hear was a voice he loved, the voice of his oldest friend, Leo Blue.

Once, when he was four and a half, Leo had tried to steal Toby's lunch, and they'd ended up sharing everything ever since — good things and things that weren't so funny. Leo lived with his aunt. Both his parents had died. All he had left of his father, the famous explorer El Blue, was a wooden boomerang. But his misfortune had made Leo Blue very strong, deep down inside. This brought out the best in him, and the worst too. Toby preferred the best: Leo's intelligence and bravery. The boys became inseparable. There was a time when people even called them Tobyleo, as if it was just one name.

One day, when Toby and his parents were due to move house, down to the Low Branches, Tobyleo hid in a dry bud because they didn't want to be split up. It was two days and three nights before they were found. It was one of the rare occasions when Toby saw his father cry.

But tonight, Toby was curled up alone in his bark hole — was this really the same Leo Blue standing just a few paces away, brandishing his flare against the dark? Toby felt his heart exploding when his best friend shouted, "We'll get you! We'll get you, Toby!"

Leo's voice rang out from branch to branch. It brought back a vivid memory.

When he was tiny, Toby had had a tame greenfly called Lima. Toby used to climb on Lima's back, before he could even walk. One day, out of nowhere, the green-fly stopped playing—he bit Toby hard and shook him like a scrap of rag. The creature had gone crazy, and Toby's parents had to separate them. Toby could still remember that look in Lima's eyes, his pupils grown fat as a pond in the rain.

His mother had said to Toby, "Today it was Lima, but anyone could turn crazy one day."

"We'll get you, Toby!"

When he heard that wild cry again, Toby knew that Leo's eyes must be as terrifying as a crazy animal's. Like ponds swollen by the rain.

The small troop was getting nearer, tapping the bark with wooden spears to feel for cracks and hollows. They were looking for Toby. It was like the White Ant Hunt, when fathers and sons set out every spring to drive the pests to the Far Branches.

"I'll make him come out of his hole."

The voice was so close, Toby could almost feel the speaker's warm breath. He didn't dare move or shut his eyes. The beating spears were coming toward him through the flame-swept darkness.

A spear crashed down, landing only a finger's width from his face. Toby was paralyzed with fear but kept his eyes glued to the patch of sky he could see in between the hunters' shadows. This time they had him. It was over.

Suddenly, night fell all around again.

"Hey! Leo! Did you let the torch go out?" an angry voice shouted.

"It fell. Sorry, the torch fell. . . ."

"You idiot!"

The group's only torch had gone out; the search would have to continue in the pitch black.

"We're not giving up now. We'll get him."

Another man had caught up with the first and was rummaging around the cracks in the bark. He was so near, Toby could feel the air moving. The second man must have been drinking, because he stank of alcohol and his movements were violent and clumsy.

"I'll catch him myself. I'm going to chop him up into little pieces. And then we'll tell the others we couldn't find him."

The other man laughed as he turned to his hunting companion.

"Doesn't change, does he? He killed forty white ants last spring!"

Toby was worse than a white ant to them—they wouldn't spare him the spear or the flames.

Both shadows were towering directly over him. Nothing could save him now. Toby almost stopped looking up at the sky, which was the only thing keeping him going. He saw the spear coming down toward him and quickly flattened himself against the sides, so all the hunter felt under his weapon was the hard wood of the Tree.

But the other man had already thrust his arm into the hole.

Toby's eyes were smarting with tears. He watched the man put his big fat hand right up against him, stop, then move it a bit higher, next to his face.

Strangely, at that moment Toby stopped feeling frightened. A sense of calm rose up inside him. There was even a faint smile on his lips when he heard a terrifying voice whisper gleefully, "I've got him. He's mine."

Silence.

The others came over. Not even Leo Blue was talking now. Perhaps he was afraid of looking his former friend in the eye.

There were four of them surrounding an injured child. But Toby wasn't afraid of anything anymore. He didn't even shudder when the man put his arm into the hole, then roared with laughter as he tore something off and showed it to the others.

Silence, longer than a snowy winter.

Toby thought he'd just felt a shred of his clothing being ripped off. After a while, words rang out in the chilly silence.

"It's bark, just a piece of bark."

Sure enough, the man was holding out a piece of bark to the other hunters.

"Got you that time, didn't I? Of course he's not here. He must be running like crazy toward the Low Branches. We'll catch him tomorrow."

The group groaned in disappointment. They hurled a few insults at the man who had pretended to find Toby. Their shadows moved off quickly, like a sad cloud. Their echoing voices dispersed.

And silence settled around him again.

It was a long time before Toby could hear the sound of his own breathing again, before he could feel his body against the sides of the Tree.

What had happened? He pieced his thoughts together very slowly.

He relived every second of that mysterious episode over again. The man had put his hand on him, but he'd felt only wood. He'd torn off a piece of his jacket and mistaken it for bark. They'd all agreed it was bark. It was as if Toby had become part of the wood. At least that was how it felt, as if the Tree had hidden him under its bark coat.

Suddenly, Toby froze.

What if this was a trap?

Of course! The man had felt him and was waiting in the dark, a few paces away. Toby was sure now. After all, hadn't the hunter said he wanted Toby all to himself? That he'd crush him like an ant? He was lurking in the shadows, waiting for Toby to come out, ready to pounce with his spear. The fear was back, curled up in a ball at the base of Toby's throat.

He didn't move. He was listening for the slightest sound. Nothing. Then, slowly, he became aware of the sky above again. His starry friend, watching over him with so many eyes.

Beneath him, the Tree was warm. Summer was drawing to a close, and the branches had stored up a gentle heat. Toby was still in the High Branches, where the sun shines from morning till dusk, filling the air with the smell of warm bread, like his mother's leaf-bread rolled in pollen grains. The reassuring smell relaxed Toby. He closed his eyes, forgetting about how frightened he was, about Leo being so crazy. He forgot that he was bait for the hunters and that there were thousands of them against one of him. A gentle wave washed over him, lulling him to sleep. He forgot everything. His trembling and loneliness, how unfair it all was, even the big WHY that had been pounding inside him for days now.

He forgot about it all. But he kept a small space free in his dreams, the only dream he would let into his sleep. And this dream had a face: Elisha's.

All day long, on the run from his enemies, he'd vowed not to think about her. He mustn't. It would be too upsetting.

He built a fortress around his heart, with watch-towers and moats. He released soldier ants into the surrounding paths. He wouldn't let himself think about her.

But at every moment, there she was, popping up in his memories, wearing her green dress. In the middle of his thoughts, she was even more real than the sky.

He'd gotten to know Elisha when he and his family had left the Treetop and moved to the Low Branches. How they met is an interesting story.

Here, with Toby asleep in his hole, let's rewind the story to six years ago, and the time of the great move.

2
Farewell to the Treetop

That year, on a September morning, while the inhabitants of the Treetop were still sleeping, Toby and his parents left.

They traveled for seven days, escorted by two grumpy porters who carried their essential items. They didn't need two men to transport a couple of small cases, a few clothes, some books, and the box of files belonging to Sim Lolness, Toby's father, but the porters' real job was to make sure the family didn't turn back.

Mr. Lolness was, without doubt, the greatest scientist of his time. Nobody knew the Tree's secrets like he did. Everyone admired him; he had made some of the most extraordinary discoveries of the century. But his incredible knowledge was just a tiny part of him. He also had a generous soul that shone like a star.

Sim Lolness was kind, warmhearted, and funny. He could easily have been a comedian. But Professor Lolness never set out to make people laugh. His imagination and originality just shone through naturally.

Sometimes, during a meeting of the Grand Tree Council, in the middle of a crowd of wise elders, he would change into his blue pajamas and settle down for an afternoon nap. Sleep, he said, was his magic potion. The Grand Council members would lower their voices so as not to disturb him. . . .

Toby and his parents had been traveling down toward the Low Branches for several days. Moving around the Tree was always an adventure. You had to get from one branch to the next on foot, down barely worn paths, and risk hitting dead ends or coming across slippery slopes. It was best to avoid crossing the leaves in autumn, as the huge brown plains might drop off at any time, whisking travelers off toward the unknown.

Not that there were many travelers. People often spent their whole lives on the branch where they'd been born. They found a job there, and made friends, and they got married to someone from the neighboring branch or the same region. So a marriage between a Treetop girl and a boy from the Branches was a rare event and likely to be frowned upon by the families involved. (This is where the expression "branching out" comes from.) And this was exactly what happened to Toby's parents. Nobody encouraged their romance. Everyone thought it

would be better for them to marry someone from their own neighborhood.

But Sim Lolness liked the idea of a genealogical Tree, with each generation developing its own branch, a touch closer to the sky. His peers thought this a dangerous idea.

Of course, the Tree's growing population meant that some families had to emigrate to the Far Branches, but this was a collective decision, with the whole extended family moving away. When this happened, a clan would choose to take over new branches in the Lower Colonies, closer to the shady, interior branches of the Tree.

But nobody went as far as the Low Branches, a land that was even farther away, right down at the bottom. At least nobody went there by choice. Not even the Lolness family, who, together with their porters, reached the wild Land of Onessa one evening, right at the bottom of the Low Branches.

They'd certainly got to know what this region looked like over the past two days. It had unfolded before their eyes as they walked—a giant maze of damp, gnarled branches. There was nobody around, or hardly anyone. Just a few Grubbers, who darted off as soon as they spotted the Lolness family coming.

The countryside was spectacular. Expanses of water-logged bark, mysterious forks where no one had ever set foot, lakes formed at the intersection of branches, forests of green moss, thick bark crisscrossed by deep paths and streams, as well as strange insects, and twigs that had gotten stuck for years because the wind had never dislodged them—it was a hanging jungle, full of strange fruit.

Toby cried all the way, dragging with him the pain of leaving behind his friend Leo Blue. But when he reached the edge of the Low Branches, which had only ever been described to him as diabolical, his tears dried up. He was hypnotized by the landscape and knew at once he would feel at home here. It was a magical place, a giant playground for games and dreams.

The farther he went, the more cheerful he became, like he had been in the good old days, but the more he could also see his mother, Maya, giving up hope.

Maya Lolness had been born into the Alnorell family, which owned nearly a third of the Treetop, as well as some lichen plantations on the Main Trunk. They were a rich family, which organized big hunts on their estates, situated on the sunny side, and held society balls that dazzled the glamorous set until dawn. On party nights, flares lit up the paths, forming garlands around the Summit. Maya's father would settle down at the piano, and everyone would dance around him. Couples wandered off under the stars.

As the only Alnorell descendant and darling daughter of the father she adored, little Maya had grown up in this festive atmosphere. Mr. Alnorell was a handsome and generous man interested in everything, and he was also sensitive, like his daughter.

But he had died young, when Maya was fifteen, and his wife had taken over, putting a stop to all the waltzes and moonlit banquets.

Toby's granny, Mrs. Alnorell, was as sad and bad as a morning spider. She hadn't been able to make her husband or daughter happy, so instead she made her accountant, Mr. Perlush, happy. In one stroke she had put a stop to all the household expenditures and begun to hoard a vast fortune. Every day, Mr. Perlush could see the revenue from the family plantations and other Alnorell businesses coming in, without a penny ever leaving his coffers.

Mrs. Alnorell loved money so much that she had forgotten what it was for. She was like a child who collects Tree-sap candies under her bed. Except that eventually the child will wake up on top of a pile of mouldy sap, while Mrs. Alnorell's money never went moldy. What went moldy was Mrs. Alnorell herself. She had turned almost green, and her manners weren't so fresh either.

Toby had been told that on finding out about the engagement between Maya and a man from the Branches, his grandmother had proclaimed, "You want your babies to be snails?"

These words had become a catchphrase for Toby's parents, Sim and Maya. They joked about it. The Branches where Sim had grown up were known for their gigantic but harmless snails, which produced the perfect grease for oil lamps. The Branch people adored their snails so much that Toby's father would often fondly call his son "my little snail," in memory of what his mother-in-law had said.

Maya Alnorell married Sim Lolness. They were in love, and they stayed as much in love as when they had first met, at a knitting lesson.

Knitting silk was something every daughter from a respectable family had to learn to do. Since Sim Lolness was already working very hard—dividing his days between the library, the laboratory, and the botanical gardens—and seeing as he just didn't have time to "meet someone special," as his mother put it, he had enrolled in knitting lessons. Unsurprisingly, he was the only boy in the class. In just an hour a week, he was guaranteed to meet thirty girls all at once—an efficient way of getting an idea about this unknown species.

The first week he observed.

The second week he invented the knitting machine.

The third week the class was canceled.

And that was the end of hand-knitted silk.

But pretty Maya had immediately understood what was hiding under the beret of this young man who had come from the Branches to study in the Treetop. She fell in love with him.

One spring morning she tapped on the door of his tiny student room.

"Hello."

"Miss . . . Er . . . Yes?"

"You left your beret behind at the last lesson."

"Oh! I . . . Goodness me . . ."

Maya took a step inside. Sim shrank back. It was the first time he had looked at a girl properly, and he was discovering a whole new planet. He wanted to take notes but realized it might not be the proper thing to do.

The truth was, to his great surprise, that he wanted to fill two or three books on the subject, but he also just wanted to look at her.

"I'm not disturbing you, am I?" she asked after a while.

"Yes . . . You're . . . You're . . . Turning my whole life upside down, if you don't mind me saying so, with all due respect, miss."

"Oh! I'm sorry. . . ."

She went to the door. Sim rushed to block her exit. He adjusted his glasses.

"No! I . . . You can stay. . . ."

He offered her some cold water and a ball of gum. The way she held her cup of water made Sim want to sketch her. But he resisted; he'd divided the ball of gum with his fingers, which kept sticking to things when he tried to pick them up.

Maya giggled to herself.

Sim reached for the walls to try and pull himself together, but he left a trail of gum all around the room.

After a while, Maya made her excuses and left, stepping over one trail and under another.

"Thanks for the beret," Sim called as he watched her leave. At which point he realized that the beret was on his head and that he had been wearing it when she'd arrived. In short, he had never left it behind.

He took off his thick-lensed glasses, put them down on the table, and fell to the ground. Out cold.

Later, he understood why he'd fainted that day—for the simple reason that if she had brought him a beret he hadn't left behind, she must have wanted to see him again.

Yes, him. Which was plenty to faint about.

A year later, they were married. It was a beautiful Summit wedding. Mrs. Alnorell agreed to spend a few crumbs of her fortune. Mr. Perlush, the accountant, sobbed as he took two golden coins from a bath full to overflowing.

"Mrs. Alnorell, we're as good as ruined," he lamented, staring at the bathtub with its contents spilling out, not to mention the hallway leading to fourteen rooms where the coffers were piled high with mountains of coins and notes.

Mrs. Alnorell behaved herself reasonably well during the wedding, but she did make fun of how awkward Sim's father was.

Being unfamiliar with the habits of high society, Sim Lolness's father was trying a bit too hard. He snacked on the spring buds meant to decorate the buffet. He lifted up the women's long dresses so they wouldn't get dust on them. After a few glasses, he was kissing everyone's hands, including the men's, and twirling his tie as if it was a candy wrapper.

ᴥ

For twenty years, the happy couple was childless, which infuriated Mrs. Alnorell.

And then one day . . .

Toby.

He suddenly came into their life, and completed their joy.

His grandmother quickly decided that there was too much Lolness in him, and not enough Alnorell. So when Toby spent his summers on his grandmother's estates, she handed him over to a fleet of nannies and did everything to avoid him. According to her, children were dirty and full of infections. She fled in the opposite direction the moment she saw him coming. In the five or six summers Toby spent there, she hardly ever saw her own grandson.

And each time she did, she had a fit of hysterics.

"Get him away from me! I'm having an attack of the vapors!" she would yelp, and Toby would be whisked off as if he had the plague.

Which was why, as she made her way farther down into the Low Branches, toward the place where she would be living from now on with her husband and son, Maya Lolness was choking back tears. She had fought so hard against her own, and her mother's, snobbery, but she felt her disgust for the dark, spongy territories of the Low Branches rising to the surface.

Her husband could see she was crying. Every so often he asked her what was wrong.

"I'm so happy to be with both of you," she tried, smiling unconvincingly. And she walked on again, wrapping her shawl around her.

Toby glanced at his father; he knew he was suffering. Not that his father would be feeling sorry for himself, because Sim Lolness could always find something to be amazed about, even a fly's intestines. No, he was suffering because he was dragging his wife and his son down with him, a part of his punishment.

The family was in exile.

These three beings, abandoned by the porters in the middle of nowhere, in the Land of Onessa, right at the end of a branch with two enormous flame-colored leaves hanging under it, this family had been banished from the rest of the Tree, condemned to decay and exile.

"Here we are," whispered Toby's father.

The branch was so damp that it felt as if they were walking on cold soup. Toby was sitting on his suitcase, wringing out his socks.

"Here we are," said Sim again, in a tight voice.

Maya Lolness was hiding her tears in her shawl.

After so much glory, honor, and success, Sim Lolness and his family were starting again from nothing.

From less than nothing.

3
The Race
Against Winter

When they arrived in Onessa, Toby and his parents quickly realized that the countdown to winter had begun. A freezing autumn had already set in, and the Low Branches were braced for a grim winter. The little family spent an uncomfortable first night outside. A damp breeze crept under the blanket where they shivered the night away.

At dawn the next day, Sim Lolness started hollowing out their home.

"Come on, son. Let's get to work."

Up in the Treetop, it would take five or six workers and a team of trained weevils six months to hollow out a modest-size house. Down here, Toby and his parents started off by clearing the bark so they could put in the front door and windows. Then they carefully carved three or four main rooms out of the wood itself, making sure not to harm the Tree or interrupt the flow of the sap.

The most desirable homes in the Summit had balconies, comfortable furniture, and two fireplaces. Some even had a rain tank, providing running water. For their first winter in the Low Branches, the Lolness family was just hoping for a small communal room with a chimney. This alone would be a huge task.

At nearly two millimeters, Sim Lolness was a tall man. He weighed a good eight centigrams. But though he was a well-built fifty-year-old, he had very little experience when it came to manual work. He could recite his times tables forward and backward, all the way to a thousand. He'd written five-hundred-page books with titles such as *The Life Expectancy of Megalopods* and *Why Don't Ladybugs Have Five Dots on Their Backs?* and *The Optics of a Drop of Water*. And he could spot a new star in a flash. But he didn't know one end of a hammer from the other, and he would have banged his finger all the way in before hitting the nail once. Anything practical Sim Lolness had to learn from scratch, with his wife and son looking on.

Toby made progress much faster than anyone else. Age seven, he was in charge of all the fussy jobs. He was small enough to hollow out the chimney, the kind of delicate task you couldn't give to digger weevils, with their jawbones sharp as machetes.

Using weevils to carve out spaces did carry a serious risk because they were capable of reducing the entire Tree to dust if they weren't properly handled. Toby's father was against the big weevil-rearing projects recently developed in the Tree and linked to the construction industry. But in any case, the Lolness family didn't have a weevil or a worker or any kind of real tool at all. Toby used a nail file, his father a bread knife. Mrs. Lolness molded sap squares to make windows and sewed together scraps of cloth to make curtains and carpets.

That autumn could be summed up in one word: *digging*. Twice a day, a bowl of thin soup restored their strength. They slept for a few hours at night but didn't even wait for daybreak before getting back to work again, in the rain.

On Christmas morning, they closed the wooden door behind them and had a good look at their work. It wasn't exactly a dream house. The floor slanted, the walls were uneven, and the windows were crooked. The fireplace looked like a triangular kennel, while the smoke went out through a corkscrew-shaped chimney.

Toby's bed was right by the fireplace, and at night he could pull a curtain across to be on his own. Among the odds and ends sewn into the curtain were a pair of boxer shorts, two shirts, and a purple slip. Toby spent many hours on his bed, listening to the sounds of the fire, watching the glint of the flames through the white fabric of the boxer shorts. Every evening, shadows and glimmers projected for Toby a never-ending and ever-changing story.

But Toby didn't tuck himself in bed on the first evening the Lolness family entered their new home. The three of them sat on his parents' bed, in front of a crackling fire. They held hands. No sooner had they lowered the door latch than the wind started gusting outside and a few melted snowflakes splatted against the panes. Winter was knocking at the windows.

The house was rickety and small, but there is no better feeling than listening to a storm from the shelter of a house you have built with your own hands. Briefly, Toby saw his mother's smile spring back to life, and he started to cry.

"Well, make your minds up." Sim sighed, seeing how emotional his wife and son were. "Are we happy here, or not?"

"I'm crying because I'm so happy," Toby insisted,

then promptly started to laugh. A tear trickled down
Maya's cheek. They looked around at one another, then
all three burst out laughing.

Oddly, Toby had fond memories of that winter. They
barely left the house, only going out to do a few jobs.
Maya would go and get a packet of leaf flour from the
larder they'd dug into the bark a few steps from the
house. Sim and his son would gather firewood and do any
essential repairs. All three of them returned to their communal room as quickly as possible, where the fire was
waiting, crouching in its corner.

Toby had given the fire a name, Flam, and he pretended it was his pet animal. Whenever he came back
into the room, he'd chuck in a piece of wood, which
Flam happily pounced on. Maya would smile. An only
child can always invent company for himself.

Then Sim Lolness would take down a big blue file
from the shelves and put it on the table. He'd wave a great
sheaf of pages under Toby's nose, place it on the table,
then fold his arms. Toby would start reading out loud.

For four months this was the pattern of their days. In
the beginning, Toby didn't understand a single word of
what he was reading to his father. For the first three
weeks, the folder on bark tectonics was complete gobbledegook, even if his father gave an occasional sigh of sat-
isfaction or a little groan, listening to these scientific
readings as if they were adventure stories.

Toby concentrated harder. He was beside himself with

excitement when he recognized a word such as *light* or *sliding*. Little by little, there were flashes that made sense. The second file, labeled "The Psychosociology of Hymenoptera," Toby soon realized was about ants. His voice became more confident. Sometimes Maya, who had taken up knitting again, looked up from her work and listened carefully too. The files contained the main body of Professor Lolness's research, and his wife could remember exactly when each of them had been written. The work on the cucullate chrysalis, for example, took her back to their first years together as a young couple, when Sim would rush home in the evenings, his beret askew, all fired up by a discovery he was bursting to tell his wife about.

Until April, they didn't see another person, and they never went more than ten minutes away from their home. Then, in the first week of April, while the enormous buds were starting to swell and crack with the rising sap, they heard a tapping at the window. At first, Toby thought he must have imagined it. Perhaps it was the last rainfall before the arrival of better weather. But the tap-tapping started up again. Toby turned toward the window and saw a bearded face staring at him. He called to his father, who hesitated before going to open the door.

An old man was standing in front of the house.

"I'm your neighbor, Vigo Tornett."

"Sim Lolness; pleased to meet you."

The name Tornett sounded familiar.

"I beg your pardon, but I believe I know you," Sim added.

"I'm the one who knows you, Professor. I'm a great admirer of your work. I've read your book on Origins. I just dropped by to say a neighborly hello."

"Neighborly?"

Sim glanced over Tornett's shoulder. He couldn't see how there could be any neighbors in a place as desolate as Onessa.

"I live in the first house, three hours' walk west from here," Old Tornett explained.

He stepped inside and took a brown paper package out of a sack.

"I live with my nephew, who's a Grubber. I've brought you some grub pâté, Mrs. Lolness."

"That's very kind of you, Mr. Tornett, but how can we accept when—"

"Please, Mrs. Lolness, what are neighbors for?"

"Could you at least stay and have lunch with us?"

"I'm sorry—I must be getting back now. But I didn't want to let another day go by without coming to see you. Unfortunately, I'm not good in this weather; I get crippled with rheumatism during the winter. I do hope you'll forgive me for not being a very welcoming neighbor, until today."

He shook them all by the hand, then departed.

And with this visit, the summer months began.

Summer in the Low Branches is a bit less freezing, a bit less wet, and a bit less dark than the rest of the year. But it doesn't stop your clothes from being damp or your feet and hands from going numb the moment you step outside. Toby's scientific readings came to an end, and he started exploring the region for himself. He would set out in the morning after drinking a bowl of black bark juice and come back in the evening, dirty and soaked through, his hair tousled, his eyes tired but shining.

Soon he embarked on an expedition to the Tornett household. He got lost five times before coming across three enormous grubs snoring in their nests. Vigo Tornett had mentioned that his nephew was a Grubber, so Toby guessed he wasn't far from his goal. At last he found the house—a low windowless structure with a wide door. A strange-looking man was sitting on the threshold. When he saw Toby, he got up and

disappeared. Old Tornett came out of the house and smiled at Toby.

"Delighted to see you, my boy. How did you find your way here?"

The other man reappeared, behind Vigo Tornett.

"This is my nephew, Plok," he explained. "And this is his house. He's been kind enough to put a roof over his elderly uncle's head these past few years. Plok, let me introduce you to—"

"Toby," said Toby, holding out his hand.

"Yes, Toby Lolness," Tornett went on. "I told you about Toby. He's the son of a great man, a wonderful scientist, Sim Lolness."

Satisfied, Plok grunted and went back into the house.

"Plok can't speak. He's been a Grubber for twenty years. He's thirty-five now."

Toby wouldn't have guessed that Plok was a day over twelve and a half.

He opened his pouch and shared some cookies he had brought with Mr. Tornett. He was surprised to be greeted man to man, like a friend. Vigo Tornett was hugely likable. He talked fondly about the region and said he was starting to feel attached to it, despite his legs complaining, making him suffer because of the damp.

"Throughout my youth I was a scatterbrain. I did some very stupid things. Now I'm old and all done in, but I can see clearly. I think I've grown up at last."

Plok stuck his head around the door from time to time to stare at their young visitor. Toby gave him a friendly wave and Plok vanished.

"How old are you, young man?" asked Tornett.

"Seven," Toby replied.

Tornett bit into his cookie and nodded.

"Same age as the little Lee . . ."

"Little what?"

"The little Lee girl, at the Border."

"What Border?"

"The Border with the Grass people, four or five hours away from your house."

Toby knew that the Grass people existed, but this was the first time anyone had mentioned them openly in front of him. "Grassies." It was the kind of rude name you didn't say in front of children.

The conversation had stopped there when Vigo

Tornett suddenly noticed how late it was and urged Toby to get home before nightfall.

When Toby lay down on his bed that evening, listening to the crackling of the embers and the clicking of his mother's knitting needles, he thought he could see the shadows of the mysterious Grass people on the white boxer shorts in the curtain. He also remembered the little Lee girl being mentioned.

When a seven-year-old boy, who is an only child cut off from other children, learns there is another child his own age living less than a day's walk away, he will do anything to find her. It's a magnetic attraction that children understand, just as lovers do.

But a whole month went by before the big day.

4
Elisha

Toby got himself well and truly lost that day. He didn't just wander off course the way he usually did: a slight detour here, around in a pointless loop there, three steps forward, two steps back . . .

"The Low Branches, my son, are full of dead ends and endless knots!" said his father, who wouldn't even risk going past the end of his garden.

Toby usually got lost at least ten times a day in the maze of creepers, on the bark mountains, and in the gray moss forests, but he was also developing an astonishing sense of direction. Yet, on this particular day, it took him several hours to realize how serious the situation actually was.

An unhappy rule applies to the walker who gets lost:

1) When you're lost, you walk more quickly

2) so each step takes you farther away from home

3) so you get even more lost.

After four or five hours, Toby stopped, out of breath, sweating, hardly able to tell up from down.

He sized up the situation, which he should have done long before. No doubt about it, he was in trouble. Night was about to fall, his parents didn't know where he was, and in any case his father couldn't have gone ten centimeters beyond his home without slipping in a puddle or falling down a hole. Old Tornett was pretty much paralised by his rheumatism. Plok never left his grubs. In short, things were not looking good. Toby couldn't rely on anyone coming to his rescue.

He was all alone in the world. *I'm done for,* he thought.

Toby sat down on a big branch. He started by wringing out his socks, which was his way of keeping calm and getting his bearings. Wet socks muddle your mind and dampen your spirits.

He squeezed his socks, watching the murky trickle of water they produced. He noticed that the water fell into a crack in the bark and then carried on its way a bit farther. He put his socks back on, focusing on where the dribble of water was leading.

He wasn't thinking about anything else now. He got up and, one step at a time, like a dreamer, followed the newly formed stream.

A tiny tuft of gray moss was floating like a boat on the eddy. Toby stared at it hard.

Other tributaries joined the sock water, and Toby had to walk more quickly to follow his gray moss boat gliding along the gigantic branch. He'd stopped being the resourceful lad who was treated like a grown-up. Instead, he was a real seven-year-old and followed his boat with the happy-go-lucky playfulness of his age.

The gutter water formed a stream, and Toby had to run to keep up with it. His heart pounding, he climbed over the splinters of wood that barred his way, then skirted around the stalks of dead leaves. Focusing on his little boat, he didn't notice the water pouring over the edge a short way off. He rushed down the bark slope and would have thrown himself over with the tuft of moss if a little bud hadn't tripped him up just in time.

Headfirst, he plummeted his full height of one millimeter, his body dangling in thin air.

"I'm really done for now," he whispered.

His life was hanging by a thread. Only his foot attached to the sticky spring bud was stopping him from falling.

Then came the most terrifying sensation. He could feel his sock slipping. Socks are always trouble. While his shoe stayed firmly stuck to the bud, Toby was sliding toward the void.

The void? Toby dared to look at the precipice below. There was something strange about that dark mass. In places, he could see intriguing bluish reflections. He was exhausted and dizzy, so it took him a few moments to realize what the void looked like.

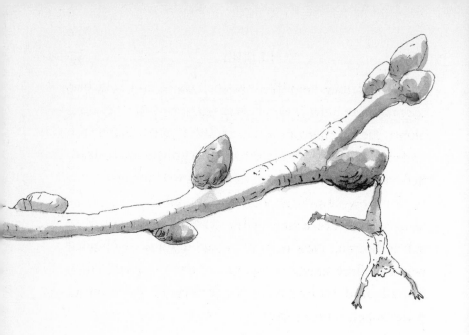

A hundred footsteps below, in the middle of an enormous battered branch, was a vast lake.

A lake hanging in the middle of the Tree. It was like a miracle.

A branch must have broken off and left a big hole in the bark, where a clear-water lake now glinted. Tall moss thickets grew close to the shore, and Toby could even see beaches of white bark with perfect coves where he would have liked to put up his tent.

The stream cascaded into the lake in a breathtaking waterfall that made the clear water foam and bubble. A fine place for his sock juice to end up.

Toby started breathing again, his heart beating to a slower tune. Curiously, he had stopped sliding. He was motionless, hanging by his foot over the cliff.

His mother told him that Grandfather Alnorell always used to say: "Fear is what makes you fall." It was a phrase his mother often repeated, but Toby had never understood it. He used to think it meant that if you startled somebody, they might fall over.

But now he understood perfectly. When you live in fear, you fall every step of the way. It is the fear that makes you fall. Now that he knew he was above a lake, he wasn't frightened of slipping—the water would break his fall. And because he wasn't frightened anymore, he had stopped slipping too.

Toby moved his hands up the length of his body, grabbed hold of a piece of coarse bark, and pulled himself up. In a few seconds, his head was level with his feet. One more try, and by pressing down on his forearms, he got himself back on firm ground. Weeks of coming and going in the Low Branches had turned him into a gymnast.

Toby was upright now, towering over this dreamy landscape and determined to explore it. He began by going to the right, following a steep passage leading all the way down to the lake.

It was even better down below. The great moss forests were reflected in the water's surface, where big water fleas jumped around. It would have taken at least an hour to swim across the vast lake. Toby had never seen anything like it up in the Heights, nor in the Summit, which he now thought of as an open-top prison. Toby didn't wait long. He pulled his clothes off and dived in.

A final ray of light managed to penetrate even deep underwater. Toby splashed around, swimming the breaststroke clumsily. The water was cold, making him gasp. He swam back quickly to where he could touch the bottom. Up to his neck in water, he contemplated the giant midnight-blue mirror.

"It's beautiful."

"Yes," Toby agreed, "it's beautiful."

"Beautiful . . ."

"I've never seen anything like it."

Toby paused. Who was he talking to? Very slowly, he turned around. He had just been talking to somebody. He hadn't imagined it. He had just answered somebody.

This somebody had brown braids and was watching him closely. She was sitting on a piece of bark peel next to Toby's clothes. She certainly wasn't any older than him, but she looked more serious and more confident. Toby had only his head sticking out of the water; he'd been caught unawares and felt embarrassed. He stayed still, eyes wide open, trying to think of a clever way to get his clothes back.

"There's only one place as beautiful as this," she said.

"Is it far?" asked Toby.

The girl didn't answer. Her hands stayed hidden under her brown cape.

"Are you the little Lee girl?"

She smiled, and Toby liked the freshness of her smile a lot. She smiled extraordinarily well for her age.

Generally speaking, people stop smiling so well when they get to four or five years old. It's downhill after that. But this girl looked as if she were smiling for the first time.

"I'm Elisha."

Toby was starting to get cold in the water. "I'm looking for the little Lee girl."

She smiled again. "Who told you about her?"

"Old Tornett."

"You'll catch a cold in there."

"Yes," said Toby, shivering.

"You should get out."

"Yes."

"You'll catch a cold."

"Yes."

She was laughing and shouting at the same time now. "SO GET OUT!"

Toby was very embarrassed, but he took a step toward the edge, then another and another. Clumsily, he walked onto the white bark beach, stark naked, until he got to his clothes, which he put on as quickly as possible.

Elisha didn't make fun of him. She just looked relieved that he was putting on warm clothes. Toby stood next to her. They were both staring at a glint on the water, far off on the lake.

"I don't know how to get back home," said Toby.

She turned her face toward him and he stared at her. She had a distinctive face. Flat and very pale, with eyes that were slightly too big for her. When she sat, her braids came down to her knees.

"I'll show you the way tomorrow," Elisha answered.

"Tomorrow?"

"We'll set out early."

"You know where I live?" asked Toby.

"Of course."

"I have to get back this evening."

"It's getting dark. You mustn't walk at night. Come with me."

She got up, and Toby saw her hands. Unlike her smile, her hands seemed just the right age for her. Toby followed her along the edge of the lake.

"Where are we going?"

"To my house."

They walked in silence, along the beach at first,

before climbing into the woods. Toby noticed that she was smaller than him and that she walked barefoot in the undergrowth. In the half-light, the soles of her feet seemed to give off a blue glow.

When she reached the top of the slope, Elisha stopped. Toby was glad to have a break because she climbed as fast as a soldier ant and he was having a hard time keeping up. The lake was starting to disappear in a black mist. Nightfall was smudging out the shadows. Elisha stared into the distance, as if she didn't take this beauty for granted. They set off again. After fifteen minutes, a delicious smell wafted around them. Toby hadn't eaten anything since that morning, and he could feel his tummy rumbling.

"We've arrived," said Elisha. "Wait for me here."

Toby noticed a round opening in the bark, where the appetizing aroma was coming from. He stayed where he was while Elisha went over to the door and disappeared inside. After a moment or two, she reappeared in the doorway and called out, "Well? Are you coming in?"

He scrambled up. The room was completely round, with no windows or chimney, just a small fire in the middle, and big squares of material hanging down in places. These brightly colored squares immediately caught Toby's eye, so it was a while before he noticed a young woman crouched down close to the fire, smiling.

"Hello."

"Hello," Toby replied.

"Are you hungry?"

"A little bit," lied Toby, who was ravenous.

He copied Elisha, who was sitting near the fire. The woman held out a plate covered with a napkin. Elisha lifted a corner of the napkin, and through a cloud of steam, Toby saw thick pancakes, dripping with butter and honey.

Toby didn't eat very neatly, but he did have a hearty appetite, which his two onlookers seemed to find funny. Finally, he pushed his plate away and downed in one gulp the bowl of water Elisha held out to him.

"I'm Toby, by the way."

This didn't appear to be news to them. Elisha and the young woman gave the impression that they already knew who he was, so he added, "I'm looking for the little Lee girl."

This got much more of a reaction from them—they

both burst out laughing. He joined in, without really knowing why.

"Do you know her?"

This time, Elisha answered.

"It's me. I'm Elisha Lee, and this is my mother."

Toby nearly fell over in surprise. This woman was Elisha's mother? She looked so young. She could only have been in her twenties. You would have thought she was her sister, with the same flat face, her braids in coils on her head.

The evening slipped by. They stayed by the fire for a long time, and Toby kept making them laugh.

In the night, using big dripping candles, Elisha took him to see the worm beetles she was breeding. Her mother sold worm beetle eggs and worm beetle wax. They needed looking after, these enormous animals, white as snow and twice as tall as Toby.

"They don't look as if they'd do any harm," said Toby, patting one of them on the flank.

"No. That one's called Lynne. The other one's Gary."

"You don't live far from the Border," said Toby. "Aren't you scared of the Grass people stealing your livestock?"

Toby had heard about this when he used to live in the Heights. One day, he accidentally caught two animal breeders talking about the Grass people. He only brought it up again now because he thought it made him sound interesting.

Elisha didn't take any notice.

"You just have to watch out for the ladybugs," Elisha explained.

"The ladybugs?"

"The worm beetles get eaten by the ladybugs, their only predators."

Back inside, close to the fire, Toby told them ladybug stories. His father was a great expert on the subject. Toby spoke at length about the ladybug with thirteen spots—very rare. Just for fun, he made them repeat the scientific name of the ladybug with fourteen spots.

"*Quatuordecim-pustulata!*"

"*Quaduorte . . . tis . . . Quatuomdecir . . . putsulana . . .*" Elisha's mother stammered.

But Elisha got it right the first time. Toby, on the other hand, tied himself in knots trying to explain about dragonflies, which had nothing to do with anything. When they were falling down with tiredness, they crawled over to the mattresses hidden behind the colored squares. Elisha chose the yellow one, and Toby the red one. By the time he closed his eyes, he had forgotten all about his parents, who would have been waiting up for him for hours now. He just heard Elisha crooning in her sleep, "*Qua-tuor-de-cim-pus-tu-la-ta . . .*"

The next day, Elisha led Toby all the way back home, but she disappeared into the bushes before Sim and Maya could catch sight of her.

This was the beginning of a special friendship. For Toby, it made life in the Low Branches blossom during those long years of exile.

5
The Moth

When Toby woke up in his bark hole, it took him a while to remember where he was. He had escaped for hours in his dreams, reliving his memories of the Low Branches and his first meeting with Elisha.

Dawn's first rays were reaching out to the Tree. Toby tried to move a little bit. His left leg hurt, but it was still responding. The rest of his body was bruised black and blue.

Usually when you wake up from a nightmare, it's a relief to see the shaft of light under the door, to rediscover a world that is friendly and free from danger. But when Toby opened his eyes after a good night's sleep, he was confronted with the nightmare of his life. In a flash, he remembered the manhunt against him. He remembered that he had lost everything. And he relived the visit from the hunters who had almost driven him out of his hole.

He would have started worrying and feeling sorry for himself again if something stronger hadn't been calling him. Hunger.

"Every brain has its key," his father always used to say. "Mine is my bed. Yours is your plate. Eat before you think, or you'll think badly."

One day when Toby was low on energy, his father had said, "See? You need food for thought." And, as with everything Professor Lolness uttered, this expression had become part of everyday speech, without anyone really knowing where it came from.

Toby pressed down on his elbows and nudged his head forward until he reached the gap in the wood. Carefully, he looked around. Suddenly, he remembered the hunter who might be crouching a little farther off. Toby froze. Even though he was starving, Toby's brain was somehow still working properly. If the hunter really was there, he would already have pounced. So Toby poked his whole head out now, unafraid, grabbing hold of a rough bump in the wood and trying to straighten the rest of his body.

He felt like a puppet. His arms and legs were as stiff as sticks attached to a rod. He'd fallen over so many times, his nose was swollen.

The cuts and grazes were painful. He had run for ten hours nonstop the day before, knocking into things, slipping at least twenty times, and scrambling back up just as often, until he had fallen into the hole where he had spent the night.

The good news was that, in spite of everything, he could still walk. His first step was accompanied by what sounded like a whimper but was actually a shriek of joy. He could still walk, and more to the point, he actually wanted to after a night of not moving at all.

The next good thing was spotting a big brown scab fungus a little way off, which would do for breakfast. Toby didn't particularly like this flat kind of mushroom on which insects sometimes laid their eggs. Usually, they had to be cooked for a long time before they could be used in a cheese dish or stir-fry.

But Toby ripped off a thick chunk and ate it raw. He had also found a tiny pond in a hollow in the bark, which he lapped up like an ant, before going back to his hole. After his improvised meal, he felt his brain getting into gear.

He pondered his plan.

Since being on the run, he had instinctively gone in the same direction. He had taken minor routes from the Summit down to the Heights, where he now was, without actually knowing where he was going. But his whole body had been leading him in this direction, and he soon realized that his goal was the Low Branches. All his survival instincts were telling him to go there. No hunter would be able to follow his trail once he was on his home ground.

His father had urged him, "Go. And don't ever stop."

But Toby wanted to believe that a safe place existed somewhere in the Tree. Plus there was Elisha. The only friend he had left, the only one who wouldn't betray him. Elisha would help him. He had to get to her. He had to. But the Land of Onessa was at least five days' walk away, and hundreds and hundreds of armed men were on the hunt for him. So he would have to travel after nightfall, when different predators—insects or nocturnal birds—were out hunting.

Toby spent the day in his refuge, sleeping and tending his wounds with strips of fresh leaf. Three times he woke to the vibrations of noisy, disorderly troops. Three times he stayed there, petrified, panting for breath, until long after the hunters had moved on.

They were still looking for him. And they were more determined than ever.

There had never been a more unfair battle in the Tree: one child against the whole world.

At nine o'clock at night in September, the Tree is already covered in darkness. That was when Toby left his hiding place for good. He knew which way to go. In fact, his sense of direction was so strong, it was as if he'd swallowed a compass. He started walking, and after a few steps, his determination to survive overcame his aches and pains; he ran along the branches the way he used to.

Toby was like a moth as he raced along the branches. Silent, unpredictable, but always accurate.

Toby knew the inhabited areas and how to avoid them. In particular, he bypassed the sprawling estates made from wood chippings, which were springing up on the outskirts of the Tree's cities.

The different groups of men hunting him, who were actually ahead of him now, sometimes pitched camp for the night in the wilderness. So Toby also kept an eye out for the glow of their campfires.

Before he saw anything, he heard the voices.

It was at a crossroads that he couldn't avoid without losing precious time. He needed to reach the other side.

Crawling on his knees and elbows, he began his

approach. About ten men were slumped around a fire that had almost gone out, where tasty-looking chunks of cricket were roasting on a spit. There must have been almost half a cricket for just ten men, and plenty of alcohol flowing.

Toby was hungry. He listened to their songs. They were beautiful—real old hunting tunes. Beauty sometimes sneaks into the hardest of hearts. Toby recognized these as songs from his childhood.

The great hunts, which had been his grandfather's pride and joy, no longer took place on the Summit estates where Toby used to spend his summers. But the governesses employed by his grandmother had sometimes taken him to the peasants' hunts that were still held on the neighboring branches. Toby had ridden on the hunters' backs, nudging their arrows in the wrong direction. He had tickled the best archers, and because he was young, people had forgiven him. Once, he had even kept a tiny fly hidden in his shirt for a whole day, so he could free it when evening came, far away from the hunters.

At dusk, he liked to stretch out under the inn table. He was only five or six at the time, and when he listened to the singing and ballads, he felt like a true hunter. He loved the songs and old stories, and the smells of food grilling and old boots that joined him under the table.

But tonight, rashly listening to his pursuers singing, he was no longer small Toby who got passed from hand to hand around the table and made everybody laugh.

This time he was the breathless prey itself, drawing near
to the hunters' camp.

He lay on the ground for some time. A rustling noise
suddenly caught his attention. It was coming from the
right, very close by. He turned his head and nearly
screamed.

Two red eyes were staring at him out of the dark.

He rolled to the side. The hunters carried on with
their songs. After burying his head in his arms, Toby
poked it back out again and dared to look at those eyes.
The noise was getting more aggressive.

It was a soldier ant.

Penned in an enclosure, it was starting to grow restless and trying to beat down the barrier. Toby noticed
another pair of eyes looking his way. And then he saw a
third ant lurking in the shadows. The scent of Toby must

have woken these three giant monsters, each of them glowing red as embers.

The hunters weren't alone. They were accompanied by these terrifying beasts. Toby was getting ready to slip away, but the sounds of the revelry suddenly stopped. The nervous ants had attracted the hunters' attention. A hairy giant, at least two and a half millimeters tall, got up and walked over to the enclosure.

"Hey! Quiet in there."

Toby did another roll in the darkness. The ants had clustered on his side of the enclosure, and the man was trying to find out what they were so worked up about.

"Falco! Enok! Shut up, will you?"

The man started walking around the pen, talking to the creatures. Toby was trying to think of what to do. He rummaged around in his pockets for a distraction. Nothing. Not even a twig to throw in the other direction. The hunter continued to pace the fence. Just behind him, the others were getting ready to join in. What on earth could be attracting the ants to this dark corner?

Toby glanced at his bandages. In less than a second, he ripped off his bloodstained dressings, scrunched them into a ball, and tossed over the fence. The ants pounced, the blood driving them into a frenzy. They were fighting each other now.

"A scrap of leaf! They're fighting over a leaf!"

The man kicked the pen and went back to the fire, to put his companions' minds at rest.

ᘒ

A minute later, Toby was already far away.

He had escaped. He wasn't going to stop. He ran full tilt, as if the ants were on his heels.

He had run like this during the six years of exile in the Land of Onessa. Whole days in the Low Branches, where distances had no meaning. He gave himself completely to the call of the Low Branches and let his mind wander.

He suddenly remembered a particular morning when young Plok Tornett had turned up at the Lolness household, unrecognizable. His face covered in mud, he kept groaning and pointing to where he had just come from. Sim Lolness tried to calm him down, but Plok's grunting got louder and louder. Still pointing toward the west, Plok grabbed hold of the professor's chin. Toby understood in a flash: the chin was his way of referring to his uncle's beard.

Something had happened to Vigo Tornett.

Toby decided to set out alone, to find out what, as fast as possible. There was no time to ask for help from the Asseldor family or from the Olmechs, friends who lived higher up. Reluctantly, his parents let him go, before ushering poor Plok inside.

It was Toby's third year in the Low Branches. He reached old Tornett's place in half the time it used to take. He knew how to navigate the risky slip-branches, shortcuts made from twigs wedged between the branches, so he didn't have to make any detours, and he darted from branch to branch, leaping from one leaf to the next.

When he got to the Tornetts' home, he didn't notice anything unusual. The fire had gone out in the hearth, and the table was set for two. It wasn't until he walked around the branch, toward the grubs' sheds, that he found the old man.

He was a sorry sight.

Tornett was lying on the bark, motionless, his clothes in tatters.

Toby was ten at the time, and he had dealt with many difficult situations, but he had never found himself face-to-face with a man in that kind of condition. He threw himself on him.

"Tornett! Mr. Tornett!"

He took the old man's bearded head in his hands.

"Talk to me, pleeeease."

Tornett didn't move; it was too late. Toby laid his elderly friend's head to rest. A cold breeze made him shiver.

"Farewell, Tornett," he exclaimed theatrically.

Just then, he felt the man's fingers pressing on his arms. More than pressing. Tornett was digging his nails into Toby's flesh. If he dug much harder, his fingers would come out the other side. Toby would never have believed an old man could possess such strength—especially one in Tornetts's condition. Toby cried out in pain, making Tornett wake up fully and release his grip.

An hour later, Toby was wiping a damp sponge over brave Tornett's bruised body. He was definitely alive and didn't appear to have sustained any serious injuries, but a fine network of grazes meant he was covered from head to toe in red streaks. As he lay on his bed in his long johns, old Vigo Tornett's scratches looked like a spider's web.

"When I was at Tumble . . ." Vigo Tornett began when he was finally able to speak. "When I was at Tumble . . . they beat me up like this and I'd done nothing. At Tumble they hit me so hard . . ."

Toby didn't really understand. Tornett was only half-conscious. The shock must have brought back distant memories. Memories of Tornett's other life, when he'd been a troublemaker. He had spoken about it to Toby. He'd spent ten years in Tumble prison. Ten terrible years that could never be forgotten.

Vigo Tornett opened his eyes fully. After a while, he explained what had happened to him this time.

Being a grubber required you to be very meticulous. Grubbing was all about knowing what you were doing. You had to take a white sheet to wipe down the grub. Next, you wrung out the sheet in a basin to collect the milk. But the grubber's most delicate task was keeping an eye on the grubs.

Everyone knows that a grub will eventually become an insect. But sometimes not even the best grubber can tell the difference between one grub and another. So it is important to pay close attention to how fast the grub matures, in order to dispose of it in time. Kindhearted Plok sometimes became so fond of his grubs that he kept them beyond a safe time limit. More than once, his uncle had rushed to help him with a grub whose shell was already cracking, its twitching antennae and jawbones starting to appear. Together they would push it into the void.

But this time, Vigo Tornett had found himself face-to-face with a rhinoceros beetle in the middle of the night. The beetle still had gloopy white shreds stuck to its shell.

Caught off guard by this first encounter, and barely out of its pupa, the insect was not in a friendly mood. It could easily have chopped Tornett up into little pieces.

The old man tried hurling himself at the beetle's head. But he had gotten caught on the beetle's single horn instead. Tornett was shaken in all directions, whipped against the boughs, and left for dead where Toby eventually found him.

From then on, Tornett only let his nephew breed small Nosodendron grubs.

Toby remembered how frightening this adventure had seemed to him at the time. He had told Elisha about it the next day, leading her to believe that he was the one who had chased off the rhinoceros beetle single-handedly, even though it was "fifty times my size".

Elisha had listened.

"What about Plok?" she whispered.

Elisha was very touched by the story of Plok, Tornett's mute nephew. Sometimes, Toby wondered if Elisha would have preferred it if he couldn't speak either. Here was the hero and savior of Vigo Tornett standing before her, and all she could do was ask about Plok.

"What about Plok? Did *he* fight with the rhinoceros beetle?"

"No, and neither did you."

From that day, Toby realized he would never lie to Elisha again.

Now, as he leaped through the night, he would willingly have entered into a bare-knuckle fight with any bloodthirsty praying mantis, rather than flee the hatred of his own people.

He ended his second night as a fugitive in a narrow hole, after chasing out a drowsy furniture beetle. He curled up into a ball to go to sleep. Day was beginning to break. It was time to disappear, like the unseen, unheard animals of the night he belonged with now.

6
Balina's Secret

"What are you doing?"

Elisha jumped into the lake, and Toby looked away, embarrassed, until she had disappeared underwater.

"What are you doing, Toby? Aren't you coming in?"

"No."

She swam a few strokes toward the waterfall that was tumbling over her now. You could hardly hear her voice under the cascading water.

"Come on, Toby!"

But Toby stayed on the beach.

Sometimes, Elisha dived beneath the blue-tinted mirror to touch the bottom. She would resurface, gasping for air but radiant, her eyelashes glistening with water droplets.

But on this particular morning, Toby barely glanced at her. His face was closed, lost in thought.

It was the fourth year of his family's long exile in the Low Branches. And life there had taken on a regular rhythm.

During the worst of the cold winters, everybody hibernated at home. Toby forgot that light even existed and locked himself away to work with his father. His body became a dormant branch, while his brain sprouted ideas.

He was a greedy learner, and he gobbled up Sim Lolness's bulky files in record time. Sometimes, Toby would work on the same subject over and over again, so as not to get through his knowledge rations too quickly. Professor Lolness knew that knowledge is always outgrowing itself. Sometimes, he likened knowledge to the Tree itself.

Toby's father subscribed to the crazy idea that the Tree was growing. It was an extremely controversial notion, and the professor's favorite subject. All the scientists argued about it. Does the Tree change? Is it eternal? Where did it come from? Will the world end? And, most important, above all: is there life beyond the Tree? These questions prompted a great debate, in which Sim Lolness always failed to agree with the fashionable viewpoint.

His book on origins hadn't been well received. In it, he told the story of the Tree as if it were a living being. He said that leaves were not independent plants but the outermost tips of a mighty life force.

Readers were shocked that a book claiming to be

about origins was, in fact, about the future. If the Tree was alive, in the same way that a moss forest is alive, then it was terribly vulnerable. They should look after this living organism, which embraced them with open arms.

As soon as spring showed its face, Toby poked his nose outside.

He stopped thinking and started sniffing things out instead.

He abandoned his heavy files and tried to follow Elisha, who was caught up in a whirlwind of projects and adventures. Together, they explored the Low Branches, until they reached the Main Trunk, and camped in the Shady Regions. They ventured as far as the Border, which completely fascinated Elisha. They made their way through marshes and discovered light-filled caves formed from deserted wasps' nests.

"Come and swim!" Elisha called out.

This time, it sounded more like an order, but Toby still didn't move from the beach. He felt sad, but he didn't really understand why. He stared at a twig that had half fallen into the water. Toby thought about his old life. The Low Branches had taught him everything, but suddenly, four months before his eleventh birthday, nostalgia for his childhood got the better of him.

He wondered about Leo. He'd had no news of him all this time.

What happens to a friendship that is catapulted to the opposite ends of the world? Toby hadn't thought about it like that before. As far as he was concerned, Leo Blue was part of Toby. Tobyleo. Nothing could separate them. One autumn evening in the Heights, they had made a vow, forehead to forehead. Toby knew that his father and Leo's father had made the same vow of friendship, forty years earlier. They had never broken it, not even when El Blue died.

Blue and Lolness: a friendship handed down from father to son, forever.

Four years had slipped by without Leo and Toby exchanging a single word. But Toby hadn't forgotten a thing. Sometimes, he would wake up with a jolt in the middle of the night; he'd been dreaming about his best friend.

In his dream, he no longer recognized Leo. His friend had turned into a stooped old man, with Leo's shorts and Leo's woolly hat, and Leo's broken tooth that always made his smile look more like a wink. Toby didn't like this nightmare.

Now, sitting on the shores of the lake, his mind was dipping back into his previous life. He would have given anything to have been able to visit his house in the Heights again, The Tufts. It had a small but perfectly tended garden, with two well-raked paths. At the bottom of the garden hung a small hollow branch that was strictly off-limits: a hollow branch hanging above the void. It was too narrow for an adult, but Toby could easily slide inside it. His father had grabbed hold of his foot one day, terrified when he had tried to explore it. Toby had scraped his face, leaving a horizontal scar on his cheek. It looked like a continuation of his lips.

Toby used to get very bored in the house and garden at The Tufts, but four years later, he dreamed fondly of that time because it had been snatched away from him. Even his Grandmother Alnorell, whom he hardly knew and liked even less, had become part of the big picnic basket of happy memories, along with dinner in the Summit, children's games, and making forts.

Elisha got out of the water, and Toby looked away. When would she understand he didn't want to see her like that? Not that she minded; in fact, she always waited as long as possible before putting her clothes back on. She was amazed when he tried to explain the reason for his embarrassment.

"It's just not what's done," was all he could come up with.

That kind of thinking made no sense to Elisha. So she amused herself instead, making Toby keep his eyes closed for hours on end, long after she was already snugly wrapped up in her cape.

But on this particular afternoon, she realized that Toby wasn't in the mood to play her game. Fully clothed, her wet hair tumbling down her back, she sat next to him.

"Is something the matter?"

"No . . ."

"Are you pouting?"

"No . . ."

"Are you sad?"

Toby didn't answer. He was thinking *YES* very loudly, but he didn't say it.

He just kept quiet.

"I understand," she whispered.

Toby glanced at her; he hadn't said anything out loud. He paused. "I've never told you the story of why we came to the Low Branches."

"No one said you had to."

No, he didn't have to. You never have to tell your friends about the big stuff in life. But the day you do, life tastes sweeter. So Toby gave it a try.

"You've never met my parents, Elisha. You always turn back as soon as we're near my house. But I know you'd get along with them. The way my mother tells stories, you'd think she was a book crammed with illustrations. And she can make pollen bread rolls too.

"My father's got very big hands. He calls me 'his little snail.' My head fits in his hands. And there's something else—he's a very great scientist.

"I'm not saying that because he's my father. I'm saying it because it's true. My father has discovered things nobody dreamed of before. Paper, for instance; he as good as invented paper. Before, people used wood pulp and it kept breaking. But if you just extract the cellulose from the wood of the Tree, you can make good paper. That's one invention, but I could just as easily tell you about the time he discovered that the lichen that grows on the bark is actually the marriage between an algae and a mushroom: two plants that decided to stick together forever. He also realized that the Tree sweats fifty liters a day! Then there are the secrets of the buds, of the flies and the sky, of the rain and the stars. He even gave me a star called Altair."

"Gave it to you?" Elisha was incredulous.

"Yes. He showed it to me and told me it was mine. That's all it takes . . . I can lend you Altair one night, if you like," Toby offered.

Elisha wanted to ask another question, but Toby was off again.

"My father has researched everything and made tons of discoveries. People used to admire him for that. But there is one discovery he'd prefer never to have made. The one that changed our lives."

They were both staring out toward the far end of the

lake, where the bark cliffs rose up. Toby took a deep breath, then began his story.

"It would have been better for my father if he hadn't gotten out of bed that day—he should have let his neurons sleep in. But as it was, he got up early, went into his workshop, and started on his experiments.

"I remember it was my birthday, and for the first time, he'd forgotten it. He stayed locked away all day long, and all night too. Not even his assistant, Tony Sireno, was allowed in.

"My mother and I kept joking, 'Is he making jam in there?' Because there was this smell of burnt syrup. But Sireno didn't seem to think it was funny at all. He didn't like being kept in the dark when it came to his boss's work.

"The next morning, my father came out of his workshop. Sireno hadn't turned up yet. My father had a big smile on his face. He sat down and drank a cup of strong black bark juice. He drummed his fingers on the table. He looked really happy, even if his eyelids were collapsing with tiredness like two crumpled pillows.

"He took off his beret and glasses, scratched his head, and asked, 'Can you hear that strange noise?'

"My mother and I strained our ears. Yes, we could hear an unusual sound coming from his workshop. We went in—there was something moving on the parquet floor of his study. And I knew exactly what it was: Balina.

"When my mother and I saw Balina walking all by himself, our eyes nearly popped out of our heads."

Elisha's eyes were wide open now too.

"I've never told you about Balina," Toby went on. "He's a miniature wood louse I made when I was small. A piece of wood with several legs. That's all.

"That morning, Balina started walking across the room. He was carrying a black box and a tiny bottle on his back. I couldn't believe my eyes. This was the best birthday present ever.

"Tony Sireno arrived. . . . He fainted from shock; my father caught him just in time. Sireno knew Balina was just a wooden toy; he'd fixed one of his legs the year before. But that morning, he saw him walking on his own.

"When Sireno came to, he heard the sound of Balina's footsteps and fainted all over again. In the end, my mother tipped a bucket of water over his head.

"I didn't really understand how important this discovery was at first. If my father could make Balina walk for my birthday, he could also fix it so that my bee, which I'd made out of moss, would be able to fly next year— fantastic! But the professor and his assistant were giving each other odd looks. My father picked up Balina and put him in a cupboard, which he locked. I didn't dare remind him that the wood louse was my present. I think Sireno must have felt a mixture of disappointment and excitement on his way home, because he still didn't know the secret magic that made Balina walk. Tony Sireno really didn't like being kept in the dark.

"Everything happened very quickly after that. A week later, Balina was presented to the Tree Council. The chamber was full to bursting. I'd gone with my mother and we sat at the very back, in the top gallery. My mother was very proud to be there. She gripped my hand. She'd put on her red hat with the veil. I was wearing a knitted tie because I'd turned seven the week before. And I had a black hat I was supposed to hold in my hands. I still can't see the point of a hat you don't wear.

"People were waiting and chattering. I saw Sireno come in. He was up in the top balcony, like us, but on the other side. He kept pushing people out of the way to get to the front. He was red, sweaty, and he didn't look happy about being up there.

"Down below, we saw my father make his way over to the platform and call for silence. He held a small box in his hands. Nobody said another word. He began to talk, and my mother gripped my hand even more tightly.

"'Whenever I come here, dear friends, I always talk to you about the Tree. I talk about how strong our Tree is. If I describe a bug, it's because it sucks our Tree's sap. If I talk about rainwater, it's because it gives our Tree life. Today, I'd like to introduce you to Balina. Our Tree lies firmly at the heart of this discovery. But I won't reveal the secret until next week.

"He looked up at the sky. The Council Chamber was built into a green woodpecker's hole in the middle of a lateral branch. It had an open roof, and the crisscrossing of branches and sky above was plain to see because we were very close to the Summit. A shaft of sunlight projected across the room, illuminating the dust particles in the air. Looking up into the light, my father spotted us right at the top. He gave a little twitch of his nostrils, which nobody would have noticed except us; it was our secret sign. The crowd was silent.

"My father put the tiny box down and opened one of its sides, and everyone saw Balina get out. My birthday present was walking across the floor, with his little black box and bottle still fixed on his back. A quiver ran through the whole Chamber. People were amazed! I even saw one of the wise elders from the Grand Council start crying. How could my Balina have such an effect on people? Balina was rewriting the Tree's history.

"There was a standing ovation in the Council Chamber; a big cheer rose up that warmed my mother's cheeks, made Tony Sireno go red with frustration and the leaves on the Tree flap all the way to the last branch.

"The following week was a nightmare. Every day, twenty, thirty, sometimes fifty people would line up outside our house to talk to my father. While they waited in the kitchen, we served them hot drinks. My mother smiled at each and every one, but she was worried about my father because his face was slowly changing.

"He wasn't talking anymore. Or eating. Or sleeping.

"In just five days, he looked thirty years older. And on the sixth day, none of the people waiting ever saw my father's study door open. My mother apologized on my father's behalf, and asked them politelyto go back home. Reluctantly, they accepted and went away.

"I saw my mother disappear into the workshop. I was busy creating a fly from chlorophyll paste, so my father could make it fly one day.

"A few hours later, my mother came out. She looked calmer now. She just said, 'Your father will speak to the Grand Council tomorrow.'

"The next day, the Council Chamber was even more packed and buzzing than it had been the week before. This time, my father had given us permission to go down and join him, close to the stage. From there, you could see all the bigwigs in their fine clothes sitting in the stalls, and in the different balconies that rose up in tiers, the crowd of ordinary folk, who'd come for the show.

"Everybody knew my father was going to explain Balina's secret. Nobody really expected to understand the complicated scientific explanation, but everyone just wanted to be there. There were hundreds of people who couldn't get in, so they had to gather around the branch instead. You could see heads poking through the big hole in the roof. There was even someone hanging from a wooden trapeze above the crowd. The spectators kept laughing and throwing tidbits up to him on his perch.

"My father made his assistant come and sit next to us. Tony Sireno looked a bit less angry than he had the week before. He was wearing a ridiculously tight shirt and sitting bolt upright. For once he hadn't been completely overlooked.

"Then came the announcement that my father was about to speak. I can remember that exact moment. People were smiling at us, at me and my mother. It was the last time anyone smiled at us in the Treetop." Toby's voice faltered. "Ever."

He glanced at Elisha. She gave him a smile. Luckily, in the Low Branches, there were smiles worth all the smiles in the Treetop put together.

By the time he was ready to go on with his story, his voice was strong again.

7
Hatred

❍"My father stood up in the middle of the hushed crowd. I felt my mother's hands go clammy. The way she was looking at my father, it was as if there was something woven between them in the air. Something only I could see.

"I remember every word he said. We were expecting a rather dry, technical explanation. I think everyone was surprised to hear my father using the same clear and simple words he always used.

"'You all know about sap. It is at the heart of your daily lives. Sometimes you can even hear it bubbling away under your feet. You make cups and plates and furniture out of it, you extract sugar from it for candies, you make glue out of it, tiles, toys, cement for your houses. . . . The sap is always there, behind the bark. All you have to do is drill a small hole, just like the greenfly that feeds on it does. In fact, I'm going to let you in on a secret—I wish I'd been a greenfly. Sometimes at night, I get dressed up in my greenfly costume, and I jump . . .'

"The nervous laughter that had started among certain levels of the public spread throughout the Chamber. Only Joe Mitch, the big digging tycoon, who was spread over two chairs in the front row, didn't laugh. He was too busy snoring. On either side of him, his sidekicks, Razor and Torn, were trying hard not to smile. My father signaled for silence again.

"'Let me get back to my stories. Stories about sap. Having never made it as a greenfly, I made my own small hole in the bark and took a look. What I saw was something that had never caught my interest before. I saw that the sap was traveling down. Nothing so extraordinary about that. The sap had been traveling down the evening before too; it had been traveling down a hundred years before, and next year, touch wood, it will travel down as well. But, being a shortsighted greenfly, I hadn't really thought much about it.'

"He looked up at the spectator on the trapeze.

"'Listen carefully to what I'm about to tell you. Listen to my reasoning here. If Mr. Clown, up there on his perch, falls off; if all the people craning their necks up in the balconies fall as well; if everyone jumps from the balconies, the result is a downward movement. Which is to say, a movement from the top toward the bottom, just like the sap. I might even describe it as a pretty movement, if the young lady with the parasol were to jump as well. . . .'

"A girl in the third gallery blushed. A few boys whistled. My father smiled in my mother's direction.

" 'So, for a while, everything falls. But after an hour or two, when everyone's piled up at the bottom of the Council Chamber, there won't be anyone else left to fall. The movement will stop. The sap, on the other hand, just goes on falling and falling. It falls the length of the Tree, and it never stops. So I asked the question you're all asking right now: where does it come from? It can't be created from nothing up in the Summit. Where does the falling sap come from?'

"This question met with a perplexed silence.

" 'Like you, I couldn't find the answer right away. At first, I thought the leaves at the Summit drank the rainwater, which then fell back down in the form of sap. But I discovered that the leaves in fact repelled moisture. Perhaps you remember my speech about how the Tree sweats?'

"Smiles lit up certain faces. I think everybody could remember the presentation in which my father had imitated a leaf transpiring by making the sound effects of a simmering saucepan.

" 'I came to the following conclusion: since it's not falling out of the sky, the sap has to rise somewhere in order to travel down again below the bark. But where does it rise? My idea was to go and see what was happening deep down inside the branch and the trunk.'

"He paused for an instant.

"'You know that, right from the start, I've been opposed to the great tunnel that is currently being hollowed out of the Main Trunk. It is, in my view, a project that is both ridiculous and irresponsible. But since the tunnel exists, I went to see it. When I got there, I was told that work had been interrupted. What a surprise! Nobody could work there anymore. At a certain depth, enormous quantities of liquid rose up from the ground, making it impossible to continue digging. There must have been fifty weevils working on that building site, fifty weevils specially reared for the project. These are extremely greedy beasts. Since the closure of the building site, they no longer had the wood from the tunnel to munch on, and nobody knew what to give them to eat. They'd bred these fifty giant creepy-crawlies but they couldn't feed them anymore! I've rarely seen such a horrific spectacle as those starving weevils in their cages. I'll end my digression by repeating my view that our world is walking on its head.'

"Mutterings were heard. Nobody had imagined the tunnel could ever be criticized. After all, its name was the Eco-Tunnel of Progress.

"All eyes were on Joe Mitch. Big Joe Mitch woke up with a jolt, rolled his gloopy eyes, and bared his teeth. Flanking him were Razor and Torn, scrawny and mean-looking. Neither of them knew how to react. Joe Mitch is a big-time breeder of weevils, and he's behind all the recent digging projects. Criticizing the tunnel means criticizing Joe, and that can be very dangerous.

"My father gave him a small bow and a polite smile, then he picked up with his speech again.

"'I put on a hard hat and went inside the tunnel. When I got to the area that had been flooded, I saw exactly what I was hoping to see. The liquid was gushing up from the ground in great spurts. That's right, it was traveling from the bottom toward the top. It wasn't water, but it wasn't sap as we know it either. I looked closely at the tunnel walls: the liquid was rising up through the wood fiber. According to my calculations, it was rising every second by the height of my son. That works out to roughly five meters per hour. I put a bit of it into a bottle and went back home.'

"This time, my father paused for a while. Everyone was hanging on his words. They'd almost forgotten about Balina's adventures. We were captivated by the mystery of the Tree.

"'I went back home and washed my hands.'

"There was an outcry from the crowd, eager to know what happened next.

" 'I kissed my wife and my son, Toby.'

"More complaining. My father looked annoyed that people were being so impatient.

" 'It's very important to kiss your wife and your son. That's not irrelevant; it's the heart of everything.'

"Back to silence. I puffed out my chest under my tie and twirled my hat in my hands. My father's voice filled the room again.

" 'So I set to work. I quickly realized that I'd just found the point where the sap rises before it falls. In the wood of the Tree, in what is known as sapwood, the crude sap rises. That's where the Tree's energy is. The life of the Tree. It gets transformed by the leaves, the air, and the light before coming back down as a different kind of sap that flows under the bark. But it originates in the rising sap, the crude sap that I had just discovered in the heart of the Tree.'

"The audience was starting to get a better idea of what he was getting at. My father continued, punctuating his sentences with silences.

" 'My only goal is to prove that the Tree is alive. That the sap is its blood. That we are passengers in this living world. This has always been the objective of my research, as you know. By demonstrating the energy contained in the sap, I could reach my goal. So I invented a small mechanism that can produce energy from crude sap, much as a leaf on the Tree does. It's something very simple that fits into a small black box. To make it, all I had to do was look at a bud, a leaf. I put my magic box on Balina's back, together with a small bottle of crude sap, and I connected this up to Balina's feet. That's all. Balina started walking.'

"From where I was sitting, on my bench, I could tell that the crowd was disappointed. My father still hadn't explained the real secret of his invention. My mother's hand, holding mine, became cold and damp. When I look back on it now, I think she knew what was going to happen.

"My father continued: 'This week, hundreds of people have come to my home. They all wanted to present me with a possible use for my invention. They were all very smart, and some were very well-meaning too. They talked to me about systems for baking bread more quickly, for traveling faster, for generating heat and cold, for cutting, digging, transporting, communicating, and mixing things; they even talked about thought systems. The Balina Method was going to change our lives.'

"The crowd applauded. They were ready to carry my father in triumph.

"But he went on: 'The only problem is that I like this life of ours, and don't especially want to change it. All I want to do is prove the Tree is a living organism. Is it right that I give everyone access to crude sap so that they can build machines that fold newspapers in four, or machines that think on their behalf?'

"No one moved a muscle. The atmosphere was oppressive. My father went very pale. You could tell he was about to get to the heart of his speech.

"'Yesterday, I spoke with my wife. I have decided not to reveal how my little black box works. I believe crude sap belongs to our Tree. I believe the Tree lives thanks to that sap. To use its blood would be to put our world in peril. Everybody is free to look for what I found. I won't stop anyone trying to discover Balina's secret. But I'd rather say no more so that one day my son's son will still be able to lean against a flower or a bud.'

"I was pinned to my bench. I didn't really understand why he was talking about my son, when I'd only just celebrated my seventh birthday. I wasn't sure what son he was talking about, but I thought perhaps this fib—making everyone believe I had a son—helped him in his explanation. Like when he told everybody he had a greenfly costume, even though I hadn't seen him wear a single insect outfit, not once.

"As for the rest of what he said, I think I understood everything and it was brilliant. Seeing as there was this big silence, I thought I'd get the clapping going. But I soon realized that I was the only one whose arms were moving in that silence. In the end, I put my hands back on my knees.

"It came from the back, almost in slow motion. It went splat on my father's face: a honey fritter.

"I don't remember much after that. Everybody was seized by a kind of madness. People were yelling, throwing things at the stage, insulting my father, pushing me, shouting in my mother's ears. What I do remember is that Tony Sireno, my father's assistant, had distanced himself from us.

"My father, on the other hand, rushed over to our bench. He protected us with his long arms, and we made our way to the exit. By this time, and egged on by Joe Mitch's cronies, even the bearded wise old men up at the front were shouting things I'm not allowed to say. The insults were getting nastier, and the first blows were raining down on us.

"I began to wonder why my father had pretended I had a son, if it made people as mad as this?

"When my mother was hit on the shoulder, my father took off his glasses and rolled them up in his beret. He was angrier than I'd ever seen him before. He went bright red, his arms and legs flailing in every direction. The crowd pulled back when they heard Professor Lolness shouting. We managed to make our exit and get back home to The Tufts. The whole house had been ransacked. The furniture was upside down, and the crockery was lying in pieces on the floor. My father held us close.

" 'I think they must have found out that I don't have a son,' I blurted.

"My father laughed through his tears. 'You might have a son one day. That's what I meant, Toby. I hope you'll have a son or a daughter when you grow up.'

"He looked so sad, I didn't want to dash his hopes.

"We stayed locked up at home for several days. My mother had asked my grandmother, Mrs. Alnorell, to put us up for a few weeks in one of her Summit properties.

"My grandmother wrote us a little note back, on a fancy card:

> *Naturally, my dear child,*
> *in your situation,*
> *please be assured*
> *it is out of the question.*

"The card was signed: Radegonde Alnorell.

"My father made lots of jokes about her first name, but my mother just cried. She must have been thinking about what had happened to us, repeating, 'It'll blow over.'

"But it didn't blow over.

"It was impossible to go out without being attacked by objects or insults. I'd started to collect the rotten mushrooms and all the different kinds of missiles that landed in front of our door as soon as we opened it.

"One day, my father was summoned by the Grand Council. Away he went. My mother and I stayed at home. When he came back, he was in his stocking feet, his face white and crumpled, like a cloud. There were peelings on the shoulders of his best gray jacket.

"The Grand Council had taken his shoes from him. This was the most serious rebuke he could receive. They

remove the shoes of criminals and kidnappers. My father
had been punished for 'dissimulation of capital information.' I had no idea what those words meant.

"He told my mother we were going somewhere very
far away. The Tufts was being seized. In exchange, they
would give us a small plot in the Land of Onessa, in the
Low Branches. That evening I went to find my friend
Leo Blue. Since the start of the Balina business, we'd met
up secretly every day, in a dry bud. This time, we spent
two days and three nights in there. Leo Blue was my
friend, and I didn't want to leave. It was my father who
found us in the end. Leo wouldn't stop clinging to my
arm.

"It all happened so quickly. Our world was crumbling. . . ."

Elisha was such a good listener, you could have followed every chapter of the story in the pupils of her eyes.
She'd had no idea about this adventure. Vigo Tornett
had simply told her that the Lolness family wasn't living
in the Low Branches by choice. And the Asseldors, who
lived right at the top of the Low Branches, were always
sighing and referring to "that poor Lolness family!"

"If you want to sleep at our house tonight, my
mother has an enormous cricket drumstick that the
Olmechs gave us. We're going to grill it, in honey sauce."

An offer like that to a little boy in pain might not
sound like much, but it was exactly what Toby needed.
Elisha knew Toby well enough by now. In fact, she knew

him so well that she added, "I'm going to help my mother get it ready. Why don't you go for a swim before joining us?"

And she stroked his hair, which was something she didn't normally do.

She disappeared into the woods. Toby was all on his own now. But the lake where they'd first met spread out in front of him, and a few moments later he was floating on his back, looking up at the canopy of branches above him. The leaves were light green and huge. Just one of them would have sheltered a hundred people from the rain. Toby could feel the waves splashing against his legs. The lake water seemed a bit salty. But he wasn't crying anymore.

8
Nils Amen

It is time to leave behind those memories—some happy, some not so happy—and return to the present, to Toby crisscrossing the Tree on his way to the Low Branches.

Toby was taking the same path and heading in the same direction as he had years before, when he was with his parents and the two grumpy porters on their way to the Low Branches. But he was alone this time, unless you count the hundreds of men and ferocious soldier ants on his trail. It would take five or six nights to get from the Treetop back to that wild country, to feel safe at last and find friends who could help him.

Toby had already walked for two whole nights, and the third one should have been easier. He had managed to reach the Main Trunk and was making his way down through lichen forests, where every sprout or shoot was

three times his height. The bark was becoming moun-
tainous and less inhabited, with gorges and deep canyons.
Lichen forests tumbled away from the vertiginous
landscape.

The troop of hunters had decided to avoid this
region. They'd taken less precipitous branches. All Toby
came across was the odd hamlet of woodcutters and a
few huts belonging to trappers.

He happened to pass close by a plantation that
belonged to his grandmother. Even though the old lady
lived up in the Summit, Mrs. Alnorell's properties
extended all the way down to the higher of the Low
Branches. This estate was called Amen Woods, after
the plantation workers who lived there. Toby knew the
woodcutter's son; they'd played together when he was
little.

Toby couldn't decide whether or not to knock on the
cabin door. He wondered if they knew about the big
hunt for him. Was there still anyone left in the Tree who
might be able to help him?

Hunger eventually made him knock quietly three
times. Nobody answered. He knocked again, but the
cabin was silent. Could he still trust a friend he had
shared a summer with a long time ago?

Toby pushed the door ajar. The house was dark, but
the remains of a fire, at the back of the fireplace, meant he
could see the edges of the room. It was a modest cabin,
home to the woodcutter Norz Amen and his son, Nils.

Toby had never been to these remote parts before,

they were too much of a diversion. But six years earlier,
during the summer before the Balina business, father
and son Amen had come up to work on a Summit estate
where Toby was spending the month of July. They were
based in a moss forest. The two children hit it off right
away. And they would definitely have seen each other
again if the Lolness family hadn't been exiled for six
years.

Toby took a step toward the table.

"Nils . . ." he called out.

Toby's eyes had become accustomed to the dark now,
and he could just make out that the room was empty. A
cloth shoulder bag was hanging on a chair to the left.
Toby went over to it. In the bag was a big chunk of
bread, a few pieces of cured meat, and some cookies. It
didn't take Toby long to make up his mind. He took the

shoulder bag and, before disappearing into the night, wrote three words on a scrap of paper left behind on the table.

> *Thank you.*
> *Toby.*

Those three words would be enough for the trap to close in around Toby again.

A few minutes after he'd gone, four men and two boys who looked about thirteen or fourteen entered the wood cabin.

"I just want to get something to eat."

"Hurry up, Nils, you clot head."

"The bag's ready, Dad . . ."

The boy who had just spoken neared the table. He lit a candle with a firebrand.

Nils couldn't believe his eyes. "The bag's not there anymore."

"Are you sure you packed it?"

"I left it on the chair."

Another man urged them to get a move on.

"I've got enough, we'll share mine. Hurry up, they're waiting for us."

"But . . . I know I left it here," Nils insisted.

"Drop it, you nincompoop. We've got to keep an eye on the woods, even if we're pretty sure the Lolness kid won't be coming this way."

The others were already outside. Nils stayed by the

chair, deep in thought. At last, he moved to follow the group. But when he got to the door, he realized that he hadn't blown out the candle. Nils went back over to the table, took a deep breath . . .

And stopped short.

Toby's note was lit up in front of him by the flickering candle.

For a few seconds, his heart hung in the balance. Should he raise the alarm? In a flash, Nils could see his friend's face again, and everything that had brought them together during their time in the Summit.

These were Nils's happiest memories, no doubt about it. The unfamiliar pleasure of having someone to talk to.

But instantly he thought of his father calling him a big sissy in front of everybody: according to him, Nils was too soft and dreamy for a woodcutter's son. He imagined how proud his father would be if he discovered the fugitive's trail. He, Nils, whose father had so little faith in him, would become the hero of the whole Tree.

So Nils called out. His father's bulky figure appeared. He saw Toby's message, elbowed Nils out of the way, and roared, "Why didn't you say so sooner, you big sissy!"

His father bounded outside, waving the note and shouting, "He's not far! We'll get him!"

Huddled in the corner of the room, Nils was sobbing his heart out; his whimpers were painful as he hit his hand against his head.

"Sorry . . . Sorry . . . Oh, no . . . Toby . . ."

A draft snuffed out the candle.

ᘓ

Toby might have gotten an hour's head start, but everybody now knew that he was following the axis of the Main Trunk. The tiny fugitive didn't realize he'd been pinpointed.

He decided to cut across toward the humid northern slopes, where his familiarity with the Low Branches would give him an advantage. He wasn't afraid of the slippery zones, which he attacked barefoot, with his shoes knotted to his belt, Elisha-style.

He'd eaten a portion of his rations and was feeling refreshed. Toby silently thanked Nils for the meal he had unwittingly provided him.

A bit higher in the branches, Nils stood up, pale-faced and desperate.

The new hunters gathered in a clearing, where they were given their instructions by Razor, Joe Mitch's right-hand man. The fugitive was a millimeter and a half tall, thirteen years old, and had a small horizontal scar on his cheek. He had to be caught alive. A bounty of one million golden coins had just been promised to the person who captured him.

When they learned the size of the bounty, the woodcutters looked at one another. They would have to work in the lichen forests for a hundred years to earn half that amount.

"And what's he done, this Toby?" inquired a bold woodcutter with very short white hair.

"Crime against the Tree," said Razor bluntly.

His answer was met with murmurings. Nobody knew what it meant, but it must be very serious if so much effort and money were at stake.

The woodcutters set off in pairs in every direction. These peaceful men of the woods suddenly felt violent, stirred up by the promise of the reward. Some carried their work axes, others hunting spears.

Meanwhile, the men who had come down from the Treetop to hunt Toby were resting in another clearing, a bit higher in the lichen woods. They were fast asleep, and deafening snores could be heard rising from the hundreds of sleeping bodies.

The horrible Torn, Joe Mitch's left-hand man, had been assigned the task of setting them back on the chase. He went over to a small group that was mounting guard around a fire.

"The woodcutters have just set out."

"Really?"

"That's what I've been told," Torn confirmed.

"Are they looking for the kid?"

"And they'll catch him too, even though you're the ones who've worn him out all the way from the top. You'd better get going before they find him. One million. Just think of that! Get a move on, boys!"

One man got up. Then a second. The gold was already glowing before their tired eyes. Word spread. Tired as they were, they roused themselves, one after another, and set off again.

A competition between the two groups had begun.

The hunters from the Treetop wouldn't think twice about setting their ants on any woodcutters who got in their way. The woodcutters, meanwhile, used their knowledge of the forest to lay traps and sabotage shortcuts. It was all-out war.

This rivalry, combined with Toby's nimbleness, meant he should have reached the Low Branches ahead of his pursuers.

But he could only move under the cover of night, while the others hardly ever stopped.

The woodcutters were particularly hardy, because they were used to crisscrossing their forest, as well as climbing the bark mountains that form the regular landscape of the Main Trunk. They were also fresher; they'd only been on the chase for a night and a day, which is why they were sure they would be the first to find Toby.

So when news of Toby's capture reached them in the middle of the second night, it was greeted with anger and surprise.

"The hunt's over!"

"What?"

"They've got him."

The announcement had been made by a woodcutter with gray eyes.

"Who got him?" the two others wanted to know.

"The men from the Treetop; they caught him after a three-hour chase. He looks pretty rough . . ."

"How did they find him?"

"He was walking at the bottom of a bark valley. He'd left the lichen bushes and didn't realize they were trailing him. There was still a little bit of daylight left. A group of men was walking on the ridgeway. They spotted the kid at about six o'clock in the evening."

"What about us? How did he slip through our fingers?"

"Well, what we do know is he gave them a run for

their money." The man smiled. "I wouldn't like to have been in their shoes. He kept them going up and down those peaks for three hours. When they finally cornered him, they brought him down into the big clearing. They were so fed up, they dragged him on the end of a rope for hours. The kid's in really bad shape. They're saying he looks like an open sore."

Nils's father laughed. "The instructions were to find him alive, but not necessarily kicking!"

Norz Amen had lost his wife when Nils was born, and he had never worked out how to behave toward his son. People thought Norz was nasty. Actually, he was just a big clumsy woodcutter who was very unhappy. But that didn't stop him from being boorish as he guffawed dirtily and kept saying, "Oh, yes! They've made mincemeat of that Lolness boy!"

Norz Amen swung his ax onto his shoulder and set off toward the big clearing with his two colleagues. They had several hours on foot ahead of them. The rumor was that Joe Mitch, fat Joe Mitch himself, was going to present the reward to the four hunters who had found Toby. The ceremony would take place in the clearing, close to Norz's house.

But Norz wasn't thinking about the Lolness boy. In fact, Norz was thinking about Nils.

He was having a few regrets.

He kept telling himself he should not have gotten so angry when Nils found Toby's message. Norz never managed to be kind to his son. He realized this as he walked along, and he turned his head so his two friends wouldn't see his eyes filling with tears.

He was thinking about his wife. A girl lighter than his ax when he hoisted her onto his shoulder. He had no idea why she had fallen in love with such a big hulking woodcutter who had trouble expressing his feelings.

Above all, he had no idea how he had survived her death.

For the first time, he realized that Nils, with his love of words, took after his mother. Norz preferred the language of rough-and-tumble gestures. A thump on the back for "I like you," a slap in the face for "I disagree."

And for the first time, Norz recognized that he blamed his son. Secretly, he blamed Nils for causing his wife's death.

Why was it that on this particular night, as he walked toward the great clearing, Norz finally understood that the tragedy had nothing to do with Nils? How did he come to realize that Nils was actually a part of her that had lived on?

Burly Norz Amen suddenly began to love his son. As if a bridge of the finest silk had been woven between them by a spider from the heavens.

How strange, the unfamiliar pitter-patter of his heart. He was even eager to see Nils's face again, after those long hours of giving chase.

If the two other woodcutters had been able to hear this giant's thoughts as he made his way to the clearing, they would have teased him and called him a sissy too.

꿈

In woodcutters' jargon, when a forest has been drastically cut back, you talk about a "pale cut" because the bark looks like a pale stain on the dark spread of the forest. But at dawn on this particular day, right in the heart of the Tree's branches, the great clearing was dark with people. Woodcutters mingled with the hunters who had come down from the Treetop. They all wanted to see the person who had made them run: enemy number one, the thirteen-year-old criminal—Toby Lolness.

Norz Amen was leaning on a lichen stump at the edge of the clearing. He was trying to catch sight of Nils in the crowd. He had made up his mind to talk to him, father to son. He couldn't see him yet. He was grappling for the right words. He would start with, "The thing is, Nils . . ."

But then it got too personal.

They saw Joe Mitch appear, flanked as usual by Razor and Torn. Torn was carrying a case that looked like it was bulging with money. Joe Mitch's hands rested just where his belly began. He couldn't clasp his hands in front of him. He was one of the few people who had never seen his own belly button, because his view was blocked by the mountain of his belly.

Joe Mitch stared blankly at the group heading toward him.

There were four of them. They had put Toby in a bag, which they were dragging. The four hunters had tried to smarten themselves up to receive their money. They had plastered their hair down with water, giving

each of them a ridiculous side part that made their hair
flop over one eye.

One of them began to address Joe Mitch so loudly,
the entire clearing could hear. His voice trembled with
emotion.

"Friendly Neighbor . . ."

He cleared his throat. Joe Mitch insisted on being
called Friendly Neighbor.

"Friendly Neighbor, here's the prey we've been chasing for days. I'd just like to apologize for the condition of
the goods—you see they got a bit damaged on the way
back."

The crowd laughed, and Norz felt obligated to follow
suit.

A cigarette butt dangled from Joe Mitch's lips. He
started chewing it like a piece of gum.

He always did that, Joe Mitch. He would light his
cigarette, chew it, swallow it, burp, spit it back up again,
relight it, chew it again, swallow it again. Charming.
Delightful, in fact.

This time, he burped it back up between his lips, took it in his fat sausage-like fingers, and used it to scratch his ear. He popped it back into his mouth, and the butt disappeared for some time.

One of the four hunters wanted to shake his hand, but Mitch wasn't even looking at him. He had sat down on a box that had disappeared under his astronomically large posterior. Razor had even stepped back a little so his boss wouldn't squash him if the box suddenly collapsed under his weight.

"What d'you want us to do, Friendly Neighbor?" asked the hunter.

Joe Mitch glanced at Torn and his suitcase. Quick slimy glances were his way of giving orders.

"Open the bag," Torn croaked.

Trembling, the four hunters bent over the sack. They paused before opening it.

One of them piped up, "We did warn you, he's a little worse for the wear. But he's still breathing . . ."

Even from far away, Norz recognized the little body they took out of the bag.

It was Nils.

9
The Crater

Norz Amen's piercing cry cut through the early autumn morning.

The crowd rose to its feet.

Norz rushed to the center of the clearing, shoving aside everyone in his path. This random violence and a cry of pain were the only ways he could express himself.

"Niiiiiiiiiillllllls!"

Most of the woodcutters had also recognized the young Amen boy as the son of one of their own. But no one grasped the real tragedy being played out. They watched an enormous crazed man running toward a blood-spattered child.

The four hunters didn't have the foggiest idea what was going on, which was probably just as well. When you're about to be beaten to a pulp, there is no great advantage in knowing about it ahead of time.

As for Joe Mitch, Razor, and Torn, they didn't flinch but just stood there, mouths wide open, staring at the sack and the child. All they knew was that it wasn't Toby.

Norz hurled himself to the ground, taking Nils in his arms. The boy's eyes were wide open. He was staring at his father. Norz was no longer ashamed of his own tears, which fell on his son's wounds.

"Nils, my own special Nils . . ."

Nils had a horizontal mark from his lip to his cheek. It wasn't a scar like Toby's, but a mark that had been painted on. Norz had remembered the description they had been given: thirteen years old, a scar on his cheek. Yes, with that brown mark, you could have mistaken Nils for Toby.

"Why?" groaned Norz Amen. "Why?"

He stood up, holding the child in his arms.

"Why?"

He put his ear to his son's face. Nils was trying to say something. His mouth moved a fraction. A barely audible whisper, a breath, escaped his blue lips.

"For . . . Toby . . ."

Norz understood in a flash. Nils had wanted to save Toby. He had deliberately drawn that scar on his face. He had tried to pass himself off as Toby. He had interrupted a child-hunt involving thousands of men. He had allowed himself to be dragged for three hours over the roughest bark to win time for Toby. He had risked his own life for that of his friend.

What Norz was experiencing right now was something very new. And it put a stop to his shouting and tears.

Norz recognized how brave his son was.

This child, whom he had never looked at closely, whom he had never really listened to, his own son was quite simply a hero.

A hero.

Norz Amen stood there, like a giant in the middle of the clearing. The crowd was hushed.

Norz noticed a faint clicking sound. He glanced round. It was the teeth of the four hunters. The chattering teeth were accompanied by a tapping noise. The knees of the four unfortunate men were knocking together, beating out a rhythm of fear.

If Norz Amen had been a hero too, he would have walked past them. "This is my son," he would have said, with a dark look, and he would have gone back home, carrying Nils in his arms. But Norz was just the hero's father. So, for a few moments, he entrusted Nils to a friend's arms. He approached the leader of the four terrified hunters, then looked him up and down. The man was still trembling and he'd started to drool.

"I th-th-think there's b-b-been some kind of mis-s-stake," he managed to stutter.

"So do I," said Norz.

There are different accounts of what happened in the minute that followed. Either Norz grabbed the leader by the neck in order to knock out the other three or he banged them against each other in pairs, like cymbals. Or he seized all four of them in his arm, like a bunch of flowers, and whacked them with his free hand. Or else they flattened themselves on the ground like a pile of slug dung before he got a chance to raise his hand against them.

Norz swore the last version was true. But the first is more likely.

Norz Amen took his son back in his arms and disappeared into the crowd.

Joe Mitch's cigarette butt took a long time to pop back up again between his lips. At one point, it was even seen poking out of a nostril. Mitch was in a thick, foul mood. Torn had taken the suitcase under his arm. Like the coward he was, Razor couldn't resist going over to kick one of the hunters who was lying there, crushed, on the ground.

Only three words were heard on the subject of Toby, three words that were spat out by Joe Mitch as they bounced on his triple chin like spittle.

"I want him."

But that morning, the woodcutters decided not to continue with the hunt for Toby, because the Amen son had been the victim of this child-chase.

That day has been remembered as Nils Amen Day. For the first time, the woodcutters chose not to obey Joe Mitch, the Friendly Neighbor. They went back home instead.

Whether he survived his wounds or not, Nils had already made a difference to the history of the Tree and to Toby's story too.

As it turned out, Nils did survive. His mission was not over yet.

The woodcutters set off into their forests. And everyone else who had been chasing Toby from the Treetop resumed their hunt for the diminutive criminal. As they left the clearing, they stared long and hard at the suitcase of money tucked under Torn's arm. Money. That is what they wanted.

It didn't occur to any of them that there wasn't a single bill in that suitcase. Joe Mitch, who was as deceitful as he was cruel, never had any intention of parting with a single coin. All anyone would have found in that suitcase were a few grisly devices to make Toby talk once he was captured.

What Joe Mitch didn't know was that on the morning after his fourth night on the run, Toby had reached the damp region of the Lower Colonies. This hefty chunk of branches was owned outright by the Friendly Neighbor. Without realizing it, Toby had entered the forbidden zone. He was on Joe Mitch's turf now.

Joe Mitch had a gang of one hundred and fifty men

at his service, plus the thousands of people who followed him because they had no choice. Those one hundred and fifty men were the dirtiest scoundrels the Tree had ever produced. A hundred and fifty pieces of scum, but equal to a hundred thousand in cruelty and stupidity. Most of them worked on Joe Mitch's enormous property.

Toby ran the risk of meeting one of them at any moment, and being chopped up into mincemeat for the weevils. But he knew nothing of this and just continued his way through the bleak landscape where the bark hung down in wasted tatters. Toby had never passed through here before on his way to the Low Branches. But he realized that the Low Branches looked like paradise compared to these gray, disease-stricken middle regions.

Toby jumped to the side and hid behind a strip of bark peel.

He had heard a noise. It was mid-morning and the first time he had continued to walk after daybreak, but his growing impatience was starting to make him take risks. He would be in the Land of Onessa tomorrow, back on home ground. Just the idea of it made him forget the dangers.

From his hiding place, he watched a gloomy-looking procession go by.

He saw the weevil first. One of the biggest weevils he had ever come across. It was bound with ropes, which were being pulled taut by a dozen men in hats. These

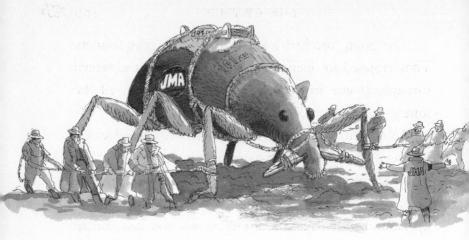

men had the letters JMA printed on the backs of their leather coats.

Toby quickly realized where he was. Even after six years of exile, he'd heard of Joe Mitch Arbor, the destruction business owned by the Friendly Neighbor.

The men called out to their coworkers as they tugged at the ropes on either side of the weevil.

"Don't let him go," one of them shouted.

"Every night a few get away. It'll just mean one more in the wild . . ."

"If they decide to count, they'll realize a weevil's missing."

"The boss has got so many, he's lost count," someone else said.

So, Toby was very close to Joe Mitch's rearing farms. He decided to follow the small group that was accompanying the animal toward the enclosure. He knew that escaped weevils were a great threat to the Tree. A weevil can dig out three times its own bulk in a day. At that rate, it wouldn't take long to reduce the Tree to sawdust.

The group reached a fence that girdled the branch. They stopped to open the vast gates and let the weevil through. It was trussed up like a sausage, with all the ropes.

Toby, who was watching from a ways off, decided he'd seen enough. Lying flat on the ground, he was about to turn and face the opposite direction when another man, also wearing a Joe Mitch Arbor hat and coat, rose up behind him. Luckily, the man was too agitated to notice Toby. He shouted at his coworkers: "There are a hundred hunters on their way. They've come down from the Treetop. They're looking for the kid. They'd better not see a weevil on the loose."

One of the men tugging at the beast used his thumb to push his hat up. Toby recognized him right away.

He'd seen the same man in the Low Branches a few weeks earlier. Just thinking about it made him shudder.

He was no taller than Toby, but he had a wrinkled, yellowish face you couldn't forget. Most noticeable of all was how small his head was, so small that his hat kept falling over his eyes.

"Open the gate, you bunch of dimwits!" he ordered.

Toby had no time to think. He was caught between the enclosure and the hunters bearing down on him. His only hope lay on the other side. He had to climb over. The man with the small head was noisily giving orders.

At this level in the Lower Colonies, the bark is soggy and rotten, and sometimes you even sink right up to your knees. So, as he crawled along, only Toby's head stuck out from the gloop of decomposed wood. He took advantage of the distraction caused by the men who were pressing against the gate and trying to open it as they got bogged down.

While the boss with the pin-size yellow head was bellowing, Toby worked his way through the mud like a maggot.

He slithered directly toward the enormous weevil, which was ten times his size. Only Toby's eyes and forehead stuck out of the goo. With just one millimeter separating them, he passed Pinhead who was busy insulting his men. Toby crawled between the weevil's legs, pulled himself up a bit, then grabbed hold of a rope belted around the beast's belly. He tugged hard and slipped his feet into another rope behind. Just then, the gate creaked open and the procession took off again.

Toby was attached to the weevil, which had started to stir.

And that was how they entered the enclosure. A mud-caked Toby blended into the animal's body. Pinhead went on giving orders while nudging his hat, which kept falling back down over half his face.

They shut the gates behind them.

The weevil and its keepers walked on for over an hour before Pinhead shouted, "Halt!"

Slowly, he went over to the animal, made the men step back, and ran his hand under the weevil's belly.

He grabbed the cord and yanked it free.

The animal could move freely again, unencumbered.

Toby had lowered himself into the mud just a moment before—just in time. From a distance, he saw the animal wade off down the slope. The men climbed in the opposite direction.

For a while Toby lay there in the mud, not moving. It was nearly midday. A disgusting smell greeted his nostrils.

The young fugitive began to regret that he had ever come this way.

A few hours earlier, he had thought he was close to his destination. But now here he was in an enclosure, hemmed in by barricades and barbed wire. How would he ever get out?

There were two options: the direction taken by the men or the path taken by the weevil. He made the same choice as the insect and wasn't disappointed by what he found after dragging himself through the mud for an hour.

There are some sights you never forget. Others are the look of things to come. Before Toby's eyes was a double effect. A monstrous vision that engraved itself on the memory forever.

Toby came to a stop on the edge of a vast hole—a gigantic crater in the branch, with open sky above it. But the crater appeared to be living: it teemed, it swayed, like a bubbling stink. An army of weevils was digging and rummaging around in the soft wood, their feet stuck in the mud. Branded on their carapaces were the initials of Joe Mitch Arbor: JMA.

Hundreds of animals were reared on this farm, and they had been mining the branches for years, digging the sordid JMA housing projects that supposedly protected the Tree from the problem of overpopulation.

What impressed Toby was the fact that he had read a description in his father's files that bore an extraordinary resemblance to this spectacle. Sim Lolness had predicted this kind of defacement down to the last detail. The crater was even described in a book that had come out six years earlier, *The World Crumbles Away,* and then in an article, "Splendor and Crumbling." Following those two publications, Joe Mitch had submitted a law to the Grand Council, banning paper, books, and newspapers. It was a so-called ecological law, to respect the Tree. But its main purpose was to silence Professor Lolness once and for all. Luckily, the law hadn't been passed on that occasion.

Toby spent a long time just staring at this horrendous sight. Now he understood the reasons for the great weakening in the Tree, which his father had noticed during his six years in the Low Branches. Simply by studying the temperature curves, Professor Lolness had discovered the summers were getting hotter. Toby reveled in those longer, lighter summers, but his father seemed worried.

"Things don't change without a reason," he kept saying.

That phrase was his golden rule.

He explained the change by way of the holes in the outer layer of the leaves at the top of the Tree. Even at

dozens of meters below, Sim Lolness could deduce the changes happening in the Treetop.

Facedown in the mud, Toby stirred from his daydreams. He wanted to start crawling again and make his way around the crater, but it felt as if he was pinned to the ground, unable to move. He kept on trying, thinking it must be a cramp. Still on his stomach, he ran his hand over the backs of his legs to massage them and get them working again.

That was when he felt something hard bearing directly down on him. Something hard, smooth, rounded . . .

He managed to turn his head a fraction and saw a boot. A boot that was squashing him into the mud. With a sweep of his arm, Toby tried to push the boot out of the way, but it wasn't on its own. There was another boot. Toby's face went *splat.*

When you find yourself confronted by two boots in the muck and you hear a stupid sniggering, you can be pretty sure there is someone in the boots.

After the boots and the laughter, Toby heard a voice. A voice he recognized. It was Pinhead, that revolting character in charge of the operation to get the weevil back into the enclosure.

"So, brat. Paying a little visit, are we?"

This time, Toby knew it was all over.

For a split second, he wondered about letting himself be suffocated in the mud, to escape Joe Mitch's men.

10
A Messenger

The powerful might of Joe Mitch and his men had continued to spread during the years the Lolness family was in exile. But Toby and his parents didn't hear anything about it. In the Low Branches, it was impossible to find out what was going on in the rest of the Tree.

Not a single letter had arrived for them in that period, nor a single newspaper. The only news they could get hold of came from the Asseldor family.

The Asseldors had lived in the Low Branches for a very long time. While the few people who populated that region tended to be relative newcomers, the Asseldors had been living there for several generations. Father Asseldor had even been born in the Low Branches. His wife came from higher up, but their three sons and two daughters had grown up on Seldor Farm, which was a place that fascinated Toby.

The farm marked the beginning of the Low Branches. It was an old house, dug out in the old-fashioned way, with big rooms and vaulted ceilings. Grandfather Asseldor had built it with his own hands. He had arrived with a New Branch dream: living together, united for a better life. He had created Seldor, a little paradise in a hostile world.

Grandfather Asseldor was long since dead, but now a father and mother and five children made the dream of a New Branch live on. It was a splendid farm. The family managed to produce everything it needed to survive. Never any more. The aim of the Asseldors was to not depend on anyone else. They sold nothing and bought nothing. But, luckily, they knew how to share.

Toby could turn up after five or six hours of walking, without giving the Asseldors any advance warning, and he always felt that they had been expecting him. There was his place, set at the big table along with the seven others. There was a remarkable atmosphere at those meal-times. Everyone sang, and joked, and drank as much as they liked. The boys, who were in their twenties, had hearty appetites. The two girls, a bit younger, weren't far behind. They dressed up for each meal as if it were a party or a wedding. They were ten years older than Toby, but he thought they were incredibly beautiful, intelligent, and witty. He talked about them to Elisha, who didn't seem all that fond of the conversation.

For an only child like Toby, the Asseldors became an

adoptive family. So it felt as if his own brother were leaving when the third son, Mano, decided to go away.

Mano had always been different from the other Asseldor children. Even physically, he seemed less robust than his two brothers, less fresh-faced and hearty than his sisters. He was less talkative at the table; he laughed less, and he ate without much enthusiasm.

Worse, he didn't play a musical instrument.

That was like someone without a shell being born into a family of snails. Music was one half of the Asseldors' life. They all sang and played superbly. Except for Mano, who could barely tap his knees in time to the rhythm.

They had tried every instrument with him, from the bango to the extraordion, but finally he'd dug his heels in and refused to give it another try. In the evenings, Toby often saw Mano discreetly leave the room while his sisters were singing like a choir of angels and the others were creating an entire orchestra with their mouths. Even Toby had been co-opted to play the marbles. He'd become the best marble player in Seldor. All you had to do was rub two marbles together to create a sound. But Mano couldn't even play the marbles properly.

One evening, Toby had seen Father Asseldor follow Mano to the front of the house.

"Where are you going?" the father asked.

"Don't know."

"What's the matter with you? Don't you want to be like the others?"

"No," said Mano.

"What is it, Mano? Take a look at your brothers and sisters. Don't they look happy?"

"Yes."

"Well, just do what they're doing!"

Mano flew into a rage. "We're here because our grandfather decided not to do what everyone was doing, but to come and create Seldor instead. And now you're asking me to be like everyone else?"

Toby stayed hidden so he could listen.

"You don't talk like an Asseldor, Mano. You don't do anything like an Asseldor."

"I know. That's why I'm leaving, Dad."

Mano's father didn't say anything. He assumed his son wanted a few minutes outside to get some fresh air.

"Don't be long—we've got the honey to harvest tomorrow."

Mano didn't turn around. Father Asseldor noticed Toby.

"He just needs to get some air," he explained.

"Yes," said Toby.

When Toby went back to visit the Asseldors a month later, there was a very different atmosphere at the table. Toby turned up in the middle of supper, on a June evening. Lola, the second daughter, got up to give him a plate. Her jolliness was a bit forced.

"Mr. Lolness, I haven't set you a place."

Lola always called Toby "Mr. Lolness," even though he was barely ten years old at the time. It made the little boy's heart swell up.

"Miss Lola, you're forgiven because you've done your hair the way I like it, with braided buns," Toby said.

The men let out a few halfhearted whistles.

Normally, one of the boys would have jumped on the table ready to challenge Toby to a duel for making advances toward his sister. Toby would grab a stick to defend himself, and it would all end in laughter.

But there was no duel that evening, and no scene of jealousy from the other sister, Lila, despite her talent for pretending to burst into tears.

The first time she did it, Toby fell for it completely

and whispered into the ear of the young lady who was over twice his age, "Don't worry—I'm very fond of you too, Miss Lila."

Everybody got the giggles after that. It was the only time Toby had felt nervous in the house at Seldor.

On this particular June evening, however, it wasn't Toby who was feeling ill at ease, but the others. Something rang hollow in the silence around the Asseldors' table. Toby soon saw what was wrong as he glanced around at the assembled family.

Mano wasn't there.

That was why they hadn't set the extra place for a passing guest. An empty plate would have been a bitter reminder of Mano's absence. Father Asseldor watched Toby, who didn't even pick up his fork.

"Mano's gone. He went up to the Treetop. He says he wants to try his luck there."

"I think he'll stand a better chance of succeeding up there," Mrs. Asseldor added. "He wasn't made to live in Seldor. I just hope he'll write to us."

Lila and Lola were unapologetically red-eyed. Both brothers stared down at their food. Toby realized it would be difficult for them to forgive Mano for leaving them like that.

Mrs. Asseldor's wish came true. After two months, they received a letter. It was full of hope. Mano told them he had found a job in sales, that he was his boss's favorite employee, and that he was hoping for a promotion.

The whole family read and reread this letter from the Treetop as if it were a message from the sky. The men didn't want to soften too quickly, but the women were instantly delighted.

"I told you so. Each to his own path . . ." Mrs. Asseldor kept saying.

And so Mano's letters became special moments in the life of Seldor Farm. The family would gather around the table. Mrs. Asseldor would perch her reading glasses on the end of her nose. With each letter, her hands trembled less, her voice grew clearer. For the letters told a tale of dazzling progress. The boss, who was getting old, had entrusted Mano with running his business. Mano had also set up a subsidiary business, which would soon outstrip the first. He was now the director of two sales companies. Mano said that he would come back to see

them soon, that he was just waiting for the right time—
and that he had a wardrobe with fifty-seven ties. The
Asseldor family weren't too sure what *sales* meant or what
you would use even one tie for, let alone fifty-seven, but
they all kept telling themselves, "Each to his own path."

Toby would often tell his parents about Mano's
adventures. It was the only news that reached them from
the Treetop. Like everybody else, Maya Lolness was very
impressed by the success of the Asseldor boy.

But Toby's father always adopted a rather stern tone.
"I'm puzzled by what you tell me. Doesn't your friend
Mano ever talk about anything else? About life in the
Heights, and what things are like for the people living
there?"

"He says that the people who want to succeed have
plenty of opportunities. He says everything happens very
quickly."

Professor Lolness didn't like things that happened
quickly, so his grumpy expression didn't change.

"I can't help thinking that, apart from the young
Asseldor boy and one or two others, there are fewer and
fewer people who are happy in the Treetop. I don't have
any information to back that up, but it's the impression I
get," he muttered to Toby.

"Sim!" exclaimed Maya. "Your son has just given you
good news from the Treetop and you're still pouting.
Why don't you celebrate something for once?"

"I'd like to very much," agreed Sim, returning to his
study.

The news from Mano was the only information that reached the Low Branches, so it was quite a surprise when a letter arrived from the Grand Tree Council.

The letter reached the Lolness home in Onessa at the beginning of August. The messenger had a tooth-less smile, a face yellow as pollen, and a very small head. It was the first time Toby and his friends had seen the hat, coat, and boots of one of Joe Mitch's men. Pinhead held out the letter.

"I'll wait over there for your answer, Grandaddy-o."

The man was talking to Sim Lolness. He had just called him "Grandaddy-o." He grabbed the professor's little bottle of walnut liqueur from the table.

Toby's father had arrived with that bottle six years earlier. He drank a single drop from it after supper every night, while staring at the fire.

Walnut liqueur was very rare. It was made from a few walnuts that squirrels had left behind in holes in the Tree. Sim had of course written a book, *Where Do Walnuts Come From?*—a poetic work on the possibility of life beyond the Tree. He had imagined another Tree some-where that produced walnuts. His exasperated colleagues had asked Sim to choose between poetry and science.

The professor didn't dare say that he had already made his choice.

So, the three Lolnesses saw Pinhead wander off with

the walnut alcohol. He sat down a little farther away and started sipping.

"That's your bottle, Dad," said Toby.

"Let him be, my son. It doesn't matter. He's walked a long way . . . "

It was years since the Lolnesses had opened a letter, and the professor turned it over for a long time in his hands, as if trying to decide which angle to attack it from.

"Come on, Toby," said Maya, leading her son outside.

"No, you can both stay."

Sim sat down, with his back to the window, and started to read out loud:

> *"Your Excellence, Professor,*
>
> *In the spirit of a scientific revival, we would be most honored to reinstate you at our Council. Time has passed on your former mistakes; the moment has come for science in the Tree to find its inspiration again. Your home at The Tufts awaits you, as does our worthy Council."*

Sim Lolness stopped. His wife and son were staring at him. They were trying to read a reaction in his expression, but Sim's face was inscrutable. So many contradictory ideas and feelings were fighting, it was like a book left out in the rain, with the ink running from one page to another. Scenes of joy, anger, sadness, anguish, hope, revolt, shame, love, and hate were being projected onto a dark puddle.

What Toby and Maya felt first was pride. They wanted to leap into Sim's arms.

But Sim continued reading:

> *"To consolidate this fresh start, you will consent, for one year only, to be observed by the Neighborhood Committees, under the supreme direction of the Friendly Neighbor, Joe Mitch."*

This last sentence prompted another downpour of contradictory messages on the professor's face. Another shower, which swept all the rest away and left only one expression glinting in Sim's eyes: fury.

He started seething, ranting and raving, cursing. Neither Toby nor his parents knew what these Neighborhood Committees were, but Toby saw his father leap to his feet.

Joe Mitch! Just the name drove the professor wild.

Sim scrunched the letter into a tight ball. He headed toward the door, which he kicked open before striding toward Joe Mitch's messenger, who was standing, half drunk, in front of the house. With blurred vision, Pinhead saw Sim draw near. He had taken his hat off, and his head looked very tiny indeed. He was holding the bottle and smiling as he swayed from foot to foot.

"Well, Grandaddy-o, are we heading on up, as in

'hitting the branch' with yer old lady and the brat? You've made up yer mind?"

Pinhead's mouth was wide open, and he was sniggering like a simpleton.

Toby saw his father deftly throw the crumpled ball of paper so that it landed in the horrible man's mouth. By the time Pinhead had realized what had happened, his mouth was already shut.

His eyes were bulging, and he was shaken by a series of jolts and hiccups. From pollen yellow, Joe Mitch's man turned pale green before going lots of colors never before seen in the Tree. He ended up as white as a fluffy cloud when he realized that he had just swallowed his message.

Sim Lolness watched him pick up his hat. Sim was bigger than he was. The man didn't dare answer him back, especially since the ball was starting to play havoc with his stomach.

"A long time ago," said the professor, "there used to be a primitive practice. People would open up the stomachs of animals to find the answers to their questions. They called them omens. Tell that to your boss. You've got the answer in your belly."

Between belches, Pinhead managed to say, "I'll get my revenge."

And he staggered out of sight.

Toby and his parents stayed in front of the house for some time. Sim took off his glasses and wiped his face.

Toby went to pick up the bottle. He held it out to his father.

"It's empty."

"That's just as well," said Sim. "It was bad for my heart."

He sat down in front of the door. They heard the sound of something snapping. He had just sat on his glasses.

For the first time, Toby realized that his father would turn into an old man one day. He was only fifty-six, but that guy had called him "Grandaddy-o," and now, sitting on the threshold, Sim looked exhausted. Maya Lolness hugged her husband and kissed him on the cheek.

"Sim, darling, I told you not to get into a fight with your classmates," she said gently.

Sim Lolness hid his face in his wife's neck and muttered, like a child, "He started it."

Toby headed off to give his parents some time alone. As he walked along a rip in the bark, a bit farther off on the branch, he thought about the letter-bearer's last words: "I'll get my revenge."

Which explains why, just a few weeks later, Toby would rather have been anywhere than under Pinhead's hard and frosty boots. His mouth and nostrils were starting to fill up with mud.

11
W. C. Rolok

The pressure from the man's feet eased off slightly, and Toby raised his head for a second. But Pinhead retaliated by pushing him straight back down into the mud again.

When his captor let him go for a second time, Toby sensed he wanted to say something.

"What your dad did to me . . . I found it a bit hard to swallow."

"Swallow . . . a ball of paper?" Toby asked cheekily.

Pinhead shoved his face back into the mud.

This time he left him down there for nearly a minute. But Toby guessed that Pinhead wouldn't let him die without inflicting extra punishments. Strange as it may sound, these punishments were Toby's chance to play for time. His only hope was for Pinhead to be even more cruel.

And that is exactly what happened.

Pinhead dragged Toby over to a bark hill that loomed over the crater. He tied him up tightly, so Toby's feet and hands were trapped. The weevils began to draw near, in groups of two or three. Pinhead produced a long whip, which he cracked to keep the beasts at bay. Toby watched as Pinhead's beaming face was made even uglier by the pleasure of causing pain.

Under that mask of mud, Toby was managing to remain calm. First, he reflected that being cruel sometimes makes you rich and powerful, but it always makes you ugly. Then he wondered what truly horrific and monstrous idea his tormentor would come up with next. Would he abandon him to the insects? Did he want to exterminate Toby, right here in the mud?

But Pinhead's idea was even nastier. It was as disgusting as he was.

He took two small white capsules out of his pocket, prompting all the weevils to turn their heads his way.

"Hey, brat-face, don't they just love 'em! We give these balls of sap concentrate as a reward to the best workers. They can smell them from miles away. Sometimes we put them inside knots of hardened wood. The weevils smash through the wood to get to the capsule."

He threw a capsule to the bottom of the crater. Twenty animals rushed off after it. A young weevil and two females were almost crushed in the fight. Toby kept his eyes on Pinhead, who was twirling his whip. "I've got one left. What should I do with it?"

Toby could have imagined just about anything except what happened next.

Pinhead continued: "It's quite simple. Nothing new. I'll just copy what your dad did with that message. I'll make you swallow the capsule, and then I'll stand far back. If these creepy-crawlies can detect a capsule that's ten centimeters below the bark, they won't have any problem finding it in your innards—even if it does mean clearing a bit of raw flesh to get in there. I'll count to a hundred—that should give the weevils time to do their work. And then I'll scrape you up. You'll be in a terrible mess, but there'll still be a flicker of life in you. Just another brat who won't curl up and die. I'll take you to Joe Mitch and pocket the million. That's the plan!"

He was laughing very loudly. And Toby was watching him. At a certain level of horror, fear cuts out. This had already happened to Toby. More than anything, he felt sorry for Pinhead. *Your instinct is to be cruel,* he

thought. *Mine is to survive.* So Toby just concentrated on breathing steadily. He was even starting to think more clearly again. He had found out there was a price on his head. He was worth a million. Not bad. He decided that a million was a sum worth defending.

But right now that million was trussed up like a parcel on a piece of jutting bark that was sawing his back in half.

Why did these words make Toby stop and think?

Sawing his back in half.

His mother had taught him how to read when he was three, teaching him that words are the enemy of darkness. If you choose to be their friend, they will help you out all your life. But if you don't, they'll block your path. Maya had explained that was why people talked about being "familiar" with a word or a language. They were like family to you.

It was a bumpy ride in the beginning, but Toby had made friends with words in the end. Every day, he saw them working miracles. They had rescued him from loneliness and boredom. They had been by his side to help him study with his father. Most of all, they hadn't deserted him during his conversations with Elisha.

Elisha was only familiar with a few words, but she dressed them up so that Toby risked tripping at every sentence. By listening to her, he had learned to make words come to life through both silence and the power of the human voice.

Words often whisper advice we don't hear. But this

time, Toby caught their message: "A piece of bark that's sawing my back in half . . ."

A mask of mud hid Toby's smile. If bark can saw through your back, it can saw through other things too. . . .

Gently rubbing against that bark ridge for a moment or two was all it took for the rope that had paralysed Toby's hands to be sawed in two.

Pinhead hadn't seen a thing. Toby wasn't much better off, but at least it was progress of sorts. He was careful to keep his hands behind his back. A few cracks of the whip had forced the weevils to retreat. Pinhead was walking over to Toby now, his face split by a smile that displayed the occasional tooth. He leaned over his victim, holding the capsule in his hand. Toby knew that if he swallowed the capsule, five hundred weevils would open up his belly to retrieve it.

This prospect made Pinhead throw his head back and roar with laughter. Close up, his aggressor's mouth was even more revolting than Toby had imagined. The stench of rotten eggs accompanied a vision of hell. Pinhead grabbed Toby's jaw and forced his mouth open. He slid the capsule between Toby's teeth.

Not missing a trick, the weevils were already starting to close in. Their feet and pincers glistened in the afternoon light.

Pinhead held Toby's mouth closed for as long as it took to swallow the capsule. It was time to abandon the boy to his fate, but he couldn't resist adding, "Enjoy your meal!"

Despite his exhaustion, Toby managed to say, "Thanks, but your capsule is disgusting. . . ."

"No, no . . . I was talking to the animals," Pinhead replied, indicating six or seven weevils just behind him.

He clearly thought his joke was hilarious and gave a hideous guffaw, providing Toby with a clear view of the back of his throat. Compared to the repulsive state of his palate and tonsils, Pinhead's teeth now looked positively respectable.

It was at precisely this moment that Toby drew on all his strength to spit out the capsule he had managed to keep in his cheek. It entered his torturer's giggling mouth at top speed. Pinhead's eyes registered astonishment and stupefaction followed by terror as he realized he had swallowed it.

His reaction made a pathetic sight. It was the second time one of the Lolnesses had pulled a trick on him. He fell to the ground. He was trying to spit out the capsule as he writhed about, pummeling the ground with his fists, whining in the mud like a child throwing a tantrum.

Toby turned the crisis to his advantage, untying the remaining ropes with his freed hands. He even managed to strip his enemy of all his clothes without Pinhead realizing what was going on. A few paces away, the weevils were becoming a real threat. Toby cracked the whip once, and the animals backed off briefly. Then he tied up his torturer with the lash.

The first thing Pinhead noticed when he lifted his head—as he slowly came around from his panic attack—was that he was pinned to the ground. Then he saw the weevils jostling for position and moving in on him. It was a sight that made his jaw wobble, seriously risking knocking out the last of his teeth.

Finally, Pinhead spotted a pair of boots right next to him. Rising up out of them was a shadow that reminded him of something. The shadow of a short man in a coat, with a hat that kept falling over his eyes so that it hid half his face. He let out a shriek, and the weevils pawed the ground.

The short man was him. Pinhead. It had to be a nightmare: the sap capsule taking effect. A hallucination. There were two Pinheads on the edge of the crater.

But when Pinhead-in-a-coat nudged his hat, Pinhead-in-his-birthday-suit recognized two sparkly eyes he detested. Dressed like that, Toby was the spitting image of Joe Mitch's man. Although it made Toby's flesh creep, he had just turned his toughest challenge so far into a chance to escape, which was a huge boost to his confidence.

"I'm leaving you the whip," said Toby. "The knot isn't very tight. You'll be able to get away. But I don't know which is worse—the weevil's pincers or your men's sniggers when you have to explain to them, stark naked, what an idiot you are."

Toby left Pinhead to his nightmare. A label in the coat's lining revealed he was called W. C. Rolok. To get out of the enclosure, this was the name Toby would need to go by.

He had no second thoughts as he put the weevils' crater behind him and climbed toward the top side of the branch. Toby had rammed his hat on snugly as he forced himself to slow down, imitating those stiff little steps taken by Rolok Pinhead, as well as copying the way he hunched his shoulders.

Toby knew how to imitate people's posture and gestures. One day, his parents had discovered Grandmother Alnorell playing funnyball behind their house in the Low Branches. Funnyball was a children's game—silly, but tricky—that involved playing ball with your hands on your feet.

Toby's parents, who were already shocked to find Mrs. Alnorell at their Onessa home (when they hadn't heard a squeak from her in four and a half years of exile) were even more surprised to see her galloping along with her hands on her feet pushing a hollow wooden ball. It was unimaginable. Grandmother had no idea what the word *playing* meant.

In fact, it was such a fantastic sight, they couldn't help giggling, then hooting, and finally choking they were laughing so hard. When Mrs. Alnorell spotted them, they tried to pull a straight face. But Maya's dimples kept twitching, and her eyes were streaming from trying not to chuckle.

When they were just a few millimeters away from Toby's grandmother, they got the surprise of their lives. Standing before them was their son, Toby Lolness, delighted with his joke.

After that episode, Toby would spend whole evenings making his parents laugh. He could imitate anybody, just by stooping or hunching his shoulders. His best number was called "Joe Mitch in his bath." His parents were astonished by Toby's memory, because he hadn't seen any of these people since he was seven.

He could also do "Mr. Perlush and the allowance." His grandmother's accountant was responsible for giving Toby his allowance during his vacations up in the Summit. Sim had given the accountant a few coins he was supposed to hand over to the boy each week. This prompted some very funny scenes in which Mr. Perlush would present Toby with a small gold coin, before hurriedly taking it back, then offering him a grain of gold that he recouped no less quickly, as if he'd made a mistake. He would hold out half a grain, but he just couldn't bear to let it go, so he put it back in his pocket instead. Mr. Perlush would end up claiming that he didn't have any spare change on him and that he would have to give Toby his allowance the following day.

This mimicry made Sim and Maya laugh a lot, but it also meant that Toby's father found out the little gold coins he had handed over every summer for his son's spending money had ended up lining the pockets of Radegonde Alnorell and her accountant.

A while later, when Toby-Rolok appeared in the midst of four men lying peacefully on the damp ground, it was

too late to turn back. So he just buried his hands in his pockets and tucked his chin inside his collar.

The four men had spread out their coats and were just finishing a nap. The moment they saw Rolok's shadow, they jumped to their feet, highly embarrassed.

"Boss, sorry, we were just having a quick break. . . ."

"A five-minute break . . . Sorry, Boss . . ."

"Boss . . . Sorry . . ." a third man repeated.

Toby knew he mustn't say anything. His voice would give him away. But his silence made each second more worrying for the others. In the bottom of his pocket, Toby could feel a notebook and pencil.

To ratchet up the tension, he took out the notebook, wrote down a couple of words as he looked at each man, and then turned on his heels.

He was breathing hard. As he walked, he glanced down at the notebook. He'd written *Be brave, Toby* four times. He leafed through the other pages. They were covered in the diligent handwriting of a five-year-old. It had to be Rolok's writing. On the first page, Rolok had written *Denunseyashun Noteboock beelongin to W. C. Rolok.*

Further on, there were sentences such as *Petur Salag has eated two sandwitchez insted of wun, he will be hangd 4 too hourz by the left fut.*

And *Geralt Binoo didunt hit the weeval rite, he will be hitted himsilf.*

Toby understood that Joe Mitch's men were driven by one thing: fear. Fear of being denounced, fear of being punished. Denounce the other before he denounces you. Hit so hard that they won't hit back.

After a few minutes, Toby had a nasty feeling he was being followed. He glanced over his shoulder. The four men had stolen up on him. Toby tried to walk more quickly, but the men accelerated. He made several detours, but they kept following him. In the end, he stopped dead, standing tall in his boots, and watched them coming toward him. With their hats under their arms, they looked like schoolchildren caught getting into mischief.

"Boss, we were just having our break. We want to apologize," said one of them.

"We didn't mean to," joined in the second one.

"We really want to denounce the others, if that helps . . ."

"Pouzzi keeps playing darts on Thing's butt."

"And Thing is too scared to say anything, because he lost his whip in the crater."

"He's supposed to be guarding big Rosebond, who knocked out one of the weevil's eyes. . . ."

Toby had started walking again. He was disgusted by these denunciations. All four of them trotted along behind him, never ceasing their pathetic bootlicking.

"We can tell you more serious stuff, Boss."

"Flannel and Magnus play soccer with Thing."

"They say things like, 'Curl yourself into a ball, then you'll roll better.'"

"Thing has to give all his supper to the Blett cousins."

"He does night duty for them, even though he's scared of weevils. . . ."

Not only was Toby suffering from having to listen to these mindless cruelties, but he was also starting to feel rather uncomfortable. A character was slowly being sketched through what they were saying: Thing. Thing, who was victimized by his colleagues, who was scared of the insects he was supposed to oversee all day. Poor, unlucky Thing. All of a sudden, Thing's situation seemed even worse than his own.

A few confessions had established a link between Toby and somebody he had never met.

"But Big Marlon's the worst. Tonight he's going to give the local farmers a fright. He's made a hole in the fence, behind the oil barrels."

Toby froze. Slowly, he turned around. The three words *hole, fence,* and *barrels* were more interesting to him than anything else.

One of the men asked exactly the question he wanted an answer to: "Oil barrels? What barrels?"

"The barrels, just over there. . . . I can show you as long as you don't tell Big Marlon I told you not to say it was me who told you not to say it was me—"

Toby interrupted by thumping him on the back, then pushing him forward. They started walking over toward the cans. The three others kept babbling as they followed behind.

"We'd have helped you too, you know? Us too."

These morons had just shed an extra two or three more years from their mental ages. They were regressing before Toby's eyes. One more try, and they'd be back in their mothers' wombs, no doubt the least harmful phase of their miserable lives.

They reached the fence. Sure enough, dozens of full barrels were piled there. Toby wasn't surprised to see CRUDE SAP written on each one. Just as he feared, Joe Mitch was already stockpiling the stuff.

All he needed now was the famous Balina black box to convert this fuel into destructive energy.

Toby clapped once. The four men stood to attention. He passed in front of each one, affectionately tweaking their ears to congratulate them. Actually, with his face covered by his hat, he couldn't see what he was doing, so he never knew if he had tweaked their ear, their nostril, or anything else, for that matter.

He made a sweeping gesture in front of him, to indicate they should disperse. Luckily, they understood and melted away, relieved to have been let off the hook. By pushing a few barrels, Toby found the hole in the fence and passed through to the other side.

Toby would have given anything to step out of his Rolok disguise and escape that shameful world. He would have given anything to run far away and save his skin.

But as he passed the wire fencing, Toby thought of Thing. The whipping boy for Joe Mitch's band of men.

The thought entered him like a poisoned arrow.

And he turned back.

12
And Another Thing. . .

Thing was sitting on a box. Big Marlon had told him to keep watch over it, and that he would have the life squeezed out of him if someone took it.

He had been guarding the box for an hour and a half. But he was starting to worry because he would have to check on the weevils soon. What was he supposed to do with the box, given that it was impossible to carry?

Thing was writing on a leaf of paper balanced on his lap. He was writing to his mother. Writing great long letters was all that kept him going, provided that no one tore them up, or worse yet, read them.

Being on box duty gave him a reason to stay there.

That's what he'd told his colleagues who had come running past him. They were all shouting out ridiculous stories. Insisting that everyone go to the crater because unbelievable things were happening there.

Thing was convinced it was a trap to lure him away. He was sure they wanted to play a nasty trick on him. One man had even shouted, "It's Boss Rolok! They say he's in his birthday suit in the crater, playing 'Whips and Weevils.' Hey, Thing, are you coming? Everyone's going over. . . ."

Really! Did they think he was a complete idiot?

So he stayed by himself in front of the main gallery, which doubled as a dormitory. It was a mild day, like a sunny interval in his terrible life.

Thing had been singled out by Joe Mitch's men from the start. He was a sensitive, polite, and sad boy—the ideal maggot to throw to an army of ants. And the ants in question were the Blett cousins—Big Marlon, Rosebond, and Flannel—the kind of unscrupulous savages Mitch recruited on the spot.

Mitch always made sure he hired a punching bag or whipping boy to be known as Thing. You could vent whatever you liked on this person, giving orders like, "Thing, clean my boots," or "Thing, give me your bread."

The chosen person had to forget his real name. Everybody would call him Thing from then on.

And so Thing had been chosen to play this tragic role, which nobody had ever managed to escape from. The story of the other Things proved a long litany of misery.

The last Thing had been caught trying to escape the enclosure. Nobody knew exactly what happened to him after that, but his little sister, Lala, the only family he had left, had received a letter announcing his disappear-ance. And the only explanation she got was two words: "Walk interrupted."

The Thing before that one had died during a game in which he was forced to eat both his shoes. He'd had a bit of trouble keeping the final lace down. The official cause of death was "indigestion."

Thing lived in dread of coming to a sticky end too. His only chance was to do everything to the best of his ability. He did whatever anyone told him to do, running from one task to another, doing the dishes for fifty people, eating his hat if he was asked to. But his col-leagues had sworn to have his skin, just like the others, and his duties were getting harder and harder.

"Finishing Off a Thing," as it was called, was a popu-lar sport inside the enclosure. It was all about pushing a Thing to his limit. Making him crack. Rolok had finished off the last two Things. He was always bragging about it, and had scratched a cross in his hat for each victim.

This Thing had made a mistake. Just one. He had lost his whip somewhere in the mud. If anyone told the boss, the game was up. So he was trying to stay away from Rolok the Terrible.

When he saw Rolok in the distance, cold sweat started trickling down the back of Thing's neck. The boss was wandering in front of the deserted gallery. He still hadn't yet noticed Thing, who turned away and huddled over his box to avoid being recognized.

So Thing had been right not to believe the others. That story about Rolok being in his birthday suit in the crater was an outright lie. Because here he was, just behind him, with his hat pushed down on his head. Still, they'd all gone off to that wretched crater. Were they setting up another trap for him?

Thing was crouching behind his box, head tucked in. Suddenly he heard a voice, Rolok's voice, addressing his back.

"I'm looking for someone called Thing."

Thing gave a muffled answer.

"That's me."

He took his time before turning around.

The next minute happened in slow motion. If there had been a witness to this scene who was familiar with life inside the enclosure, they wouldn't have believed their eyes.

Nothing like it had ever taken place there before.

Thing turned his head slowly.

There was Rolok standing in front of him, his hat pushed down almost to his chin. Thing cowered. But Rolok began to stagger backward, as if having a dizzy spell. Thing blinked. What on earth was Rolok up to now?

Next, Thing saw the short man come to a halt and whip off his hat. Shock and astonishment! It wasn't Rolok's yellow face under that hat at all. But a likable and familiar face. The face of a thirteen-year-old boy—Toby Lolness, the boy from the Low Branches, the most wanted fugitive in the Tree—Toby!

Thing stood up. His body drew itself up to its full height for the first time since he had entered the dreaded enclosure. He even opened his arms wide.

But the most extraordinary was still to come. To begin with, Toby just stood there, totally taken aback, but little by little his face lit up. A stunned smile spread across his eyes and then his cheeks.

In one jump, Toby leaped into the open arms.

"Mano, is that you, Mano?"

Thing held him tight.

"No, Toby . . . it's not me anymore."

They stayed like that for a while, hugging each other. Neither of them had held a friend in his arms for a long time. It was as if the air crackled around this simple gesture. Time was ticking dangerously by. It was broad daylight in the middle of the afternoon. Someone might show up at any moment, but they felt protected.

Eventually, Toby whispered, "What are you doing here, Mano Asseldor? Your letters . . . In your letters you said . . ."

"Yes," said Mano in a choked voice. "Didn't my family enjoy those letters?"

"But you made it all up!" exclaimed Toby. "You're slave to Joe Mitch's worst slaves. . . . You lied!"

"Toby! Weren't they happy to get those letters?"

Toby fell quiet. Mano had invented the whole story so his family could keep on dreaming. He had failed everywhere, wandered around for weeks on end, begging for a bowl of sapwood porridge. And then he'd been hired at Joe Mitch's. The last stop for outlaws and dropouts.

As he wrote those letters, he had made up another life for himself working in sales—a glorious life. The life he would like to have lived, the kind that makes your parents, your brothers, your two darling sisters proud.

"I'm taking you with me, Mano," said Toby.

Mano didn't say anything.

"I'm taking you with me. I'm going back to the Low Branches. Everybody will be so happy to see you."

"It's too late," Mano replied. "Leave me here. . . . Don't say a word to anyone. Forget you ever saw me."

Toby pulled back sharply from his friend.

"Never! I'll never leave you. Hurry up—they'll be back soon. Rolok will raise the alarm."

"No."

"Hurry up, Mano. They're coming. I know how to get out of here. We'll be at Seldor tomorrow."

"You don't know about shame, Toby. It's worse than death."

"That's not true. Nothing could be worse than here."

Toby tugged Mano's arm. The sound of shouting started to rise up from the crater in the distance. They couldn't stay where they were. Toby grabbed a wooden club that was lying on the ground in front of the dormitory. Holding it with both hands, he raised it up high and brought it crashing down on Big Marlon's great box. It smashed into lots of tiny pieces. Stunned, Mano watched him and cried out, "The box!"

"Since fear seems to be the only thing that motivates you."

"What am I supposed to say to Big Marlon?"

"Up to you. I'm leaving. Good-bye, Mano."

He started running, but Mano called him back: "Toby! Wait."

Toby stopped. He saw Mano bend down, pick up the club, and violently smash the remains of Big Marlon's box. Mano was raining down blow after blow, without stopping, until there were just tiny scraps left on the ground, and still he kept on going. Toby grabbed his arm.

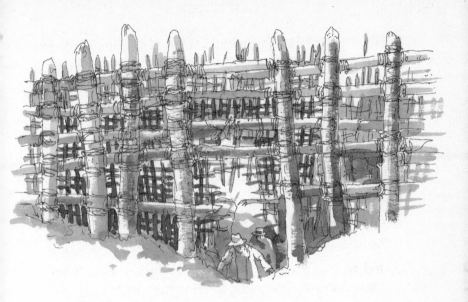

"That's enough. Come with me now."

The pair set off. The shouting behind them was getting nearer. But when they made it through the hole in the fencing, they paused for a moment.

"Thank you, Toby," whispered Mano.

Toby had taken off his coat and hurled it to the ground. Mano did the same. They threw their hats into the air.

"We're going home," Toby said simply.

And they raced toward freedom.

When the men chasing Mano Asseldor and Toby Lolness reached the hole in the fence, they were ordered to pause their search. Rolok reassembled his troops.

There were ten rows of four or five men. Rolok appeared before them, dressed in a bathrobe that reached his ankles and kept tripping him up. Rolok wasn't yellow anymore; he was transparent. His purple lips were as tight as a fly's behind.

He passed in front of the troops, who were desperately trying to keep a straight face.

Rolok had categorically refused to explain how he had ended up without a stitch of clothing on him in the crater, surrounded by the herd of weevils. The only thing he admitted was that Toby had been involved. They had gotten him out of there on a stretcher, and the rejoicing troop had accompanied their boss all the way to the dormitories.

Now he was trying not to faint with embarrassment in front of his assembled men. And, above all, in front of Joe Mitch, who appeared in the entrance to the tunnel, framed by his two shadows, Torn and Razor.

Joe Mitch had traveled down from the woodcutters' clearing to find his enclosure in a state of near chaos. He was speechless with anger and having trouble breathing; in fact, he would have gladly strangled someone.

Razor gave him the news that Thing had also disappeared. Everybody grinned as they turned to face Big Marlon, who was bright red and squirming in his seat.

His smashed box had just been discovered. He had always led people to believe that it was full of weapons and knives, but the tiny bits and pieces that had been found revealed the remains of toys for small children: a top, some dominos, moss dolls, a card signed *Mommy* and, in big flowery handwriting, *For my darling Marlonnikins, who still likes playing with his toysy-woisies.*

Big Marlon no longer had the same effect on his colleagues. In fact, he didn't seem nearly so "big" now that he'd been made to look ridiculous.

Another man stepped forward, with a coat in his hand. He held it out to Joe Mitch.

"We found this behind the fence too. Toby Lolness must have used it to make his getaway. There's a label with a name on it: W. C. Rolok."

Joe Mitch signaled to Torn, who took the coat. All eyes were on Rolok, who looked like a spat-out candy, stuck inside a bathrobe.

Torn interrogated Rolok: "Does this ring any bells?"

"I . . . I . . . Yes, that's my name, I think . . ."

"No!" exploded Mitch.

He made for Torn, shaking his head. "No," he kept spitting, as he snatched the coat and stared at the label. His big fat jowls flapped as he moved left to right.

"Yes it is!" insisted Rolok. "I swear that's my name."

"No," Mitch snapped back.

"But, Friendly Neighbor, you know perfectly well that I'm Rolok. W. C. Rolok, your head of weevil farming."

Joe Mitch was already heading off. And Torn and Razor were keeping their distance from Rolok.

"Pleeeease," whimpered Rolok, "have some pity! Who am I, then? Who am I? What's my name?"

Joe Mitch turned around one last time. Belching as only he could, he answered.

One word was enough: "Thing."

13
The Black Widow

Joe Mitch's weevil farm was only a few hours away from the Low Branches, which meant that Mano had spent the past months very close to the paradise of Seldor, and to his family. But he had been separated from them by the highest rampart of all: shame.

Now, as they made their way toward the Low Branches, Mano was starting to get his hopes up again. He was even learning a real lesson in confidence and bravery from Toby, his young guide.

Every now and then, however, he couldn't help seeing this boy in a different light, as he twirled between the branches ahead. Who was he exactly?

The Toby who Mano knew came from the Treetop. He had turned up in the Low Branches when he was barely seven, with his parents and nothing else. Mano had watched this Toby-of-the-Low-Branches grow into a bold, nimble boy, a will-o'-the-wisp, who was curious about everything and who would turn up at Seldor with shining eyes. But there was a third Toby, the one everybody had been talking about for days now.

Mano had heard the rumors about the most recent events in the life of the Lolness family. He had learned that they had gone back up to the Treetop, but he didn't know why. And then he had found out about the tragedy, the so-called treason of the Lolness family." People were talking about a "plot against the Tree," about an "unpardonable crime." The Lolnesses had betrayed the rest of the Tree. They had been condemned to die, but the Grand Tree Council had intervened to reduce the death penalty of the three guilty parties to life imprisonment. If he was found, Toby would have to rejoin his parents in captivity. But most people expected a harsher sentence to be imposed, because the Grand Council was gradually losing all its influence over the Neighborhood Committees.

One day, the Lolness family would be executed, no doubt about it.

While he stopped to catch his breath, it occurred to Mano that he might be following a dangerous terrorist. But when Toby turned to face him, Mano saw the same bright pair of eyes he had always seen. Toby was a thirteen-year-old boy who jumped around barefoot and was alert to his companion's every hesitation, pointing out the dangerous slip-branches, and letting him drink first when they found a puddle. In the end, Mano had to admit he trusted Toby more than Joe Mitch and his infamous Neighborhood Committees.

When he had arrived up at the Heights three years earlier, lost and without a penny to his name, Mano had witnessed the rise in power of the Neighborhood Committees.

At the time, these consisted of just a few community groups who, on seeing the increase in the Tree's population, had gotten together to defend their areas of the branches. Joe Mitch had been quick to get behind them. He was a fat weevil farmer, incapable of pronouncing words of more than one syllable. But after six months of lessons, he had learned a five-syllable word—*so-li-da-ri-ty*—a word that was long but magical. Joe Mitch hung around the branches saying "solidarity" over and over again, and shaking people's hands.

As a matter of fact, what Mitch actually said was more along the lines of "sodilarity" or "sorryladdity," but it all sounded the same to the crowd.

One day, even though he'd only just arrived in the Heights, Mano had managed to shake Joe Mitch's hand. It had made a big impression on him. A recent, starving immigrant, Mano had shaken the fat, limp, sweaty hand of success. Yes, Mitch had something. He was close to the people.

Joe Mitch had then proposed his Popular Plan for Friendly Neighborhoods to the Neighborhood Committees.

At the start of each branch, he offered to dig huge Welcome Housing Projects for free. As it turned out, these were just a series of holes, like worm-eaten wood, where all the people on the housing list were dumped. That way, life in the traditional neighborhoods wasn't ruined. The Neighborhood Committees would collect half of the rent, the other half was payable to the builder's company, Joe Mitch Arbor.

A glance at the election results showed that everybody was enthusiastic about this generous proposal. Conveniently, those who weren't so enthusiastic weren't invited to vote.

Joe Mitch's weevils flooded into the branches to dig the Welcome Housing Projects. Mano picked up a bit of work on building sites during that period. He even got to eat a meal from time to time, and to sleep in a dry place. This was when he was slipping sentences into his letters such as *My assistant's calling me—I'd better go* or *I've got a young lodger at the moment. She's an economics researcher whom I've taken under my wing.* All made up. If he'd been honest with his family, he would have written *Today, I boiled the end of my belt. It didn't taste so bad. I miss you. I want to come back home.*

The final stage of the Mitch Plan had the Grand Tree Council in its sights. Little by little, Joe Mitch was managing to weaken the Council and make it look ridiculous.

Since Joe Mitch himself was part of the Council,

people thought his outspoken criticism was very brave. They would say things such as "Joe Mitch speaks for the people. He takes risks."

Finally, he resigned from the Council. As he walked out, he spat on Councillor Rolden. A few idiots even insisted it was really brave to spit on a ninety-eight-year-old man who was a symbol of the Old System.

No sooner had Joe Mitch spat than everyone stopped listening to the Grand Council. All eyes were on the Neighborhood Committees, which drew up new laws on a daily basis. This was when Joe Mitch was named "Friendly Neighbor." He presided over all the Neighborhood Committees. The motion to ban books and newspapers was finally voted in.

Mano quickly understood Mitch's method. It went against everything his family had taught him at Seldor. But hunger and fear outweighed everything. He became a volunteer at Joe Mitch Arbor.

And so Mano became a slave to fear. Compared to him, young Toby, who was being hunted down, with a ransom on his head and troops on his heels, was freer than a butterfly.

Night fell. When you're as low down as Toby and Mano were in the branches, you hardly notice changes in the moon. But from the pale glimmer that lit their path, Toby guessed it had to be in its first quarter. The last few nights had been pitch-black, so now the moon would be waxing for the next two weeks. A distant rumbling announced a thunderstorm. The shadows around them were exaggerated by lightning. The moon was already disappearing.

Toby pulled his collar up. Behind him, he heard, "Toby . . ."

"Yes, Mano?"

"You don't have a tie I could borrow, by any chance?"

Toby couldn't believe his ears.

"A tie, Mano?"

"When you're in sales, you wear a tie. I need a tie to wear at my parents' house."

Toby stopped in his tracks.

"Mano—"

"I'll tell my family I've taken a few days off to come and visit. I don't want to tell them the whole truth right away."

Toby had figured out what was going on. "You're not going to start lying to them again?"

"I . . . um . . . I'll tell them the whole story one day."

Mano was interrupted by a crash of thunder. The storm was heading their way. Toby turned back to face him.

"Are you saying that I risked my life for a liar, and that right now I'm helping a liar get back home? Is that it?"

"I'm not doing it for me," Mano explained. "I just don't want to give them a shock."

"Fine, Mano. I'm sure you know what you're doing. Good luck!"

Mano was looking down to see where to put his feet. When he looked up, he was all alone.

"Toby? Are you there?"

No. Toby wasn't there. The shadow of a gigantic dead leaf passed over Mano. He was alone, in the middle of nowhere. He had no idea where he was, or where he was supposed to be going. In a split second Toby had melted into thin air.

"Pleeeease Toby," Mano called out. "Pleeeease, come back . . ."

His voice rang out in the darkness.

"Tobeeeeeeeeeey!"

His only answer was the whistling of the wind. Mano collapsed against the bark. A drop of rain drenched him. Another fell right next to him. Mano stayed where he was, unable to get up or take a step. It was raining harder now. The storm was rumbling.

When you're less than two millimeters tall, a raindrop is a very big deal. Mano was soaked through in less than a second. He stood there, sobbing, on the very spot where Toby had deserted him.

"I'll tell the whole truth, Toby. I won't lie ever again. . . ."

At first, he didn't hear the humming noise coming toward him. Thirty seconds later, they arrived in a buzzing din: a cloud of mosquitoes seeking shelter from the storm. When they saw Mano unprotected on the branch, they clustered toward him. Mosquitoes, along with a few other insects and birds, ranked among the most dangerous predators in the Tree. A single bite was enough to drain a hearty grown man of all his blood.

Right now, there were fifteen of them buzzing around Mano. Mosquitoes with proboscises as sharp as blades, who were so excited by the warm blood flowing in Mano's veins that they had forgotten all about the wind and the rain.

Lost on his branch, defenseless, while lightning flashes ripped across the sky, the poor boy saw his last breath coming. The beating of mosquito wings made the raindrops fly in splashes. A watery haze was enveloping this bloodthirsty army.

Where had Toby gone?

Mano was just barely keeping them at bay by shrieking and waving his arms and kicking. But one of the mosquitoes managed to attack him in the stomach, tearing through his clothing and grazing his skin.

Suddenly Mano saw a wave of water surging toward him, along the bark, with Toby's red pants occasionally visible. The mosquitoes rose slightly to let the torrent of water through.

"Hold on, Mano!"

Mano saw a hand coming out of the water, which grabbed him and dragged him in its wake. Toby and Mano rolled down the slope of the branch for several seconds, unable to breathe.

Then they couldn't feel anything underneath them anymore. They were suspended in midair.

Toby's short life, culminating in this fall, flashed before his eyes. He decided it had been a good life, after all.

He had experienced a lot, for a thirteen-year-old. He thought about his parents, who wouldn't hear any more news about him. And about the Asseldor family.

He thought about Elisha.

A month earlier, she had said good-bye on the shores of their lake.

Elisha didn't like farewells. She was wearing her green dress that came down to her ankles; when she stood in the water, she had to lift the hem. Toby had rolled his pants up to his knees. They couldn't look at each other, just at the water and the circles forming around their legs. Elisha didn't make any big declarations.

"Are you leaving?"

"Yes, but I'm coming back."

"You say that now. . . ."

"I mean it—I'm coming back," Toby insisted. "I'm going up to the Treetop, to my grandmother's place in the Summit, and then I'm coming back."

"We'll see."

"Elisha, don't you believe me?"

Elisha let go of her dress, as if she didn't care how sopping wet it got anymore. She even took another step in the water. Toby stayed behind a bit. He imitated the sound a cicada makes. It was their secret code.

"When I come back, I'll make the same noise. There'll still be one cicada left singing in autumn. Me."

Elisha's reply had been harsh.

"You know what? There'll be plenty of cicadas in the Low Branches next summer. Life doesn't just stop."

Elisha was like that sometimes. Stabbing you with her words. She did it when she was sad.

Toby didn't say anything else. He floated a small bright red shell that he'd found, then he walked away. The shell drifted slowly toward Elisha. She picked it up when it washed up in the folds of her dress, which looked like long beaches of green silk as they rippled on the surface.

Elisha didn't return home until it was very late. She held the red shell in the palm of her hand.

Toby remembered Elisha's last words. "Life doesn't just stop." He kept saying them over and over again to himself as he went careering into the void.

The downpour had ended. A distant echo of the storm still rumbled in the Tree.

Several minutes went by, then Toby started asking himself a few questions. He felt as if he were lying on a mattress of air. It was a very comfortable kind of a fall. Was this what happened when life stopped?

It's not so bad after all, he thought. Then he heard a voice.

"Toby . . ."

And he had company too! What a nice surprise.

"Toby, it's me, Mano. Can you hear me?"

"Yes. Are you still falling?"

"No, I think we've stopped. But I can't see anything."

Toby tried to move his hand. Something was restricting his movements. A bit farther off, Mano was starting to panic.

"What on earth's going on?"

Then Toby shouted, "Don't move, Mano! Whatever you do, don't move!"

Mano froze.

"What's the matter?"

"Don't move a muscle."

Mano didn't dare say another word.

"We're in a spider's web. We've landed in a web."

The web that had saved their lives would become their tomb if they couldn't get out before the spider returned.

With every movement, they risked being in even more danger. Each vibration might alert the spider to the fact that there were two tasty steaks in her shopping bag.

Toby sized up the situation as calmly as he could. He knew all about spiders. He knew how to recognize the fine mesh of a black widow's trap. His father had written his thesis on selected arthropods, with three chapters dedicated to the lethally dangerous black widow.

Sim's research had led him to encourage the use of spider's silk in the Tree, because it was finer and stronger than any plant-based twine.

But what had particularly stuck in Toby's mind was that any prey caught in the web had only a few minutes to play with before the spider detected its presence.

Toby tugged on one of the web ropes. He wound it around his wrist. He needed to amass enough rope without weakening the supporting structure. While he was working, he gave Mano instructions.

"Cut out the web around you. You need to snap the threads off, cord by cord. Just leave the ones that are supporting you."

Mano did as he was told. He still had his Joe Mitch Arbor knife.

Toby managed to wind in a thick reel of silky rope. The wide loops of the bare meshwork were all that surrounded him now. He attached the end of the rope to one of these loops and let go of the reel. It only took him a few seconds to make his way across the web and lower himself down the rope.

He could hear Mano's voice above him.

"Toby, I've almost cut it all."

Toby called back, "I'm down here. When I give the word, drop. Don't waste a single second. When I shout, you let go."

"But I'll be falling into the void."

"Do as I tell you. I'll catch you. Jump when I give the signal."

"I can't."

"You can, Mano."

"I'm frightened."

"Yes, Mano. At last you've got a real reason to be frightened. Use it to jump."

And Toby started swinging on the end of his rope. Every two seconds, he swung directly below Mano, like the pendulum on a clock. He calculated that he had to give the signal just before, in order to catch Mano as he fell.

Mano was dangling above the void. He knew he would never be able to jump. He had to tell Toby. He needed to say, "You go, Toby. I'd rather stay here. You can tell my family the whole truth."

"Toby . . ." he whimpered.

Mano could feel a shadow hovering just behind him, which was odd, because he knew nobody could have come near him without making the web vibrate and giving himself away. Nobody had the aerial skills to pull that off. Nobody.

Except, perhaps . . . black widow! She was poised right next to him.

Mano heard Toby's signal.

He let go.

14
Seldor Farm

It was a typical early morning at Seldor Farm.

Lola and Lila had heard the storm rumbling in their sleep. They got up without making any noise, so as not to wake their two brothers. The boys had worked deep into the night with their father, making a hundred jars of winter preserves from a mushroom that they'd found on the far reaches of their land.

After a downpour, the girls always went over to the Ladies' Pond. This was the name Grandfather Asseldor had given to a polished bark ditch that filled with clear water every time it rained. It had become a communal bathing area for the women of Asseldor.

Lola was rubbing herself down with a sponge.

"It'll be too cold for this in a month, so I'm making the most of it."

"I bet Mano's got a real bathroom at his home in the Treetop," said Lila.

"I bet he has servants to scrub his back and people who pour bowls of hot water over him."

This was their favorite game: imagining the life of their brother Mano.

The Asseldors had been brought up never to boast. So if Mano's letters were always positive, it meant that in reality things were even better. He said he had two houses, so he probably owned four. He wrote that he had a hundred and seven pairs of socks, so he must have at least a thousand.

"It's such a shame we can't write back to him. He never puts his address on his letters," said the elder daughter.

"I'd like to tell him about Lex," replied Lola.

Lex was the only son of the Olmechs, a neighboring family in the Low Branches.

Lex had followed Mano's whole story, and now he too dreamed of going into sales up there, like Mano. He also dreamed of taking Lola, the younger Asseldor daughter, with him.

Lola and Lex had been in love for a year and a half. It didn't go any further than holding hands when they went on walks together, but even that made them feel dizzy. It was easy to fall in love with Lex, whose velvety eyes made him so handsome, and it wasn't hard to be seduced by Lola, with her dark-red hair and moon-like pale complexion, not to mention her hands as delicate as pieces of frayed cloud. Shy and good-looking, they made an old-fashioned couple.

Lex hadn't told his parents he was in love, or discussed his plans to go away. The Olmechs were counting on their son to take over the small family business—a leaf mill, which was famous for its fine white flour.

"Mano will explain to Lex's parents," said Lola.

"Yes," said Lila.

Lola was looking at her big sister, who was just as beautiful as she was.

"Isn't love strange? Why was I the one who fell in love with Lex, and not you? All of a sudden, something just happens between two people. Lex and Lola. Lola and Lex. And the rest of the world doesn't matter anymore."

"Yes," said Lila.

Lila knew exactly what her sister was talking about. All of a sudden something just happens between two people . . . and the rest of the world doesn't matter anymore.

Lila had also been head over heels in love with Lex—for the past five years. She had never dared tell anybody. Especially not Lola. Or Lex. She wouldn't even know where to begin. "Um, Lex, I think I . . ." or "Lex, there's something I want to tell you . . ." or "Lex, if I told you that . . ."

A year and a half earlier, in a matter of hours, her little sister had snatched handsome Lex from under her nose. Just like that, without thinking about it, simply following her heart. Perhaps she hadn't even said any-thing at all. Perhaps she just brushed against Lex's hand.

Lila didn't blame Lola. And she didn't blame Lex either. She blamed herself. But it was too late. Now, in the Ladies' Pond, Lola was sure to start talking about Lex, as if Lila needed convincing that he was kind and good and strong. Lila knew this better than anybody; it was why she hadn't been able to sleep well for the past five years.

She changed the subject.

"I bet we don't recognize Mano when he comes back."

"Maybe," said Lola dreamily.

They wrapped themselves in their blue towels and ran toward the house. It would soon be October, and it was almost cold. They were shivering. They both entered the big vaulted room, where a fire was crackling away. They stopped in their tracks, flabbergasted.

Everybody was standing up, motionless, like a paint-ing.

Their mother was holding a steaming kettle. Their two brothers were just behind her, leaning against the wall. Tall Father Asseldor was backlit as he stood by the window.

Someone else was sitting on the hearth in front of the fireplace, swaddled in a blanket. The steam from the bowl of herbal tea he cupped in his hands clouded this person's face.

"It's me, Mano."

The two girls reeled backward. Silence ran the gamut of those dark vaults. Lola was the first to go up to him.

"Mano?"

"I want to ask your forgiveness."

On a board, next to the window, was a great thick album into which Mrs. Asseldor had carefully glued all of her son's letters. On the front she'd written *Mano in the Treetop*, as if it were the title of a novel.

And here was its author, poor and stripped of everything, huddled in a blanket. He had made it all up; he was like one of those insipid writers who lack any of the vibrancy of their heroes.

The father spoke.

"Mano lied to us. For years now he has been deceiving himself and deceiving us. He's made all the wrong choices. Except one—he's decided to come back to us. That choice doesn't change what's happened, but it will make up for it."

Mano put his bowl down, and he held his head in his hands. Yes, he had come back. That was what mattered. Life could get back to normal. But his father continued in his beautiful, deep voice.

"I want Mano to go away again one day."

General consternation. The entire Asseldor family turned toward the head of the family.

"I want Mano to make his dream come true. And his dream isn't to be with us."

"Yes it is, Father!" Mano sobbed.

"No. You're saying that because you're frightened. And fear . . ."

Father Asseldor grabbed the album and hurled it into the fire. The flames shot up. Then he tried to regain his composure. At last, Lila and Lola noticed Toby, who was sitting in a dark corner of the room, next to the bread bin.

"Toby!" said Lila. "Is that you?"

"He brought us back our Mano," explained their mother.

And Father Asseldor added, "For the time being, Mano and Toby are in danger. There are people looking for them. We've got to hide them. Mano will go away again, once it's all over."

"Hide your son first," said Toby. "I'll manage. You can't have two fugitives in Seldor. It would be dangerous for your whole family."

But Lila objected. "We can't just abandon Toby. . . ."

Lola couldn't say a word. She looked at Mano. Then at the dancing flames. Her dream was shattered, and so too was that of her sweetheart, Lex.

Milo, the older brother, piped up. "At least Toby never lied to us."

Toby paused.

"Your brother deserted Joe Mitch's army. If they ever find him again, he'll be executed. I'm the one who made him leave his post. And I'm asking you to take care of Mano."

Silence again. The album was almost burned to cinders now. Mano heard his father's voice.

"Behind the flames in the fireplace, there's a square plaque. And behind the plaque, there's a tiny ventilated room. Only one person can hide in there. They'll be on the hunt for you for several weeks. You can't both stay in that hole."

"Hide Toby," croaked Mano.

"No," muttered Toby. "I just want to rest for a night and then I'll go down toward Onessa, to get back home."

Milo stepped out of the shadows.

"I'll take you to the Olmechs. They're just an hour away from here, if that. You can spend the rest of the day there, and the night too. Nobody'll go looking for you there."

Lola gave a little shudder when she heard the Olmechs' name. Her father seemed to have his doubts.

"I'm not sure you should involve the Olmechs in this story. I'm very fond of them, but—"

"Dad," Milo cut him short. "If the hunt is on for Toby and Mano, we might even get a visit today. We've got to hurry. The Olmechs have a cellar where they store their leaf flour, under the floor of the main house. Toby can sleep there for a night."

Toby stood up.

"I'm off. I don't know the Olmechs well, but if you think we can trust them . . . I don't need you. Thank you, Milo," he told the Asseldor brother. "I'd prefer not to tell them about Mano being back."

Lola sat down on a chair, relieved. Toby wasn't going to talk to Lex about Mano. She would tell him all about it later.

Lola wrapped some bread, grasshopper rolls, and other fried delicacies in a tea towel. Toby slung the bundle over his shoulder. He hugged each member of the family in turn.

When he got to Mano, he said very quietly, "Remember your promise." And he took his friend's hands in his.

Then Toby was out the door.

Gathered around the window, the Asseldor family watched him head off until he disappeared at the end of the bark path.

ॐ

Mano had made a promise to Toby. He had sworn an oath with his forehead pressed against Toby's, which is how things are done in the Tree.

It had happened in the spider's web, just after Mano's big jump. He'd been caught at the last moment by Toby, who was hanging from his rope.

One on top of the other, they made their descent down the silk cable. After a few minutes, Mano had said, "We've made it to the bottom."

"Perfect," replied Toby, "climb onto the branch."

"But—"

"Hurry up!"

"There's no branch. . . ."

The rope was far too short. The branch was still lower down, and quite a ways. What was to be done? If they let go of the rope, their bodies would smash into smithereens on landing. If they climbed back up, they would soon be face-to-face with the spider.

Time was ticking away. They were dangling in midair and starting to run out of stamina. Toby spoke first.

"In times of grave danger, it's a good idea to make some promises. And our chances are so slim, we should make them serious ones."

"If we survive," said Mano, "I'll . . ."

Mano hesitated; he was trying to understand what had changed in him.

"If we make it, I'll never be the same again."

He had climbed back up to Toby's level, and their foreheads were touching. He opened his eyes.

"If we survive, I won't be frightened of anything ever again. . . . I'll be the kind of man who's always braaaaavvve. Aaaaaaaaahhhhh!"

He had cried out in utter terror. There, bang in front of him, was the black widow's giant sucker, ready to gobble him up. The spider's hard eyes drilled a hole in the darkness.

Hunger had made her go after them, and she was now at the end of the thread she was weaving in order to lower herself. Her legs alone were fifty times the size of Toby.

Mano was the first to react.

"Climb back up, Toby. I'll take care of her."

He had got out his knife and was waving it around like a windmill blade.

Toby called out, "I'm staying with you."

He took a long hard swing, and the black widow must have realized that her snack wasn't going to let itself be swallowed like a defenseless cookie. She retracted her legs when Mano's knife got too close, but instantly shot them back out again, like arrows.

She was a hairy monster of a spider, and getting increasingly agitated. But Toby still called out, "She looks like my grandmother!"

It wasn't a fair fight. The spider must have been offended by Toby's comparison, because she lashed out mercilessly with her legs. She was going to knock them out, kill them, and suck them up, drop by drop, with her sticky sucker.

"What was your promise again?" roared Toby.

"To be brave!"

As Mano sliced the air with his knife, Toby caught his eye. "So far, you're keeping your promise, Mano!"

One of the spider's extended legs lashed out against the friends' silk rope. There was a sudden jolt. Toby and Mano slid down at least a millimeter. A second later, their rope dropped another level. The black widow was poised to attack.

"Move, Mano. Wiggle around as much as you can! We have to pull on our rope!"

The rope was starting to drop in violent jerks. Toby realized that the web their rope was attached to was unraveling—just like when you pull on someone's knitting. The spider had no idea what was going on. She lay there, watching two appetising morsels of meat disappear below her.

At last, the rope unwound like a ball of yarn. The spider tried to climb back up before her web was reduced to nothing but a gaping hole.

By some miracle, the two friends bounced on a leaf and came to a halt. Mano looked at Toby in the shadow.

"Where are we?"

Toby squinted to see more clearly, but it was the gentle smells of dampness and mushrooms that meant he could announce, "We're here. We're in the Low Branches."

An hour later, they reached Seldor.

When Toby left Seldor a bit later, on his way to the Olmechs' mill, he deliberately took his time. The landscape of the Low Branches made him forget how tired he was. Crickets darted across his path. He dislodged a big fly laying its eggs. He walked with his arms open wide so he could fill his lungs with the air from his own country again. He slid between vines, recognising green bark hills and watery caves.

Eventually, he allowed himself to think about his parents. His spirit lifted, and his chest swelled.

Sim and Maya Lolness were prisoners, chained somewhere in the Heights. Would they ever see the Low Branches again? Toby wanted to believe they would.

He whispered to his parents across that great divide, "I'm fine. And I'm waiting for you."

It was a postcard written on the air. Toby imagined a warm breeze rising, or else the secret flow of crude sap, carrying his words up there.

And sure enough, up in a stinking dungeon, a man turned toward his wife. He looked painfully thin. His ripped shirt was buttoned all the way up. He was standing tall on a rotten twig. Through the bars, he could see a guard in a hat snoring in front of his moss beer.

The woman held her hands together on her dirty dress. Her eyes were dry because she had no more tears left.

The man said, "My pretty Maya . . ."

The woman didn't answer, but the words felt like a warm shawl over her shoulders.

"Mother Maya, I think our son is doing well."

He put his arm around his wife's waist.

Sim Lolness was smiling.

15
The Mill

When she saw Toby, Mrs. Olmech let out a series of shrieks and quickly climbed onto a chair. A funny kind of welcome for an exhausted thirteen-year-old friend.

Toby had arrived at about ten o'clock in the morning. He was expecting to find everybody at home. When it's been raining, millers don't go out to collect leaves for grinding. Damp leaves produce a sort of porridge, which bears no resemblance to the fine leaf flour used to make white bread and dainty cakes.

But Mrs. Olmech was all alone in her kitchen. She was busy sponging down the leaf cart. It was gray, a sort of box on wheels, with one opening at the top and another underneath to unload the chopped leaves into the cellar.

Eventually, she stopped squealing.

"But . . . what . . . what are you doing here?"

Toby ran his hand across his face.

"I'm sorry to trouble you, Mrs. Olmech. I need your help."

"I . . . My husband isn't here. I don't know. . . . What do you want, little one?"

"What about your son? Isn't he here either?"

Mrs. Olmech got down off her chair.

"Lex left this morning; he'll be back tomorrow. He went to get the egg supplies from much lower down."

Toby gave a start.

"Right at the bottom?"

"Near the Border . . ."

"Ah . . ."

"He's gone to the Lee household. Elisha Lee and her mother."

"Ah . . ." Toby said again.

"We're stocking up for winter. The worm beetles have laid their eggs. But, tell me, what are you—"

"Are they well?"

"Who? The worm beetles?"

"Elisha and her mother . . ."

"I think so. I don't really know."

Toby gave a long sigh.

"What do you want, little one?" asked Mother Olmech, leaning over him.

All of a sudden, Toby felt the urge to take to his heels and run straight to Elisha. He was silent for a moment. His eyes grew heavy and he stumbled.

The woman pushed a chair toward him. He remained upright, clinging on to the back of the chair. The tiredness was kicking in now. Mother Olmech said, "I thought you were in the Treetop. People have been talking about the Lolness family. They say you've had problems."

"I need to rest until tomorrow," Toby blurted.

"Well, the thing is, that's not very convenient for us; we've only got two beds, you see."

If he hadn't been so exhausted, Toby would have remembered that Lex's bed was free, which meant there had to be another reason for Mrs. Olmech not welcoming him, but instead he said, "I don't want a bed. I just want to sleep in your cellar."

"But . . ."

"That's all I'm asking for . . . please. I'm . . ."

The chair was shaking in his hand.

". . . tired."

Mrs. Olmech pushed the leaf cart away to reveal a trapdoor in the floor. She opened it without saying a word. Toby slid halfway down. Before disappearing, he put in a last request.

"Roll the cart back over the trapdoor. Don't tell anyone I'm here. I beg you."

Mrs. Olmech stared at the boy's washed-out eyes as he whispered, "Thank you."

The trapdoor closed over Toby's head. He heard the cart being pushed back into place. A nice smell of flour greeted his nostrils. It reminded him of his mother and her warm bread. Thick buttered slices.

One crumb later, he was asleep.

Toby had no idea what time he woke up. While he was sleeping, he thought he'd heard footsteps and raised voices above. He remembered someone flaring up into a temper, as if Father Olmech had been angry with his wife when he got back. But Toby put it down to a bad dream because the house seemed calm enough now.

Toby yawned and stretched. In the darkness he slid the bundle he'd brought from Seldor toward him. He wolfed down everything with great relish. He recognized the taste of the delicious Asseldor ingredients, the picnics they used to give him in the good old days, for the road: crusty turnovers, lice crisps, grasshopper pâtés so good that they would make a grasshopper weep.

Toby realized that he hadn't made a promise when

the spider was bearing down on them. The pleasure he got from his meal made him vow to learn how to cook one day.

He heard the cart being wheeled again. The trapdoor creaked and swung open. Toby saw the head of Mr. Olmech appear. There was a big smile on his face.

"Are you all right, little one? Lucille explained you wanted to rest here for a while. Stay as long as you want, little one. Would you like to eat something?" he asked in a gentle voice.

"Thank you, Mr. Olmech. I've got what I need."

The father closed the trapdoor but quickly opened it again. "In an hour or so, Lucille and I are going to set off, to collect leaves before night falls. When we come back, we'll give you something hot."

He shut the trapdoor. The cart slid back into position. Toby didn't move in the pitch black of the cellar.

Less than an hour later, the Olmechs put on their work vests and tucked their scythes into their belts. They slid the cart forward again and rapped three times on the trapdoor; Toby's distant voice greeted them.

"We'll be back soon," said Father Olmech.

And they left.

Mrs. Olmech went ahead, with her husband pushing the cart behind her. Just a few paces from the mill, there was a bulge in the bark, which marked the end of the garden.

There, a hit squad of fifteen men was waiting.

The Olmechs felt their legs buckle. Mrs. Olmech turned to face her husband. He made his way over to the group. They were all wearing coats and hats.

"Well?" asked one of the men.

Father Olmech answered, "I . . . Everything's as we agreed."

"The little one is in the cellar," his wife added.

The man rubbed his hands. He wasn't even looking at Mr. Olmech. Mrs. Olmech took a step forward.

"What about the money? When will they give it to us?"

Her question was greeted with loud guffaws as if it were the punchline of a joke. The hit squad encircled the house.

The Olmech parents went on their way. They were pushing the cart with crestfallen faces, sweating profusely.

"What have we done, Lucille? What have we done?"

Joe Mitch's hit squad was made up of his best men—which is to say the worst. The cream of the bullies.

Fifteen men who had been through prime training now assailed the mill from every angle, agile as dancers in tutus but a lot better equipped. Every window, every door, every exit was guarded. One man even hung off a windmill blade.

Joe Mitch would be very pleased. Everything looked set for a capture at last.

It only took a second for a flamethrower to rip out

the door. Four strapping men rushed in. They had crossbows on their shoulders. They surrounded the trapdoor. A fifth man arrived to open it. The others maintained security on the outside.

The trapdoor sprung open with the blow from the club. The four crossbows were aiming into the black hole of the cellar. Not a sound. Toby must have fallen asleep again. All the hit squad needed to do was scoop him up.

The chief was the first to jump in. He raised his torch and saw the huge pile of flour that filled most of the room. Nothing else.

The man smiled. He'd anticipated everything. He got a few men to come down and join him. Using pitchforks, they began to forage around in the flour, waiting for the yelp of pain that would signal the fugitive's presence.

They spent an hour down there, with different groups taking turns shifting the flour in search of Toby.

By the time the hour was up, it looked like there were fifteen snowmen down in the cellar. The men were coughing. Their mouths were lined with dough, and their lungs were clogged. The flour clung to their eyes, their tongues, their ears. It crept into every orifice.

The commando didn't cut the dashing figure he had upon arrival. His head was covered in flour, and he was sneezing over his torch in a corner of the cellar. Suddenly, looking up, he discovered a few lines scrawled in charcoal on the wall. He raised his flame. They were four lines from a well-known nursery rhyme:

> *I went down to the mill*
> *To give my belly a fill,*
> *But I didn't find bread—*
> *I found white lice instead.*

He stared at the words Toby had written clumsily in the pitch black of the cellar.

His stooges came to join him, whiter than the lice and more floury than the bread in the song. They read the rhyme too. They watched their boss frown like a poor clown and stamp his feet in fury.

After walking for a few minutes, the Olmechs stopped their cart at a bend in a dead branch. They sat down on a knot of wood. The rain from the day before had left puddles on the ground.

"We've done something dreadful, Lucille."

"We've betrayed a twelve-year-old child who wanted to hide in our home."

Mrs. Olmech started sobbing.

"What will we tell Lex? He'd never have let us do it."

"Twelve years old?" asked a voice out of nowhere.

Toby had decided it was time to get out of the cart. Astounded, the Olmechs slid to the ground in unison. Toby's lightly powdered head peered out of the cart.

"A twelve-year-old?" he asked again.

It was like a scene from a puppet show, except that Toby had no desire to laugh. He fixed the millers with a stare that would have made the hardest wood shatter into a thousand pieces.

His anger had been building up for an hour now, ever since Father Olmech had said that they were going to collect leaves. Collect leaves? On a rainy day? Did they think he was stupid? He'd instantly realized what was going on and had slipped inside the cart via the trapdoor.

Toby was still grinding the poor millers to a pulp with his stare.

"I'm not twelve. I'm thirteen. Even rotten old branches should be able to count."

Toby decided that what was in store for the Olmechs was punishment enough. He didn't need to add anything. Joe Mitch's wrath was the price they would have to pay. Toby leaped out of the cart.

"So long."

And off he went as night fell.

஺

All Toby's trust in his fellow beings, all the hope he had left, could have crumbled after the episode in the mill. But Toby still had the light of Elisha glowing ahead of him, so he decided not to make any more detours. He would go straight to his only friend.

Earlier, he had thought about stopping off at Onessa and going to his parents' house—for one more look at the place he should never have left. But he knew now that he couldn't risk stopping again.

By the middle of the night, he was close to where Elisha lived. He crouched down on the bark embankment, placed his thumb on his teeth, and chirped like a cicada. No movement from the house. He tried again three times.

She was probably asleep. Toby didn't dare keep trying. He headed off toward a moss coppice, crossed it, reached a grainy bark slope on the other side, and suddenly stopped when he saw the view. There was the lake, under the soft light of the setting crescent moon.

A sense of peacefulness rose up inside Toby, and he glided down the slope. His feet found familiar footholds. He was as light as a feather, skimming the glowing wood with his feet.

Toby sat down on the beach.

A few big leaves had fallen into the lake, forming idyllic islands. Five nights earlier, he had been in a hole in the bark, looking up at the sky. Now the Tree was taking on its autumn colors. A russet-colored light spread across the sky.

His adventures could stop here.

He would wait for his parents by the shores of this lake. They would turn up one day with their little cases, their coats over their arms.

"Here we are . . ."

"It took a while, but it's over now," his mother would say. "Life goes on, you know."

Toby was half dreaming as he lay there in his cove. But in a corner of his heart, the whirlwind of adventures still to come was already beginning to stir into action. It was just that this gentle dream was much more appealing, and he wanted to snuggle inside it, as if under a blanket when it's snowing outside.

Just then, he heard a very odd noise for an autumn night. A cicada. Toby's eyes shot open. He'd waited so long for this moment. A shadow passed over him.

"Are you dreaming?"

Elisha's question came with a tinkling laugh that somersaulted all the way through Toby.

"Yes, I'm dreaming."

Each second was as full and delicious as a honey fritter.

"And does your dream end happily ever after?"

"That depends on you."

PART TWO

16
Refuge

When you peel off a maggot's skin (which is kind of like pulling off a big sock) to make a sleeping bag or plant protector, it leaves a sticky white substance behind.

The Grass people were covered in this repulsive gloop, and their skin looked as if it had been boiled for too long. They came whooping and leaping out of the undergrowth. Elisha stopped swimming and stared at them: three Grass people were waving their arms around as they threw a wide-meshed net over her. Then they hauled the net onto the beach.

Toby wanted to rush over, but his feet wouldn't move from the branch. He was trembling like a leaf. When he tried to call out, he produced a tiny whisper nobody could hear. Elisha had stopped struggling in the net now. She had surrendered to her captors. She gave Toby a little wave good-bye. She didn't look sad.

When Toby finally managed to tear himself away from the bark, he let out a big cry and woke himself up. The night was silent. Toby pulled his blanket over him.

His nightmare had left him chilled to the bone, soaked in a frosty sweat.

For the last month, Toby had been sleeping in a hole in the bark cliff on the other side of the lake. The cave was reasonably wide and high, but a fly wouldn't have been able to slip its leg through the entrance.

Elisha had settled him in there on the first night.

When Toby crawled into the cave for the first time, after clambering up the cliff, he had complained. He had been dreaming of Elisha's mother's delicious pancakes, and the thick mattresses in their colorful home. But Elisha had managed to convince him that he shouldn't let anybody know his whereabouts, not even her mother, Isha Lee.

And she was right, because the next morning one of Joe Mitch's patrols knocked on the Lees' front door.

Elisha went to open it. Her mother was busy with the worm beetles. When she heard them rapping, Elisha slipped on a nightshirt over her clothes and rumpled her hair to make it look as if she had just been woken up. There were two men at the door. The others must have been waiting higher up.

"Hello," she said.

Elisha gave the biggest yawn she could manage. The two men stared at her. She was twelve and a half, but you couldn't tell from looking at her. Her clothing made the

visitors step back. Was this a child in front of them, or a scantily clad young woman?

Unsure what tone to adopt, they didn't say anything. But not being gentlemen, they quickly reverted to their base nature.

"We've got to do a search!"

Elisha smiled.

"I once taught a bug how to say hello, so I should be able to manage with two cockroaches. . . . Hello," she said again.

The cockroaches in question were very surprised. In the normal course of events, they would have squished this tiny louse of an Elisha against the door. But Elisha was Elisha, and you wouldn't want to squish her.

In fact, she was the one crushing them with her huge almond-shaped eyes that were spinning like lassos. They took another step back.

"Hel-lo," one of them stammered.

"We've got to do a search," the other repeated fool-ishly.

Elisha looked at this second man as if she felt sorry for him. Then she turned to the first. "Man-who-says-hello, you can come in, but I'll have to ask you to leave your animal outside."

The man who had said hello watched his colleague blush. He stepped inside the house. Elisha banged the door behind him. The rude visitor stayed outside, dazed.

Elisha sat down on the ground, close to the fire. The man realized it wouldn't take long to search the house, once he had seen what it looked like from the inside. He pushed the colorful partitions aside and lifted a few mattresses before rejoining Elisha.

"I . . . Thank you, miss. I've finished my searching."

He was discovering the joys of being polite. And once he'd started, there was no stopping him. "I have greatest . . . delightings in thankings you . . . for your receptional . . . if I can allow you to express me like that."

Elisha was trying not to crease up with laughter. Pushing an ember into the fire, she managed to say, "Please feel free, dear Clot."

"Clot" was a name her mother used. Elisha didn't even know what it meant. The man looked flattered. He started nodding and making little bows.

"Forgivings for waking you, miss. We won't opportu-nity you again with another pesty search. . . ."

He was walking backward now. Elisha was hiding her

tears of laughter. He was really getting into his stride. "I am your humble Clot . . . your devoted Clot, missie."

Finally, he left, closing the door ever so gently.

Elisha ran over and glued her ear to it. She heard the man calling out to his companion.

"Well? Are you proud of yourself, you badly-brought-up good-for-nothing? You'll never be called a Clot by a young lady who's just risen from her bed!"

"But—"

"No buts."

"Sorry—"

"Sorry who? We say: sorry, Clot."

"All right, Clot. Sorry, Clot."

When she told Toby about the visit, the cave echoed long and loud with the sound of their laughter. They played around, saying, "I am your humble Clot," as they bowed all the way down to the ground.

And so Elisha's life was divided between time at home and time spent with Toby. Two or three times a day, she would say to her mother, "I'm for a swim in the lake. I'll be back soon."

Because she worked hard the rest of the time, her mother let her go.

On the way, Elisha would pick up a small bowl that she hid in a hollow near her house. She popped the left overs from each meal in there. Luckily, her mother had said one morning, "If you're doing so much swimming, you'll have to eat more."

So Isha gave her daughter bigger portions every day.

Elisha took the bowl to Toby; he hadn't lost any of his appetite. They would exchange a few words, and sometimes she would give him a snippet of local news. "Did you know that the Olmechs' mill has been destroyed?"

Toby hadn't told Elisha about his stay at the Olmechs', because he didn't want to condemn those poor people by revealing their act of betrayal.

"Lex found the mill ransacked. His parents had disappeared. People think they've been arrested by Joe Mitch's men. Lex set out to look for them. Now there's no news of him either."

Toby listened, and thought, *Those poor people; they've baked their own happiness just as you would a cake: a drop of fear, a handful of lies, a lot of weakness, and a sprinkling of ambition. And now their son has to swallow all of that.*

On several occasions, Toby saw groups of hunters skirting the lake, so he tended to go out only at night.

He would climb down his cliff at dusk. He walked on the shores of the lake, skipping pebbles across the water and raising a foam that looked like the moon's surface. He would do a few somersaults on the beach, to stay limber. He played funnyball by himself, kicking around a ball of compacted sawdust. Sometimes he would lie down and spend part of the night under the stars, despite the increasingly biting cold.

Before the first rays of daylight, he would climb back up to his lair.

Now and then, Elisha would join him in the middle of the night. When she had managed to sneak out without waking her mother, she would catch up with him on the shores of the lake.

It was on one of these occasions that Toby asked her about the Grass people. She kept avoiding the question, pretending to hear a faraway noise, or saying she had seen a shadow swimming toward them.

But Toby wouldn't give up, so she gave him a vague kind of answer: "I don't know, really. . . . People talk. You shouldn't believe a lot of it. They live down below, on the other side of the Border."

After his brief and terrifying return to the Treetop, Toby had discovered how important the Grass people were. He had heard very little about them when he was small, but now everybody talked about the Grass people. According to Mano Asseldor, there had been a review of the case of Leo Blue's father, the famous El Blue, the explorer who had been killed crossing the Border. At the time of his death, when Leo was very small, no one had been able to find any explanation. But now, no doubt about it, the Grass people were to blame. They had assassinated El Blue. The Neighborhood Committees were sending out alarmist messages through public criers. People feared an invasion, but there was no actual mention of the "Grass people." Instead they just talked about "the threat" in a mysterious sort of way.

"Still, people are saying that—" Toby added.

"But they've never seen them!" Elisha interrupted him.

"Have you?"

"Let me tell you something," Elisha continued. "The first time I came across a mayfly, I screamed I was so scared. I thought I was going to die, because people said mayflies eat children. Mayflies make a lot of noise and they nibble away at our branches, but they wouldn't harm anyone! You shouldn't always believe what people say. If someone had told you I was an ugly wild animal, we'd never have been friends, and you'd have told everyone you met about the ugly wild animal who lived near the lake."

"As far as mayflies go," said Toby, sounding very serious, "I'm happy to believe they're not as bad as people say. And maybe the Grass people aren't either. . . . But I wouldn't like to cross paths with an Elisha!"

Elisha pretended to be furious and jumped on top of him so that he toppled over onto the bark, then she jumped on top of him again, pinning down both his arms. She was surprisingly strong. Laughing, Toby begged her to stop. Elisha's hair was tickling his neck. She let go and slid down to join him.

They stayed lying on the bark, side by side. It felt safe, like the good old days, getting lost in an abandoned bees' nest, which they pretended was their very own fairy-tale castle. They would run through golden corridors leading into chapels where honey stalactites hung down. The nest was Elisha's favorite place. Deserted by its swarm of killer bees, it had become a paradise, like the shores of the lake without Toby's hunters.

They listened to the waves lapping, the sound of the wind shaking the bare branches. The lake had drowned the last leaves. You could no longer see the rounded backs of water fleas that slept on its surface in summer.

They drifted off. Elisha was curled up in a ball. Just her arm stuck out of her cape, digging into Toby's shoulder, but Toby would never have dreamed of complaining about such discomfort.

And so November slipped by, with almost too little to worry about, warm enough to make you forget how close winter was and that you had to prepare for it.

Then winter arrived without warning, in one night, and this is where the story should have drawn to a close. The fitting ending would have been: "Winter stole Toby away, and he was never heard of again." But the outcome of a story always hinges on a tiny detail, and so it was that one detail changed the course of Toby's story.

This "detail" was actually eight centimeters long and had a wingspan of ten centimeters. This detail traveled at twenty-four kilometers per hour, cruising speed. Sim Lolness had proven, in one of his old research projects, that this detail could link the Tree to the moon in one year, nine months, twenty-eight days, and seventeen minutes.

This detail dropped dead in front of Isha Lee, on the first day in December.

It was a blue dragonfly.

In its mouth was a mosquito, still alive, which it had

been trying to kill in mid-flight. The dragonfly died suddenly and peacefully, like most dragonflies at the first genuinely cold snap.

Isha Lee stood there, dumbstruck. Its giant frame was twitching on the ground in front of her. She didn't even see the mosquito remove its hooks from the beast and set off at a zigzag, with a lisping buzz. Isha wasn't thinking about the tragic fate of the dragonfly, which had died like a plucky old lady staring retirement humorously in the eye.

Isha was thinking about something else.

She was thinking that winter had arrived. Right now.

And a winter that mowed down the fastest insect in the Tree (twenty-four kilometers an hour) with its first kiss would be a merciless winter.

Elisha's mother left the oversize insect's skin where it was and went back inside her house. She took a big cloth bag and emptied half her larder into it. Next Isha ran over to the two new worm beetles, Kim and Lorca. They were the fourth generation of beetles to lodge at the Lees' since the Lolness family had first arrived in the region, six years earlier. Next to them, a shed kept the last eggs of the season safe. She stuffed at least half of them into the bag and set off toward the moss woods, by the path that led to the lake.

She strode purposefully, her load over her shoulder, advancing against the freezing wind that had just seized the Tree. When she reached the viewing point, she surprised her daughter, who was on her way home.

Elisha stopped in her tracks and stared at her mother. They looked like two slightly embarrassed reflections of the same person.

"So, Elisha, have you been swimming?" her mother asked.

"Yes, Mom."

"Not too cold?"

"No, Mom."

"Are you sure?"

"Yes . . ."

Isha gestured toward the lake. Elisha turned around to see.

The lake's surface was entirely frozen over.

"So? It doesn't hurt too much when you dive in?"

Elisha's cheeks were red. She was chewing her lips.

"I didn't go for a swim today, Mom."

"What about yesterday?"

"I didn't go then either . . . or the month before that."

"Where is he?"

"Who?"

Isha wasn't angry, but she was starting to get impatient.

"Quickly! Where is he?"

The cold wind was spreading, and night was about to fall. Elisha shivered as she looked at her mother.

"He's up there."

Isha Lee overtook her daughter, raced down the slope, skirted the lake, and started climbing back up the other side. Elisha struggled to keep up, even though her mother was carrying a heavy bag.

Toby was busy drawing on the cave walls. He was painting with a russet-colored piece of mildew, the kind you find on the edge of the lake at the end of autumn. He was drawing a flower, an orchid.

A flower had grown in the Tree a long time ago, or so the story goes. Out of nowhere, an orchid had taken root in a branch in the Heights. It died on the first day of December, long before Toby was born, or his parents, or his parents' parents.

Since that time, a Flower Festival was celebrated

every first day of December. A crowd would throng onto the branch where the orchid had grown. No statue or monument marked the spot. The flower had simply been left to dry, and so it had kept on changing, with the wind and the rain, gradually shriveling.

But when Toby had gone back up to the Heights, the dried flower had been razed to the ground. A Joe Mitch Arbor housing project was blossoming in its place.

So Toby was busy painting the memory of that orchid when someone rose up behind him.

"Elisha!" he called out, proud of his work. "Look!"

He went over to her. But it wasn't Elisha. It was Mrs. Lee, beautiful Isha Lee, who was putting her bag down on the ground, utterly exhausted.

"Hello, Mrs. Lee," said Toby.

Elisha ran in just behind, even more out of breath than her mother.

"This isn't a game anymore," said Isha Lee.

"You found out," said Toby, stating the obvious.

"Yes, I found out! From day one! From the night when I heard a cicada singing in autumn and I saw Elisha sneaking out of the house."

"And you didn't say anything?"

"The only thing I'd have said is that you shouldn't take me for a brainless louse. Apart from that, what was there to say? I just had to continue on as if Toby was there, count him in for the meals, and let Elisha look after him."

Elisha and Toby were stunned. They had thought they

were the smartest people in the world, but now they realized that luck and someone else had been on their side.

"Now, you must be very careful. The cave could
become inaccessible at any moment. If it snows, Toby
will be cut off. We need to find him a winter hiding
place. I'm thinking of the worm beetle shed. We'll need
to get it ready tonight. In the meantime, Toby, you stay
here. I'm leaving you this bag. There's enough to hold
out for two whole weeks, in case something happens.

She went to the cave entrance. At the last moment,
she turned around and looked up at the flower.

"What's that, my Toby?"

My Toby. Nobody had called him that for weeks. He
felt a little twinge in his heart as he thought of his parents.

"A flower," he answered.

Isha stopped for a moment. That word seemed to
affect her.

"It's beautiful. . . . I'd forgotten it was like that. And I
grew up surrounded by flowers."

She went out. Toby thought about what she had just
said. Where could you grow up surrounded by flowers?
Elisha stayed a few seconds longer. She was looking
down with a contrite expression.

"Your mother's a very good person," said Toby.

"Yeah, she's all right," Elisha uttered faintly. "So,
um . . . I'll see you tomorrow."

Elisha left through the hole.

"Till tomorrow," said Toby.

᠀

When Toby tried to stick his nose outside the following morning, it was met with a wall of snow. Despite digging all day, nothing shifted. The snow held him hostage.

It was December 2. The thaw would start in March.

Four months.

And he only had food supplies for two weeks.

So . . .

17
Buried Alive

In the Treetop, a gust of wind or a ray of sunshine is enough to sweep away the snow. But in the Low Branches, it clings like a big white caterpillar and doesn't leave until spring.

At first, Toby was extremely angry.

Ending his days like this! Having escaped every kind of dark evil imaginable, was he now going to be killed by an innocent blanket of snow? He kicked the heavy door of ice.

His feet hurt after a few kicks, but there wasn't even a dent in the door. He fell to his knees. The hope was draining out of him. All he had left in him were pain and anger.

"Come back, Toby. Come back. . . ."

He kept saying the same thing, over and over again, but the hope was leaking away. The starry sky, which had always helped him, was no longer above his head. All he had was the cave's cold walls and ceiling. One bag of food could never last four months. He would end up like an emaciated twig that would snap. Toby sat there for a while, weak and limp. Maybe not having to fight anymore wasn't such a bad thing, after all.

He might never have gotten up again if he hadn't thought about his parents. He'd been waiting for them for the whole autumn, like a little boy perched on a chair at the meeting point for lost children.

Suddenly, an image came to him. It was a small hut on the edge of a huge field, home to an abandoned fair. Old scraps of paper littered the ground. Everything was deserted. There was a sign on the hut: LOST PARENTS OFFICE. And if you took a closer look through the misty window, you could see Sim and Maya Lolness inside, sitting on stools. They looked as if they had been waiting for centuries, with their hands on their knees.

Toby realized that he had nothing to wait for; he was the one who was being waited for.

They were counting on him.

Instantly, without gaining so much as a thousandth of a millimeter, he felt tall. He got up slowly, like someone miraculously cured.

Yes, his situation was dire, but at least he knew that. "Forewarned is forearmed," Grandmother Alnorell always used to say to her accountant, Mr. Perlush, to get him to keep piling up the treasure. For once, Toby heeded old Radegonde Alnorell's advice. He tried to anticipate what would happen.

First of all, he sat on the ground and took off his socks. He put them by the fire to dry. Amazingly, the fire was still going. He would be able to get wood by digging away at the floor and pulling off the splinters. He had seven matches left. He put the precious box to one side. Luckily, the fire wasn't smoky. There must be some unseen vents in the Trunk, which allowed the smoke to escape and fresh air to enter. So Toby had no trouble breathing.

Air, heat, light—all that was missing was a bit of food.

He emptied the bag, item by item. There were more than a hundred rations.

Toby counted how many days there were between now and the first day of April. One hundred and twenty. So he should eat one ration per day, for four months. One egg, one biscuit, one chunk of dried fat, or one lichen leaf.

Toby made a face. It was going to be pretty tight. Tight? Total starvation, more likely. A horribly painful and certain death.

Feeding a thirteen-year-old an egg a day is worse than giving a hollow wooden ball to a team of eleven weevils for a game of funnyball. They'd immediately swallow the ball, which is when the referee should start worrying about his own safety.

Toby watched his socks drying by the fire for a while. He saw the orchid on the wall dancing through the flames. His gaze slid to the floor, and the small pile of russet-colored mildew he had left. He frowned, stood up, and went over to the pile.

It had doubled in size.

The previous evening, he had drawn a charcoal circle on the floor. This was his palette, where he'd smeared his improvized paint. And now here was the mold spreading all around. It had definitely doubled.

Toby stuck his finger in the mildew. He stared at it in disgust. It had the consistency of slightly greasy powder. Quickly, he stuffed his finger into his mouth. He chewed for a long time, and had to admit that it wasn't so bad. It tasted of crushed mushroom. He took two more fingers' worth, then a generous thumbful, and went back to the fire.

Toby was proud of himself. Like all living organisms, the mildew never stopped growing, so he had an unlimited supply of fresh food (if you can call mildew fresh). Together with a chunk of meat or an egg, and some melted snow to drink, this meant that he would get a full meal each day.

He tripped over the word *day*. What does day mean when you're in a black cave? How can you tell what time it is without the sun? His grandmother had a clock, which chimed every hour. There were only two or three clocks in the whole Tree. Everyone else relied on the sun, or the quality of the light. But how could he tell what time it was, here, in this hole? Was there a single thing in this cavern that was governed by time? He thought it over for a while.

Toby gave his belly a poke. Got it!

His stomach ran like clockwork.

When he was hungry, his stomach grumbled as nois-ily as a clock striking the hour. So, at first he thought he'd be able to tell what time it was according to when he felt hungry. It seemed the perfect solution. One rumble, two rumbles, three rumbles. Luckily, his thinking didn't stop there.

Toby had enough supplies to hold out for a hundred and twenty days, but not for a hundred and twenty rumbles. Even if he only felt hungry every twelve hours, he would have finished his supplies by February, mean-ing a diet of one hundred percent mildew through until April. That would be tight. No, he couldn't just listen to his stomach.

He kept on thinking.

He had to know what time it was. What was there in this hole that changed with time?

He looked at the mildew again and grinned. Not only was it going to feed him, but it would be his clock too.

Toby drew a second circle around the first one he had made the day before. In twenty-four hours, the russet powder had extended from one circle to the other. All he had to do was remove what was outside the small circle. When the mold reached the second circle, twenty-four hours would have gone by again, and he could have his next meal. With the powder he removed every day, he would have enough to feed himself.

And so Toby's winter began. With air, water, warmth, light, food—and a sense of time. Enough for the four months ahead. He spent the next two days feeling very excited. He was going to survive after all. He would see the light of day again.

But when he celebrated the third day with a small hard bread roll and a plate of mildew, and he calculated that he had one hundred and seventeen days left to go, he realized that we can't survive on air, water, heat, light, food and a sense of time alone.

What was it he was missing? What keeps us alive more than anything else?

Other people.

This was the conclusion he reached.

Other people keep us alive.

Two more days went by, during which Toby looked for other signs of life. But there wasn't even the tiniest snippet of a hint of a beginning of other life in the cave. Not so much as a funny-looking insect he could have chased around the fire. At one stage, he tried the mildew again. Sometimes he hoped this would become his companion, since it was alive just like he was. It was growing just like he was. Maybe it even had a soul somewhere in that russet-colored heap.

But after talking to it for several hours, in the warm tones of an old friend, he realized he would go completely crazy within a week if he continued like that. He called out in the cave, "Toby! Stop talking to that pile of mildew! Toby! Do you hear me?"

The echo prolonged the sound of his voice. He felt a lot better. Still, he went to apologize to the mildew, explaining that he didn't have anything against it personally, it was a huge help to him in many ways, but he wouldn't be talking to it again.

Toby dug away at the wood for a while, extracted a few splinters to get the fire going, then went to sit down.

And that was when he thought about Pol Colleen.

Pol Colleen was a silly old fool. Or that was how people referred to him, even though he was neither old nor crazy. There are some words like that, which don't really mean anything: *simpleminded* people often have lots of complicated things going on inside their heads; and *bigwigs* can just as easily be small, plus they probably don't wear wigs either.

Pol Colleen had one distinguishing feature: he lived on his own. All alone. He lived on a branch on the farthest tip of the Low Branches, on the east side. He drank dewdrops and ate the maggots from a small colony of midges that had settled near his home. Toby had gone that far only once. Colleen had smiled at him over his shoulder. He didn't yell at Toby for being there. He didn't say anything at all. Toby had watched him. He looked happy.

He sat at a small desk and wrote. He never stopped. Once a year, he went to get his supplies from the Asseldors, who were happy to give him paper. He made his own white ink by squashing young maggots. The paper he used was dark gray, so his long manuscripts looked like summer skies after a storm.

Pol Collen wrote from dawn till dusk. One spring day, after writing and paper had been banned, Pol Colleen disappeared.

Now Toby contemplated his painted flower on the wall. He needed to be working at something, like Pol Colleen. In addition to air, water and all that, he needed a project. He made a new palette in one corner of the cave and put a handful of mildew taken from his meal there. From that day on, Toby dedicated himself to his project.

On the walls of the cave, he began to paint the world

as he knew it. He was painting the Tree. His work took the form of a giant circular window around the orchid: dozens of scenes, landscapes, and portraits, all linking and overlapping. The geography didn't bear any relation to what you would find on a map, because it was the geography of Toby's imagination. When he was painting the Tree, Toby was drawing himself, in the great stained-glass window of his memories.

Close up, you could make out different characters, some familiar, others not, as well as real and imaginary insects. There was young Nils and his father, and Sim, Maya, and everyone else too, including Rolok astride a snail, and the Asseldor sisters leaving the Ladies' Pond in their white dresses. There was the Grand Council Chamber, like a teeming crater, full of weevils in neckties. There were forests, bright and shady branches, Razor and Torn depicted as Grubbers, raising a big fat grub that looked suspiciously like Joe Mitch. In one corner, a portrait of Leo Blue showed him with two faces, one smiling, the other scowling. Higher up, detailed landscapes unfurled: a perfect copy of the Lolness family's former home, The Tufts, and its garden with the little hollow branch at the bottom.

Day after day, the painting spread over all the walls of the cave, drawn in mildew red and charcoal black. When he had finished one particular painting, Toby held his flaming torch over it, in order to set the colors and prevent the mildew from blurring the outlines.

᪥

Depending on what he was painting, Toby had happy days and sad days. At night, he stopped dreaming. His dreams were on the wall, in the glow of the fire.

There was one scene that Toby painted through tears. He spent several days finishing it. It took place in a small, clean living room belonging to Mr. Clarac. Zef Clarac was a lawyer in the Treetop. Toby drew the scene with great precision, without adding anything or leaving anything out.

It was the scene that had determined Toby's fate. But in order to understand it, we need to go back in time to find out everything about the curse on the Lolness family.

Everything.

Three weeks after the message from the Grand Council had been delivered by Pinhead-Rolok, another letter arrived for the Lolness family. Somebody slid it under the door one morning: a black envelope. Toby gave it to his father, handling it the way you would a fragile object.

Sim Lolness put it on his desk. He called his wife. Since he'd been living in the Low Branches, he had learned how to work with his hands, because he had to. He had become very adept, and had even recently made a new pair of glasses with lenses from recycled fly wings. It was a very time-consuming job, but one he couldn't avoid, after sitting on his last pair.

The new glasses weren't dry yet, so for now he was working with a big magnifying glass, which tired his eyes. He asked Maya to open the envelope and read the letter.

When she had the piece of paper laid out before her, Toby's mother didn't say anything at first, then she burst into tears.

Sim and Toby were very worried. What new drama was about to befall them? They each imagined the worst catastrophe possible. Seeing that Maya was incapable of reading it aloud, Sim passed the letter to his son. Toby glanced at it and felt reassured. The letter didn't contain anything serious. He put it down again, relieved.

All this playacting was starting to make the professor lose his temper.

"Read-me-the-let-ter!"

Toby gave his father the news: Grandmother Alnorell was dead. Radegonde was no more.

Sim Lolness let out a big sigh. Phew! That was all. He kissed Maya on the forehead, as if she had just lost a thimble, and went outside into the garden.

Toby went to sit next to his mother. He felt awkward. He wanted to say something, but he didn't know what.

He could have said, "Don't be upset—she was old, after all," or "Don't worry—she was silly anyway." Luckily, he knew better. He stayed there for a long time, sitting next to his mother in silence.

From watching her that day, Toby realized that when you mourn somebody, you also mourn what they didn't give you. Maya was mourning the mother she'd never had. From now on, one thing was certain: she would never have a perfect mother in her life. And that was why she was sobbing.

It was as if, up to the last minute, you hold out for a gesture or a word that will make up for everything. As if death also kills the gesture that was never made, or the word that was never said.

Toby thought of it as the final example of his grandmother's wickedness: "When I was there, I hurt you, and now that I'm gone, I'm hurting you too."

You could call it the double effect of Radegonde. Even when she was dead, she made you suffer.

The next morning, Maya packed her suitcase.

18
Good Old Zef

"It's completely out of the question!"

The professor wasn't joking.

"Going up there all by yourself! Crossing the Tree in your flimsy skirt, with your suitcase and shawl! I'd rather tie you up in the middle of an ant nest and cover you in honey! No, no, and no again!"

Maya Lolness was gentle-natured and considerate toward her husband, and as kind as she was attentive, but enough was enough. With the back of her hand, she sent an inkwell flying, knocked over Sim's desk, and then calmly said, "Since when did you decide for your wife, Professor? I'll do exactly as I please."

Toby, who had been woken up by the noise, rushed into the study in his pajamas.

"I knocked my desk over," said Sim, trying to downplay the situation to his son.

"No, I trampled on it because you were stepping on my toes, Sim, dear." Maya put him right.

Toby smiled. He knew all about his mother's darker side. Even an angel's feather can poke an eye out if you mishandle it. But when he saw the suitcase, his face dropped.

"Toby, I'm leaving," said Maya. "Just for two weeks. I'm going to spend some time close to my late mother, and then I'm coming back. Look after your father."

"I'd look after your own backside, if I were you," muttered Sim.

When goaded, his temper was no better than hers.

"And as for you, Toby, look after the house. I'm leaving with your mother," he added.

Maya was speechless. She saw Sim piling up a few papers and stuffing them into a bag. A quarter of an hour later, they were standing on the threshold and giving Toby last minute bits of advice.

"Ask the Asseldors, if you need anything. We'll let them know when we pass by their place."

Toby kissed his parents. Maya was overcome because she hadn't spent more than three days apart from her son in six years of exile. So just to get her fill of being mom, she said things like "Don't catch cold," and then she buttoned up the top button of his pajamas.

That evening, the Lolnesses reached Seldor Farm.

They knew what a magical welcome the Asseldor family always offered, but they were still surprised to see two places nicely set on the big table. The others had already eaten. They were playing music in the adjacent room. While Lola Asseldor warmed up their soup, Sim and Maya went to listen to the concert. They pushed open the door. There was the full orchestra lineup with a special guest soloist playing the marbles: Toby Lolness.

Sim and Maya stared at each other, flabbergasted.

After keeping up a steady pace for just over four hours, Toby had reached the farm in time for lunch. He had spent the afternoon kneading the bread with Lila and Lola, chopping wood, and smoking cockroaches. Smoked cockroach, finely sliced, tasted a lot like smoked cricket, he discovered, but with an added hint of aniseed.

And now Toby was playing the marbles in front of his astonished parents.

The music stopped, and Toby made an announcement in the silence.

"I'm coming with you."

Sim opened his mouth to protest, but the concert immediately started up again. By the time the music came to an end, Maya and Sim had already been asleep for a while. Toby thanked the Asseldors.

The next day, all three of them set off together.

They made it back up to the top in seven days.

It was an excruciating journey.

Not that they suffered from exhaustion, however, nor the dull rain that made everything damp at the start of this September. In fact, they moved as energetically as

Leo Blue's boomerang, heading out quickly to get back quickly. No, the pain they felt on their climb back up to the Treetop was sparked by the landscape unfolding on either side of them.

Sim had foreseen things accurately, and the Tree was in a pitiful state. Six years had gone by, and a lot of sawdust since they'd last seen the Heights, which they no longer recognized. Every area of the wood was staked out, and it looked as worm-ridden as a waffle. Pale heads popped out of the holes to watch the passersby.

Of course, there were still a few beautiful wild places that were unpopulated, but the villages were all under siege from the Joe Mitch Arbor housing projects, which were turning the branches into sieves.

The leaves were few and far between, even though autumn hadn't yet arrived. The famous hole in the layer of leaves discovered by Professor Lolness was no longer the delusion of an old madman. The Tree's climate warming up, the risk of flooding during the summer, the gullies being formed in the bark—these were real dangers. Toby finally understood why his father had been so obsessed by these factors.

When evening came, the Lolness family couldn't rely on anybody for hospitality. In the course of their previous journey, years earlier, they had been turned away from the refuges and barns where they sought shelter.

"I could understand it in those days," said Sim,

"because people genuinely believed I'd made a mistake. But today, they reject us for no reason, except that they don't know us. They won't open their doors to anybody here."

In the distance, they sometimes saw convoys of weevils, which made Maya shudder. They also came across men in hats, leading red ants on leashes with big studded collars around their necks. The Lolness family turned their heads until they had passed by. They were traveling incognito.

One night, they stopped and pitched their tent at a dead end on a branch. A bit farther off, a man was taking a nap. The sun had barely shone all day. They lit a fire and invited their neighbor to share some grilled toast.

"I don't have anything to give you in return," said the man.

"Of course you don't," Maya replied. "We'd just be happy to share with you."

"I don't have any money, so there's no point."

The Lolnesses didn't understand.

"I don't have any money," the man said again, refusing the piece of toast.

Sim Lolness rummaged around in his pocket and gave him the only coin he could find as well as the piece of toast. The man stared at him, then grabbed the piece of toast and the coin and ran off.

This kind of encounter happened again and again. The Lolness family no longer understood how this world worked.

On the sixth day, when they were getting close to their goal, Sim, who had brought his new glasses with him, asked Maya to show him the letter.

"I didn't even get to read it, in all that fuss. . . ."

The truth was, Sim had been fretting about the letter for several days. Could there be a link with the letter from the Grand Council, mentioning Joe Mitch's Neighborhood Committees? He had even wondered if it might all be some kind of trap that had been set for his family. He took the letter out of its envelope.

The signature alone put his mind at rest. The letter was signed by Zef Clarac, Esquire, the Treetop lawyer.

"Good old Zef . . ." he whispered, grinning.

Zef was Sim's oldest friend. They were born on the same day and had grown up together. Along with El Blue, they had formed an inseparable trio. Zef Clarac was a hopeless student and an oddball, but everybody was incredibly fond of him. He had made himself an exemption card, which he flashed at all his teachers. As a result, he was excused from every subject, and he stayed in the playground from morning until evening. Huddled over his exercise books, young Sim would watch Zef through the window. The two friends had been inseparable until Sim met Maya. From that day on, Sim Lolness chose not to see young Clarac anymore.

Sim was frightened. For Maya.

He found it hard to admit the truth—Zef was a total charmer. Everybody fell for him. He could have made a patch of black ice blush red. And because he was worried, Sim had never told Maya about Zef Clarac.

One day, Zef had sent a note to Sim, saying he didn't blame him for keeping his distance.

"If I had a friend like me," he wrote, "I wouldn't have introduced him to my wife either."

Sim wasn't proud of his behavior, but he did at least keep up with what was going on in his friend's life. Zef Clarac had become a lawyer by mistake: a silly story of a sign carved in error by a craftsman. Zef had ordered a sign saying WIPE YOUR FEET, but in a mix-up he had received a smart LAWYER sign instead, which he hung above his door anyway. It was shorter, but just as useful for keeping his house clean.

His friends referred to him as a lawyer as a joke in the beginning, but then passersby began to knock on his door. He answered them politely. And since the passers-by were mainly female, he became a lawyer of some repute in the Tree.

On September 15, at eight o'clock in the morning, Maya, Sim, and Toby Lolness were trying to catch a glimpse of a house through the bars of a gate. They were in the Heights, and the house called The Tufts. They had made it. They walked all the way around the fencing. Everything was locked up.

On a hook near the door, Maya noticed the soft shape of Sim's beret, which hadn't been moved in six years. In her memory, she replayed the scene of the young Sim turning up one evening in the knitting class, with his thick glasses and beret.

Next, they headed to their appointment with Clarac, in the winter greenhouse at the far end of the park belonging to Grandmother Alnorell. The greenhouse was at the end of a branch, some distance from the house. Lit only by the light above the door, the greenhouse resembled an empty theater. Everything had stopped growing a long time ago. A few empty pots stood in corners. A fine leaf dust covered the floor.

Presiding over this scene and laid out on trestles was a long box fastened with two chunky padlocks. Even Mrs. Alnorell's coffin looked like a safe.

A footstep rang out at the end of a corridor. Sim recognized the tottering gait of Zef Clarac. The professor shuddered. He looked at his wife. Would she be able to resist? Zef appeared in the doorway.

He certainly wasn't physically attractive. Any normal woman would have preferred a long intimate waltz with

a wood louse grub, rather than shaking hands with Zef
Clarac. He looked like—it was difficult to say—like an
old cheese, but less firm.

Zef was extraordinarily ugly. Exceptionally ugly. In
an ugliness competition, he would have wiped the board.

Toby, who had heard the story of Zef's exemption
card from Sim, couldn't help thinking that he should
have been exempt from being born, from living. He
should have been exempt. He must have suffered so
much, from his earliest childhood, when he had to show
himself to others or walk in public.

Maya looked discreetly away, so
as not to be sick, but Zef Clarac
opened his arms wide.

"I was expecting you."

And suddenly the decom-
posed mushroom turned into
Prince Charming. When his face lit
up, Zef was a demigod. He gave off
all the warmth, generosity, and sparkle
you'd ever hope to find in a person.

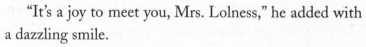

"It's a joy to meet you, Mrs. Lolness," he added with
a dazzling smile.

Maya walked toward those arms and buried herself in
them. She would probably still be there if her husband
hadn't given Zef a warm hug.

"My old friend Zef!"

Maya was ejected like a tiny insect being flicked out
of a bowl of soup. Next it was Toby's turn; he shook Zef's

hand. The eyes Mr. Clarac fixed on him were bright and lively. For that specific moment in time, Toby felt he mattered to this stranger more than anyone else in the world.

Sim intervened again. He was already regretting ever having come.

Luckily, Toby and his mother remembered that Grandmother Alnorell was there too. Walking farther inside the greenhouse, they went to gather around the coffin.

Maya was thinking about her mother.

Toby was thinking about Maya.

Sim was thinking about leaving.

"There are certain times in one's life . . ." Zef began.

This banal opening was made with such conviction that it was coated with a fine veneer of gold. Zef was a magician. The three visitors turned toward him.

Zef moved swiftly on to the practicalities, which lowered Maya's and Toby's heart rates again.

"Well, there we go. I felt it was a good idea to write to you immediately. Mrs. Alnorell died the day after the departure of her accountant, Jasper Perlush," he explained.

"He left?" asked Maya.

"Temporarily," Clarac explained. "He spends two weeks in September dealing with 'awkward customers.' He travels around the Tree with two giant men, Venge and Losh. Two excessively violent, burly men. Venge has enormous fingernails, which make his hands look twice as big and which he sharpens to needlepoints. Losh

doesn't any teeth left. He lost them in a fight. He has razor blades instead. When he smiles, everybody laughs too. . . ."

It was Zef Clarac's turn to smile now. And it wasn't a pretty young girl's smile. His teeth were scattered randomly around his gums, like a handful of seeds. But Zef's eyes were so clear, you could see his soul laughing at the same time.

"Big Mitch lends those two, Losh and Venge, to Perlush. Every year, in September, the three of them set out to confiscate the property of your mother's debtors. It's a sordid trip that gives them a lot of pleasure. The Fortnight of the Awkward Customers . . ."

Maya shuddered. Her mother hadn't behaved any better in her absence.

"No, dear lady, please don't think your mother turned into a monster. Perlush manipulated her. She was just an unhappy old woman."

He dabbed his tearful left eye and continued in a serious tone of voice.

"Perlush is due back tomorrow, and he'll want to get his hands on the Alnorell fortune—"

Sim interrupted, "Good for him—thank you, Zef. We'll leave you now. . . ."

He was already pushing his family toward the exit.

"Thank you for everything. It was a pleasure to—"

Suddenly, Sim felt a heel on his toe; his wife's forceful side was coming out again.

"Could you let Mr. Clarac finish, Professor?"

Zef coughed and hesitated in front of his friend, who was hopping from one foot to the other. Toby looked at his mother. She continually surprised him. He adored her.

"At least let me explain how she died," Zef went on.

He took a tiny object out of his pocket.

"She choked on this."

"Poor woman," said Sim flatly. "Why don't you give it to us—it'll be our inheritance. See you later. . . ."

"Yes," said Zef. "Your only inheritance."

The Lolness family, who had no desire to inherit anything, were nonetheless astonished.

"Great, it's all worked out perfectly," blurted Sim. "We'll take this . . . object, and we'll head back. Agreed, darling?"

Sim walked up to Zef and held out his hand to collect the tiny object. When he had it between his fingers, he gave his glasses to his wife and collapsed like a piece of clothing falling off its hanger. He was out cold, a small white heap in the greenhouse dust.

Zef, Maya, and Toby rushed to him. But Zef didn't seem to be surprised by Sim's reaction. He slapped him gently, saying, "I'll explain. . . . Wake up!"

Maya held out her hand. Sim's fist was firmly closed around the object. Little by little, the color returned to his cheeks. His eyelids twitched.

"The Tree Stone . . ."

His hand relaxed and his palm uncurled. There indeed was the Tree Stone.

19
The Tree Stone

There was nothing magical about the Tree Stone. It couldn't grant you eternal life or make you smart. It didn't make you invincible or invisible. It didn't give you special powers to see through a wall, or a dress, or into someone's brain. It didn't help you fly, or talk to insects, or shout out things like, "The Force of the Tree is with me!" It didn't turn into a goblin that hopped from foot to foot, or a plump fairy, or a sword, or a dragon, or a lamp, or a genie. Its only power lay in its price: the Tree Stone was very expensive.

It was expensive because it was rare. The only stone in the whole Tree. It was kept in the Council Chamber, tucked inside a splinter of wood where it had always been. It belonged to the Tree.

The Council was responsible for keeping it safe, and the reason was very straightforward. The Stone guaranteed that the Tree would always be the richest and that nobody would ever seize control of it. It was the Tree's treasure, a guarantee of its freedom.

"But it's priceless!" exclaimed Sim.

"Dear friend," said Zef, "our friendship is priceless, and so is your son, but the Stone has a price, a very specific one. Four billion."

This time, none of the Lolness family fainted or felt shocked. As far as they were concerned, money was like Mano's tie collection. They couldn't care less about it.

"This is what happened: Perlush convinced Mrs. Alnorell that her fortune was in danger, with bandits likely to steal it. She needed to be able to keep an eye on it, to sit on top of it in order to keep it safe. So Perlush advised her to buy the Stone."

"Buy the Stone . . ." repeated an incredulous Sim.

"She had exactly four billion and twenty-five cents in her coffers. The Council agreed. Mrs. Alnorell bought the Stone and sat on top of it."

Sim frowned as he handed back the Stone that had been incubated by his mother-in-law.

"Of course, Perlush is under Mitch's thumb," Zef the lawyer went on. "And he was banking on getting the Stone back when the old lady died. But Perlush and Mitch had forgotten that Mrs. Alnorell loved money. To the point of distraction. She had gone along with Perlush because the Stone was a sensible size that would allow her to put her plan into effect."

"Her plan?" asked Toby.

"The day after Perlush's departure, your grandmother heard a noise. She thought it was the robbers that she was so afraid of. She picked up her Stone, intending to swallow it."

Toby's eyes were as big as saucers now.

"That was her plan, young man—to carry her fortune to her grave. A fortune that could be swallowed. The noise she heard was just my friend Dr. Pill, who dropped by every evening to give her an injection in the left buttock. She was in terrible pain from sitting on the Stone, so the doctor was treating her with injections. Pill heard a choking sound. He forced the door open. Too late! The Stone was jammed in her throat. She died without suffering."

Zef left a respectful silence.

"The doctor extracted the Stone with a pair of tweezers. He came to find me. I preferred to settle the matter discreetly by informing you."

Sim was thoroughly perplexed now. He was chewing a ball of gum nervously. The money didn't interest him, but the Tree did. Allowing Mitch to gain possession of the Stone meant giving him absolute power over the Tree and condemning it to the worst kind of destruction.

Maya had taken the Stone. It was very beautiful, like a button-size ball of sap, and perfectly transparent, with all the colors merging as gleefully as a group of children splashing around in the water. Toby went over to take a look.

A few minutes later, the family had made their decision. They had to leave right away. Nobody would ever know they'd been there. Zef Clarac, Esquire, would take care of Mrs. Alnorell's funeral by himself. They slid the coffin inside the stem of a feather, in keeping with the traditions for important families. A dignified death for an old lady who didn't deserve it.

The plan was simple. When Perlush, Venge, and Losh turned up the next day, the lawyer would welcome them with his big smile and tell them the old lady had died from choking on an unidentified object and that her body was now floating somewhere above the clouds. He wouldn't mention the Stone. Zef would undoubtedly have to spend a very unpleasant fifteen minutes, but, as he said, what's a quarter of an hour out of a whole lifetime?

The Lolness family had to set out immediately. They shouldn't stay a second longer. Sim slipped the Stone into his pocket.

"I ask only one thing of you," said Zef Clarac. "Come by my place before you leave. I'll give you some provisions for the journey. And, Mrs. Lolness, you're welcome to use my bathroom to freshen up. . . ."

Here we go, thought Sim, indulgently, the worm charmer is on the offensive. Run for cover! Women and children first!

"You're too kind, my good friend Zef," he said as calmly as possible, "but we have to be going. Thank you for everything."

"Please," Zef persisted. "I live just two twigs from here. Please do me the honor. You can't set out again just like that."

"No, really, I mean it," repeated Sim, who was starting to get irritated.

Zef turned to Maya, "Mrs. Lolness, may I call upon you to exert your authority?"

"That wouldn't be appropriate," she answered.

"Gracious lady . . ."

Zef had released his last two arrows, and they struck their target. He held his hand to his heart, and his gaze made the beholder impossibly dizzy. Mrs. Lolness surrendered. *He's irresistible,* thought Maya. *He's incorrigible,* thought Sim, starting to chew his ball of gum again. He had always known that Zef's devastating charm would lead to his own downfall.

So after paying their final respects to Mrs. Alnorell's remains, all four of them set out together. Sim followed at a distance, dragging his heels. The neighborhood had changed a lot. Before, the Summit had been one of the most beautiful places in the Treetop, with plenty of fresh air circulating among its tender branches. The plots between the houses were gangrenous now, swarming with busy people, and there were passageways randomly carved out on every side.

Nobody really noticed the four of them, because nobody really noticed anybody anymore. The world had changed.

"Things don't change without a reason," grumbled Sim.

Toby could see small posters on the walls: GRASS PEOPLE = DANGER.

They soon arrived at Zef's home. There was his well-polished LAWYER sign. Clarac spent rather a long time looking for his key under a piece of bark. He found it in the end.

"That's strange—I never normally put it there."

Sim, who hadn't registered what had just happened, kept on grumbling, "Things don't change without a reason. . . ."

And he was right.

Zef opened the door and stepped inside, followed by Maya and Toby. The entrance hall consisted of a small room with a second door that was closed. This must be the lawyer's waiting room. Sim was still on the doormat, wiping his feet and joking loudly.

"I'm wiping my feet, Zef Clarac, Esquire. You should put up a sign telling people to wipe theirs too!"

Zef, who wasn't crazy about people talking about the story behind his sign, signaled to him to be quiet. But Sim wouldn't budge from the mat. Toby and Maya didn't understand the professor's joke, and Zef hurriedly pushed them inside. He ushered them into the spacious living room, where they stumbled on a scene which, months later, it would take Toby three days to paint on the cave wall, a scene that made him weep with every brushstroke of his trembling fingers.

There were a lot of people in Clarac's living room. Eight, not counting the new arrivals. The first person they noticed, mainly because his backside was taking up the entire sofa, was Joe Mitch.

When he saw them come in, he gave a smile, or the closest he ever got to one. In any event, you could see one or two yellow teeth on the side, behind the cigarette butt. The sound of his jowls flapping was followed by a rumbling noise from the bottom of his throat. Yes, this probably was his way of smiling.

Just behind the sofa were Mitch's two revolting sidekicks, Razor and Torn. They were a few years older than at the time of the Balina incident, but the advantage of already looking like a corpse is that you never seem to age.

A little to the right, perched on an armchair,was Mr. Perlush, whose feet didn't quite touch the ground. He looked like a creepy wax statue. Next to him, Toby was disgusted to see the figure of Tony Sireno, Sim Lolness's former assistant, who was bright red with embarrassment. He had chosen his camp. He had gone over to the other side. Finally, on either side of the door, two distinctive shadows were already framing our friends. Even though he had never seen them before, Toby had no trouble recognizing Venge and Losh. Venge was scratching his belly button with a fingernail as big as a scythe. Losh had a piece of raincoat between his teeth. It was the same material as the raincoat hanging from the living room coatrack, at the back on the left-hand side. Very high up—a green raincoat.

Zef recognized the coat hanging on the wall. It belonged to his frien, Dr. Pill. There was little doubting the owner, since the doctor himself was still inside it, dangling, unconscious.

After a lengthy silence, which was only natural among people who hadn't been expecting to meet up in this way, Joe Mitch made a long hissing noise between his teeth.

Razor rushed to translate. "We weren't expecting to find you in such good company, Mr. Clarac. What a surprise."

"And indeed a joy," Perlush added.

Mitch let out a "Grrrrrrr . . .," which shut Perlush up until the end of the conversation.

Razor picked up again. "Well, I do believe we've got the professor here too. Good news. . . . I could only see the old bag and the brat."

Sure enough, Sim had appeared behind Maya, Toby, and Zef. Later on, he wondered if he would have done better to flee before being spotted. But at the time, it didn't occur to him to desert his wife and son. He even stood in front of them and cast a dark look at Tony Sireno, whom he had just recognized.

Razor explained, "To be frank, we were only expecting Mr. Clarac. One of your friends, namely Dr. Pill, has just confirmed that Mrs. Alnorell has died and that the lawyer is handling this affair."

Zef stared at Pill, who was hanging from his collar on the coat hanger. He knew the doctor well: if he had given anything away, it could only have been under the vilest torture, and he already forgave him for it. But Zef himself was trembling with guilt and horror at having unwittingly led the Lolness family into this trap.

"So we were waiting for you to tell us where the corpse is, and of course the 'affair' in question. We'll handle everything, along with Mr. Perlush."

Sim spoke up. "My mother-in-law's body is in the winter greenhouse. It should be treated with respect. As for her affairs . . . they revert to my wife, who is her only daughter."

Normally, when an entire room bursts out laughing, the atmosphere is blissfully happy, like a foretaste of eternity. But when Joe Mitch's six stooges burst out laughing, Toby wanted to cover his ears. In the end, it was Joe Mitch himself who silenced his stooges.

He got Torn and Razor to help him up from the sofa. A crane and pulley wouldn't have been out of place.

Once standing, Mitch was so exhausted that it took him nearly a minute to catch his breath. He took the few steps that had separated him from the professor and came to a stop in front of him. Mitch stared at Sim, as if there were something on his nose, and then, raising his fingers to the professor's face, he grabbed Sim's new glasses and crushed them in his hand. He threw the broken remains of the glasses onto the floor, then returned to the sofa and collapsed into it, gratified.

Sim hadn't moved. Maya closed her eyes. A tiny tear nestled in the corner of one eye. But she gritted her teeth and kept telling herself, "Don't cry. Don't cry."

The tear must have heard her silent instructions. It briefly popped out, only to disappear back inside again.

Toby and Zef hadn't taken their eyes off Sim.

Torn spoke first. "The Friendly Neighbor has a great sense of humor. He likes these little teasing games, which make life more fun, and—"

Mitch let out a loud "Rhhhaaa-glglglgl-burpb . . ." that was difficult to decipher.

Torn cleared his throat and continued. "You've got five minutes to give us two things: the Stone and Balina's black box."

Sim tried to hide his surprise. He glanced at Tony

Sireno, who was shifting from foot to foot, embarrassed, in front of his former boss.

So, this riffraff still had their minds set on the black box. . . .

What the professor didn't know was that they were so set on it that, guided by Sireno, ninety researchers had been scratching their heads over the question for the past six years. It was Joe Mitch's obsession. He wanted the secret of that black box.

Torn asked Losh to count down five minutes. Losh looked shifty and signaled to Venge, who was biting his little fingernail. Neither of them knew how to count to five. They looked pleadingly at Perlush, who started counting the seconds.

"One, two, three, four, five, six, seven, eight, nine, ten . . ."

The four people under interrogation stared straight ahead of them. Toby glanced briefly at the body of Dr. Pill hanging from the coatrack. He was still moving.

The five minutes went by very quickly. Nobody said a word. Losh was sharpening his teeth by grinding them against each other. He sensed he was going to have to take action. Impatience was making white foam appear in the corners of his mouth.

When the time was up, Mitch growled. Torn offered a simultaneous translation, "All right, then, we'll have to search you ourselves." And he roared, "Search them!"

Venge didn't know whom to start with. "The wart first," Razor said.

Venge almost wavered, but Zef Clarac had already stepped forward.

It could only mean him. Ever since he was very small, he had always been the wart, the monster, the scruffy one, the blister, the pimple, the stain, the eyesore, or the stinking pile of garbage. Zef Clarac smiled. He had chosen to be a glittering monster, a radiant pimple, a flamboyant wart.

Toby noticed that in front of Joe Mitch's hideous gang, Zef looked like a prince.

Venge almost hesitated to go up to someone with so much pride. In the end, he put his revolting hands on Zef and started searching him. They didn't find anything except his house key, so Losh pushed him to the other side of the room.

Maya stepped forward.

"It's my turn. Is there a woman to search me?"

A few sniggers greeted this question. Mitch mumbled, "Puss-y-kin-ska."

"Get Pussykinska in here!" Torn shouted.

Losh disappeared for just long enough to usher in someone who had been standing guard outside. She had problems squeezing through the door and had to stoop and tuck in the folds of her generous curves.

There was only one way to describe Pussykinska—she was a human mountain. This aside, her face was quite kind, and she had a bowl haircut. She wasn't the least bit scary. Maya smiled at her. Pussykinska went up and delicately searched Maya's pockets, her hems and linings, concentrating hard throughout. She shook her head at Razor. Maya Lolness joined Zef on the other side of the living room. Pussykinska left discreetly, which was no mean feat for her.

Next they frisked Toby in the same way. After which, Razor looked at Toby and said in disgust, "The worst is when scum breeds small scum."

Instinctively, Toby answered back, "Small scum? I wouldn't say you're that small. . . ."

Razor was slow to catch on, but Sim Lolness rushed over and gave Toby a great whack on the back of his head. Toby's hair flew up.

"Don't insult the gentleman!" Sim shouted.

Trembling, Toby instantly raised his head and rushed over, with his back to the wall, to join his mother. He felt groggy and he looked distraught. Maya stared, wide-eyed. It was the first time Sim had ever hit their son.

Everyone looked from Toby to his father. The professor was losing his wits. Losing his soul.

They had won.

This great scientist, this unique man, was going to crumble because of them. Maya saw her husband sink to the ground until he was kneeling with his head in his hands.

"I can't go on. . . . I give up. I'll tell you everything. I'll give you everything."

Sim Lolness's shortsighted eyes were shedding warm tears.

Toby's face hardened.

Never let a child see his own father in the act of betrayal.

20
The Hollow Branch

Everyone in Zef Clarac's living room was in a state of shock. Even the Mitch camp looked stunned by Professor Lolness's disgrace.

Joe Mitch was already picturing himself as the master of Balina's secret. The crude sap reserves he'd been stock-piling would be put to use at last. By employing mechanical weevils, the Tree would be destroyed twice as fast.

Joe Mitch's projects were simple. They revolved around one thing: holes. Ever since he was born, Mitch wanted to make holes. Little ones, big ones, holes every-where. It was like a disease or an itch. He dreamed of turning life into one big hole. For this crazy project, he needed a lot of money.

By telling all, Sim Lolness would be making the only dream inside the big black hole of Joe Mitch's brain come true.

Fifteen years earlier, Joe Mitch had still been a modest Border guard.

The Border consisted of a simple line around the Main Trunk, at the base of the Low Branches. Mitch lived in a stinky lair with two weevils he'd trained. After El Blue died crossing the Border, Joe Mitch took advantage of the general unrest to put his weevils to work. He started digging a deep trench within his surveillance area.

The Grand Tree Council congratulated this young unknown Border guard who gave up his free time to digging for the security of the Tree. Only Professor Lolness and a few old crazies raised any opposition to his initiative. Sim made a speech entitled "Cut-throat," in which he talked about how the trench along the Border was cutting the Tree's veins and endangering it. People called out, "He's got talent but he really goes over

the top, that Lolness. Soon they'll ban us from cutting bread so we don't hurt any poor little slices!"

Joe Mitch enjoyed his first taste of success and started breeding a few weevils, which he hired out so that houses could be dug.

And so Joe Mitch Arbor was born. The business started growing, like a baby ogre. But once it got hold of the Balina Method, that ogre would grow up.

When she saw Sim collapse, Maya's tears welled up again. And this time, they rolled down her cheeks, sneaking into the corners of her mouth, soaking her collar. Zef held out a handkerchief, which she didn't even see.

Toby kept his icy gaze fixed on his father. He was witnessing the Lolness family pride cracking in every direction.

Torn went over to Sim Lolness and put a hand on his shoulder.

"Take heart, Professor. You're a brave man."

Toby saw his father shudder. A compliment from a swine is about as palatable as delicious cream served up in a dirty ashtray.

Sim took a deep breath.

"Before explaining where the Stone is, I'm going to lead you to the black box."

"Just tell us where it is."

"That's impossible. I'll have to come with you. You'll never find it without me."

Razor looked at his boss, who seemed to be snoring, despite the fact that he was wide awake. Joe Mitch shook his head.

"You're not leaving here," Razor said.

For this bunch of idiots, a scientist like Sim was a sort of wizard, capable of vanishing into thin air, or slipping through their fingers as soon as he left the room. Sim didn't look surprised by their reaction. But when he spoke, he sounded annoyed.

"In that case, my son will have to take you there."

Toby reeled. His father was crazy. Toby hadn't seen the black box for what felt like centuries and didn't know anything about it. His father must have gone crazy. Mitch mumbled something else even more inaudible. Torn and Razor leaned over the sofa, ears straining to catch what he was saying. Mitch gave each of them a flabby wallop.

Razor whimpered, "The Friendly Neighbor consents. Your son will go with Venge and Losh."

Losh smiled, slicing his lips with his teeth. The blood oozed into his spit. Venge was snickering, "We . . . wee-wee . . . wee-wee . . ."

Toby could make neither head nor tail of what was going on any more than Maya could as she watched her only son about to be sent out by his unhinged father on an impossible mission.

But a simple glance from Sim, who was wrinkling his nose the way he tended to on important occasions, made Toby think that his father must be giving him a signal.

There was a glimmer of hope after all. Toby understood that the first part of his mission was to play for time. He reminded himself that the only one of the four not to be searched was his father, who still had the Stone in his pocket. The professor's breakdown might be a trick. All was not lost.

Like a good babysitter, Venge held out his killer's hand to Toby. Toby refused to take it and put his hands in his pockets instead. He went ahead of the two creeps. At the last moment, he turned round again. Toby saw his mother in floods of tears, which made him melt. Then he turned to his father, who was gently scratching his cheek. The professor said something very silly: "And don't go injuring yourself again."

It was idiotic, pointless, ridiculous.

But as he walked out of that door, Toby was sure about one thing—his father's look was that of someone saying farewell. A look that meant, "Leave, my son. And don't ever come back."

For now, Toby was being followed at a distance of a quarter of a millimeter by two psychopaths. It was going to be difficult to shake them off. But his little brain, free as the air, was working overtime.

There could be no worse situation in the world than the one Toby found himself in now. Since his father had led him here, however, and since a few clues gave him hope that Sim hadn't actually gone crazy, there had to be a meaning to all of this. For the time being, he walked tall on the branch with no idea of where he was going.

His father's golden rule kept going around and around in his head, "Things don't change without a reason." This had to be the key.

Why had the professor changed so suddenly?

With the grim escorts galumphing behind him, Toby started by trying to understand Sim's odd behavior. First of all, slapping Toby; next, the promise to surrender his secrets; and finally, that last sentence: "And don't go injuring yourself again."

No matter how hard Sim tried to be a normal dad, tactless as the next, he never said cheesy things like "Be careful," "You'll get all dirty again," or "Don't go breaking your leg, now." So if he was talking like that for the first time, there had to be a reason for it.

"Don't go injuring yourself again." Odd advice when you're sending your son to the front line. Toby appealed to the words to shed some light. And instantly the words showed him the way.

The only time he had really hurt himself was at The Tufts, in that little hollow branch at the end of the garden. He still had the scar on his cheek. He thought back to his father's gesture, scratching his cheek as he gave advice. Toby smiled to himself.

The garden at The Tufts. That was where he had to go.

He turned and found himself face-to-face with Venge and Losh, who were peering at him.

"I made a mistake. It's this way."

Losh made the blades of his teeth glint. He didn't like

being taken for a ride. Venge warned Toby, "Wotchit-kiddo."

Which can be roughly translated from Venge-speak to mean, "Be careful, young man."

They stepped aside and let him pass between them.

To get to The Tufts, they had to cross a second branch and turn right under a few leaves turned gold by early autumn.

They got to the gate, which was still padlocked.

"It's here," said Toby, who was panicking about reaching his destination so quickly.

He thought the business of opening the gate would give him a few more minutes to play with, but Losh had already taken a big bite out of the chain and Venge sent the gate flying.

"There we go!" they said in unison, like a pair of out-of-tune choristers.

Toby walked round the outside of the house. He saw his father's beret hanging up. He saw the broken window panes, the ripped curtains, the garden running riot. Wild grasses had taken root in the bark dust. Venge's swaying hands acted as a makeshift pair of shears.

What now? wondered Toby. *What now?*

He knew the black box wasn't there. What did his father expect him to do?

He was standing opposite the little hollow branch. In front of him, under his feet, was the hole where he'd had his accident. This was the end of the garden. He couldn't go any farther.

If he turned around, he would be reduced to a finely shredded pile at the feet of Losh and Venge. Equipped to smash anything, but with only one brain between the two of them, these crackpots weren't renowned for being patient.

Toby racked his brain one last time. His father had sent him to the only place that was previously out-of-bounds to him. It was here that Sim had caught Toby at the last moment, when he was very little. And his father had said to him, "I'll be relieved when you're a teenager. You'll be too big to fit inside the hollow of this dead branch. But for now, don't get too close to it."

Behind him, Venge and Losh were getting restless.

"Well, kiddo?" said Venge.

"This is it," Toby answered flatly.

"Issit?" asked Venge.

And they laughed for a good minute or so, going, "Issit? Zit! Zit, zit, zit! Issit?"

Such sophisticated humor could have kept them occupied for at least an hour. But when they tried to catch their breath, between hiccups, Toby was already in the branch's hollow.

They stopped dead and leaned over the hole.

Toby hadn't hesitated for a second. He was only just thirteen, so it was his last chance to pull off such a trick. He entered the forbidden branch. This was his father's plan. No doubt about it.

He could see his guards' heads above him.

"Wotchitkiddo," Venge said again.

But Toby had disappeared inside the little branch.

Venge wanted to slide his head in, but it wouldn't fit. So he stuck in his hand and arm instead. His fingernails shredded the tunnel walls. As bad luck would have it, Toby was injured twice by Venge's nails, once on each shoulder. He was bleeding. Venge looked at his colleague. Losh was stamping his feet. He elbowed Venge out of the way, stepped over the hole, and positioned himself on the far side.

Lying down on the branch, Losh started gnawing away at the edges of the hole with his teeth. Each snap of his jaw made chunks of wood go flying up.

Rarely had so much energy been demonstrated by somebody sawing through the very branch he was lying on.

Back on the side of the Main Trunk, a perplexed Venge was watching the scene, and it reminded him of a joke. But which one?

At the first cracking sound, he remembered which joke it was. Losh looked up. From the expression of terror on his face, he also appeared to be familiar with the joke about the idiot who—

Crrrrrrrraaaaaaaaaccccckkkkk!

The branch had just broken off, making the most hideous noise. Clinging on for dear life, Losh headed for the unknown, calling out, "Tooooo-o-beeeeeeyyyy..."

Venge watched him fall, hitting branch after branch before he disappeared into the depths of the Tree.

All he could say was, "Gosh, Losh..."

It took Venge a while to realize that Toby had disappeared along with Losh. But he just kept on saying, "Gosh, Losh . . . Loooshhhh . . . ," in a very distraught kind of way.

A patrol sent out that same evening by Joe Mitch found Venge at the bottom of the garden at The Tufts, still standing at the point where the branch had broken off. Mitch's men went up to him slowly, so as not to frighten him. When they questioned him about what had happened, he just kept saying, "Loooshhh . . . ," in the same way the head of a decapitated person might, remembering the rest of its body. The men from the patrol took one more step toward him.

"Loooshhh," Venge croaked one last time.

And he leaped into the void.

But the name he called out as he fell, which echoed and reverberated into the distance, wasn't Losh's. Venge was shouting out, "Tooooo-o-obeeeeeeyyyy . . ."

The soldiers leaned over, terrified. The noise mobilized the entire neighborhood.

A millimeter under the crowd's feet, with a seat in one of the dress circle boxes to catch the show, someone whispered to himself, "Poor Venge . . ."

It was Toby.

When he had crept inside the hole in the branch, he had noticed that the tunnel of worm-eaten wood forked two ways. Instinctively, he had taken the healthier-looking fork, heading uphill. Here, he had twice come under attack from Venge's claws. Then he had seen the branch snap off altogether with Losh's body clinging to it. In midflight, poor Losh caught sight of Toby and called out his name in despair.

Toby clung on in his hole. With the terrifying abyss straight ahead, he had a tiny space in which to lie low and wipe the blood from his wounds.

From there, he had heard Venge's despair at the loss of his colleague, and then the sound of the patrol arriving. Finally, he had witnessed Venge's swan dive. Cruel chance determined that Venge would also notice Toby as he fell past him, but it was too late, he couldn't do anything except cry out a harrowing, "Tooooo-o-beeeeeeyyyy . . ."

Within a quarter of an hour, a crowd of onlookers was squeezed onto the branch. They held up torches and oil lamps. Luckily for Toby, they quickly erected a safety rope where the branch had broken off. But the crowd kept pressing forward. Rumors were spreading. Accident or suicide? What had happened in the abandoned garden? They'd heard Venge's final cry. Then nothing.

Foiling all the security, a daring boy ventured into the darkness at the end of the broken branch. He scrambled down between splinters of ripped wood, a torch in his hand. He looked younger than fifteen, with a tough expression, and his jaw was square and thickset. His deft movements didn't make a single rustle.

Toby saw him suddenly appear in his hiding place. He hesitated for a second.

"Leo? Is that you, Leo?"

The boy pulled back, and then, slowly, brought his torch near.

"Toby?"

The two friends stared at each other. After six whole years of separation, the best friends in the world had found each other again, by chance, at the end of a branch in the Heights. Tobyleo, joined at the hip.

"Toby . . . you came back."

"Help me, Leo."

Leo raised his torch higher. Toby could see the changes in his face: as strong as ever, but there was something jagged about it too. Like shards of broken glass. Leo looked at the wounds Venge's nails had made on Toby's shoulders.

"Help you?" he said.

"Yes, Leo. I'm in danger. Don't ask me to explain. I just need to get back to the crowd."

A few years earlier, Leo wouldn't have hesitated for a second as he did now.

"Help me, quickly," Toby asked again.

"Follow me."

They clambered across the section of broken branch. When they reached the top, Leo blew out his torch. Some men were trying to keep back the more curious members of the public. Finally, the boys found a spot where the rope slackened. Toby and Leo easily blended in with the crowd. They pushed their way into the swelling throng. Toby lowered his head.

"You want to stay hidden?" asked Leo. "Why?"

"Good-bye," said Toby.

He hugged his friend and disappeared.

Leo stood stock-still in the bustle. He felt strangely uneasy, a deep-seated sense of guilt. For years, the wicked seed of doubt had been growing inside him.

"Don't trust anybody," the Friendly Neighbor's men always said. And Leo did as he was told.

Above all, Leo Blue feared the threat of the Grass people. This fear, cultivated by Joe Mitch, added to the terror that, since childhood, he had associated with his father's death. El Blue had been killed by the Grass people and no doubt their master plan was to ambush and finish off the rest of the Tree's population.

Leo had to be on his guard against everybody. What did he know about Toby Lolness anyway? Not much, not anymore.

A friend? This person he hadn't seen for six years?

Yes, that was it—he had just helped a stranger. A complete stranger. The weight of his mistake just got heavier.

Joe Mitch arrived a few minutes later. He had entrusted the Lolness parents, back in Clarac's living room, to a dozen maniac guards who never took their eyes off them. Mitch stepped onto the broken branch, flanked by Razor and Torn. The crowd parted to let him through. He sat on his folding chair for a long time, staring into the void.

And then Joe Mitch had his idea. Voids always inspired him.

He signaled to Razor and muttered something to him in gibberish. It looked like he was sucking his ear. The crowd was packed in tight all around.

Razor glowed with delight. The boss was brilliant. Primitive but brilliant. Razor coughed and asked for silence.

"Fellow Tree-dwellers, the Friendly Neighbor has spoken! Listen to his message. A crime has just been committed against the Tree. The Lolness family, who have withheld Balina's secret from us, have chosen to abuse their exile by selling this secret to foreign powers! Dear Tree-dwellers and neighbors, consider the crime of the Lolness family. From now on, the vermin known as the Grass people will control Balina Power!"

The crowd was silent for a moment before erupting with anger. In this furious madness, a fourteen-year-old lad remained quiet a few seconds longer. . . . Then he raised his fist higher than anyone. It was Leo Blue.

There was a fixed look of hatred in his eyes that set them ablaze.

When Joe Mitch entered the living room once again, Zef and the Lolness parents were trembling. Mitch plonked himself down on the sofa, which made a noise like a balloon being deflated. There were some things greedy Mitch couldn't resist saying himself: "He is deeeeeeaaaaaad . . ."

Sim and his wife looked at each other.

Toby.

Dead.

Their exhausted eyes searched for a last glimmer in the other's gaze.

But there was nothing left.

Zef was crying. But his faint mewing didn't even reach the ears of the Lolness parents.

None of them saw the imposing figure of Pussykinska come back in, pushing Leo Blue ahead of her. Caught off guard, Mitch turned to face the newcomer, who said, through gritted teeth, "I saw him. He's alive."

Sim and Maya Lolness felt their whole skin tingling with a warm feeling returning them to life.

And so the long manhunt for Toby began.

21
Infernal Tumble

It had been the worst winter for Elisha.

She had set out for the cliff ten times, battling against the cold and snow. Ten times her mother had rescued her, racked with exhaustion, tears frozen around her eyes. The cave was halfway up the cliff of snow, which looked like an unassailable glacier.

By February, everybody thought the thaw was on its way. There were a few fine days. The families in the Low Branches paid each other visits, but the lake and the cliff remained out of bounds.

A week later it was snowing again and the Lees' hopes were smothered under a white coat. March was icy cold, and by the first day of April it was still impossible to reach Toby's refuge.

On April 10, the sun shone again. A gentle warmth enveloped the whole Tree. The water trickled and dripped around the Lees' house.

Isha spoke softly to Elisha. They were both crouching on the threshold of the round door to their home, watching the rays reflected in the puddles and streams.

"All you can do is hope. . . ."

There was nothing else to do, given that Toby had been imprisoned for four and a half months with just a meager bag of food. Basic math or a cold look at reality was all it took to realize that he didn't stand a chance. But hope glowed in Elisha's heart, making her believe in the impossible.

On April 16, Elisha managed to plow a path as far as the lake, and from there on to the cliff. She was at the foot of a damp snow wall, looking for a way to climb up, when she heard a voice calling out. She was about to bellow, "Toby!" when four shady characters suddenly rose up next to her. They were drenched in melted snow, from their hats to their boots.

"We've been calling you for the last two hours, little girl. We followed your footprints in the snow."

It was one of Joe Mitch's vile patrols, already back out on the hunt for Toby.

"What are you doing here, kid?"

"And you?" asked Elisha.

"We're looking for the Lolness boy. Answer the question! What are you doing here?"

"I live nearby, with my mother. I wanted to see if the water bugs were back out on the lake."

It was the first excuse that came into her head. But it

was easy enough to satisfy the lightweight brains in front of her.

"If you find Toby for us, I'll marry you," said a hunchback, whose pimple-pocked nose nearly blocked his eyes.

"Now, there's an incentive. I'll keep my eyes peeled."

She blew on her hands to warm them. A little cloud of white steam formed between her fingers.

Big Nose walked up to her.

"Can I give you a kiss while we're waiting?"

"I don't deserve it yet—wait until I've found this Lolness boy for you, and then it can be my reward," she said, pulling back.

Big Nose was very pleased. Elisha pretended to turn for home. When she'd taken a few steps in the snow, she heard them saying something about the professor and his wife. The four men were talking very loudly. What they said nearly struck her down. She didn't have the strength to continue walking.

But she made it back home in the end, then collapsed in her mother's arms.

The next day, at midday, Elisha stood in front of the mass of snow blocking the entrance to the cave. She chipped away at it all afternoon, keeping an eye on the shores of the lake. By six o'clock, Elisha's tiny hand scraped its way through the last snow rampart. Her arm was on the other side. She stopped. No sound came from the interior.

She dug furiously, crying out angrily, making the snow fly all around her. She wasn't scared of anyone anymore. Daylight snuck its way into the cave, and Elisha followed it, on her hands and knees.

The fire was still warm.

Coming from the bright outdoors, Elisha couldn't see anything. She called out feebly, "Toby . . ."

No answer. Elisha didn't know where she was putting her feet. Her eyes still hadn't gotten used to the dark. She detected a bundle of wood in front of her. She took it in her hands and walked back to the hearth, with its hint of red. She threw the wood onto the glowing embers. Tall flames shot up at once. Elisha followed their journey with her eyes.

That was when she saw the ceiling and walls sparkling with light. She had discovered Toby's masterpiece. The huge painted fresco stretched out in red and black over every surface of the cave. Elisha couldn't take her eyes off it. She felt as if she were inside Toby's glowing heart.

"Do you like it?" asked a weak voice.

She rushed toward the sound.

"Toby!"

There was Toby, lying propped up against the wall. He was pale. His cheeks were hollow and his mouth dry, but deep in his eyes still glowed a steadfast comet.

"I've been waiting for you," he said.

Toby had never seen Elisha cry before. She made up for lost time that day, as she pressed her forehead against Toby's chest.

"Stop it, stop it! What's there to be sad about? Look, I'm fine."

He offered her a handkerchief splattered with red paint. Elisha couldn't stop crying. Toby felt her wracking sobs as she clung to him. In the end, she buried herself in the handkerchief, reemerging with reddened cheeks. Little by little she calmed down, then looked up toward the arched ceiling.

"It was to keep me busy. Some people paint their tombs so they can lie down in them. But for four months, I painted windows so I could see the outside world."

Elisha stared, wide-eyed. Yes, it was like a window to the world. She walked over to the wall, with her paint-smeared face.

"Elisha . . ."

"Yes?"

"I'm a little hungry."

Toby hadn't eaten anything except mildew for seventeen days. Elisha disappeared outside immediately.

Toby cried in despair, "Noooo! Don't leave me! Come back!"

Elisha rushed back inside, worried. Toby couldn't stand to be left on his own for another second. She had just gone to get the food parcel she had brought with her.

"I'm staying now, Toby. Don't be afraid."

She unwrapped the paper, which was soaked in butter. At last, Toby smiled. There, in front of him, was the biggest pile of honey pancakes he had ever seen.

It was three days before Toby could stand again. He had managed to exercise regularly during his four and a half months of imprisonment, to keep his body from seizing up. So it wasn't long before he was agile again.

He spent some time being a moth on the shores of the lake, flapping his arms and hopping around. Elisha never left him now. Toby needed this shadow watching him run in the moonlight.

Tucked on a ledge, above the cliff, they sat down at last. Toby could feel the springtime bubbling away underneath them, in the night. He breathed deeply to make up for lost time. Elisha told him about what had been happening over the winter.

Over at the Asseldor household, Lola wasn't doing at all well. From the moment Lex had set out in search of his parents, she had insisted on lying down on a little mattress in the main room at Seldor, and she hadn't moved since. She ate almost nothing and stopped talking, so the whole family had found out about the secret bond between Lex and Lola.

At first, her parents tried to shake her out of it.

"It's just a crush—there's no need to make a big drama."

But after a week, they realized it was more than a crush. She was actually prepared to die for this boy who had gone away.

They were immensely patient with Lola, and no doubt their patience helped prevent her flame from going out altogether.

Lila, her sister, was never far away and slept by her bedside, holding her hand. She understood everything about her pain; she was living it too.

The last news that Elisha had dated back to February. Lex hadn't reappeared, but Lola's condition had stopped getting any worse. Her eyes were open, and she was able to eat a little breakfast. Her brothers sang every evening in the room next door, and Lola might be seen tapping a finger in time to the music.

Her big sister kept watch over her, silent and discreet.

Elisha told Toby this story among others, but what she wasn't saying weighed heavily on her conscience: what she had heard Joe Mitch's men utter by the shores of the lake.

On the fourth day, Toby spoke about his parents.

"I thought about them all through the winter. There's no point in waiting. They won't come looking for me."

"Maybe you're right," said Elisha fervently. "You shouldn't wait for them anymore."

"If they don't come looking for me, I'm the one who's got to go looking for them."

Elisha gave a start.

"Go where?"

"Back up to the Treetop, to find them. Rescue them from Mitch's paws."

Toby had been watching Elisha while he talked. She had lowered her long eyelashes and was looking at the ground. She wanted to speak. That was when he realized that she knew something.

"Toby . . . I overheard something about your parents."

Toby shuddered and tried reading Elisha's look.

"They've been sentenced to death," she went on. "They'll be executed on May. 1"

Toby grabbed Elisha by the shoulders.

"Where are they?"

"That's not the problem. You've got to protect yourself."

"Elisha, where are they?"

He was shaking her.

"Please. Look after yourself, Toby. The hunt is still on for you."

"Elisha—"

"Toby, I've got an idea where you might be able to hide."

"I'm leaving; I'll be in the Treetop in three days. It's

April 21. That'll give me a week to find them. Good-bye, Elisha."

He let go of Elisha. He turned.

"Listen to me!" shouted Elisha.

"They'll be dead in ten days if I don't help them. I'm going to the Treetop."

"Toby, they're not up there!"

Toby turned around again.

"Where are they?"

"They're at Tumble," whispered Elisha. "They're at the fort at Tumble."

Toby went pale. Tumble was just a few hours' walk away, which meant his parents were very close. And yet Toby felt himself wavering.

He knew something about Tumble from old Vigo Tornett, who had spent ten years there and who could never bring himself to talk about it.

If anyone said "Tumble" to Tornett, first his lips started trembling, then his whole body. Ten years of captivity at Tumble destroyed a man.

By his own confession, Tornett had done some stupid things in his youth. Toby didn't know the details. But Sim Lolness, who was better informed, admitted that Tornett hadn't always been the gentle and benevolent man who lodged with his grubber nephew. In fact, to be brutally honest, Tornett had been one of the worst brigands in the Tree, a bandit of the highest order.

He had gone on to spend ten years at Tumble, when the prison was still controlled by the Grand Council. If it had looked like a vision of hell back then, that was a picnic compared to what Tumble had become under Joe Mitch's control.

Aside from the question of surviving inside the fortress, one thing was for sure: you would never escape from it. Nobody ever had, and nobody ever would.

Tumble was a ball of mistletoe dangling in thin air. It was a parasite growing in the Tree, sucking out its sap and drinking its water, attached to a branch by a single creeper, which was kept under surveillance by ten armed men. At the first sign of mutiny, all they had to do was cut the link and the prison would be plunged into the void. They called it the Final Plan.

In a flash, everything Toby knew about the prison at Tumble came rushing back to him. His hopes were dashed.

A sleepless night followed, in the silence of mourning, on the shores of the lake.

By dawn, Elisha felt almost relieved. She had told the truth, and Toby didn't look as if he was going to take up an impossible mission. He knew enough about what people had said on the subject of the ball of mistletoe.

Ten days to get a clumsy scientist and his wife out of that trap—Toby would need at least ten years. Just to get in.

Unless . . .

Elisha prayed that an idea, which had just crossed her mind, didn't occur to Toby. She chased it away by batting her eyelids and saying, "No, no, no" deep down inside.

But Toby's face was already a different shade. There was nothing she could do. Between their two hearts was a shortcut, with thoughts flowing freely along their narrow shared branch.

Toby looked into Elisha's eyes. He had decided to give himself up to Joe Mitch.

Elisha shuddered.

"If I turn myself in," Toby explained needlessly, "I'll be taken to Tumble in a matter of hours, so half the journey will already be done."

"You'll do the other half in your coffin!"

It took a whole day and night for Elisha to realize that Toby wasn't going to back down. If he didn't risk everything for his parents, the rest of his days would be meaningless. His life would be like an ornament on a mantelpiece. It wasn't about succeeding. It was about risking his life for them.

Idiots would call this honor. Toby called it something else. Love, maybe, even if he couldn't bring himself to say it.

As she listened to him speak, at the back of the painted cave, Elisha put Toby's feet on her knees and, with a strand from a feather soaked in blue caterpillar ink, she drew on the soles of his feet, a vertical line, a barely visible mark from his toes all the way to his heels.

Toby didn't put up a fight.

"Is that my war paint?" he asked.

He thought back to his childhood and remembered how when he was little, he and his friend Leo Blue would sometimes paint signs on their hands and faces. Leo had always been a moody, occasionally violent child. The death of his mother when he was very young, followed by that of his father two years later, had left a terrible scar, but he wouldn't talk about it, not even to his best friend.

The last time Toby had seen Leo, before the winter, in the little hollow branch, it seemed to him as if the wound to his heart had become infected.

Elisha was quiet. Her braids brushed against her eyes.

Toby knew that she had the same blue marks on the soles of her feet, and that they could only be seen at night when they gave off a bluish light.

"Is it a secret?"

Elisha nodded and put down the strand of feather on the edge of the inkwell.

"I've got a secret too," said Toby.

And he told her about it.

When he'd found himself all alone on the end of the broken branch, and he'd heard Venge wailing for his lost colleague, Toby had tried to think through his father's plan, so he wouldn't forget anything about the three clues he had been given.

1) He had been able to explain his father's false treachery easily, because its only purpose was to help Toby escape.

2) At the last moment, he had also decoded those words of warning: "And don't go injuring yourself again," which had signaled the hollow branch at The Tufts — the place where he was small enough to escape his guards.

3) But he still didn't understand why Sim had raised his arm against his own son, when he ordered him to speak politely to the cretinous Razor. Again, it was completely out of character for Sim, so Toby needed to find a sign or a meaningful clue in that too.

An hour or two later, when Toby was already on the run, and Leo Blue had walked into Zef Clarac's living room, Joe Mitch had thrown a tantrum under the maternal eye of Pussykinska. *Toby still alive?* Mitch couldn't stand the idea.

Joe Mitch's tantrums were like a bad case of gas. He gripped his belly, turned bright red, and made a thousand mysterious noises, which sounded like a cross between farting and bleating. His cigarette stub accidentally shot from his lips like a rocket being launched. It landed in

Pussykinska's cleavage, and she crushed it subtly by sticking out her chest.

When he had calmed down again, Joe Mitch lay still for a few minutes. Then, very slowly, he turned his bulbous eyes toward Sim.

There were certain matters on which Mitch never allowed himself to be caught out. He remembered full well that Sim Lolness hadn't been searched. The diversion Sim had tried to create wasn't enough. The Tree Stone was there. . . .

Mitch gestured toward Torn, who pounced on the professor.

Maya was watching her husband. Toby was alive, but Mitch was still going to take possession of the Stone. She would of course have given twenty such priceless Stones in exchange for her son's life, but the power bestowed on Mitch by this fortune would spell catastrophe for every life hanging in the balance of the Tree.

Torn was searching Sim frantically. Even when he was stark naked in the living room and two men were going over his clothes with a fine-tooth comb, there was still a big smile on the professor's face. His plan had worked.

They didn't find anything except two balls of gum and a pencil. Razor squashed the balls of gum with his shoes. There was nothing inside them. The gum stuck to his heel. Razor hopped from foot to foot, trying to get rid of the gum that was now gluing him to the ground. Faced with this absurd spectacle, Mitch's eyes were rolling furiously in their sockets.

Sim smirked.

At exactly the same moment, during his desperate flight, Toby had run his hand through his sweat-drenched hair and found a ball of that same gum right there, stuck to the back of his head, in the place where his father had hit him so hard. Mixed in with the sticky substance, he could feel something much harder. He pulled it out of his hair—there, stuck between his fingers, was the Tree Stone.

Now, four and a half months later, in the cave by the lake, Toby took the Stone out from the hem of his pants and showed it to Elisha, who still had a bit of caterpillar ink on her hands.

"Here's my secret," he said, holding the Stone between his fingers. "My father entrusted me with it. I'm going to hide it here, in this cave by the lake. If something happens to me, you'll know where it is."

He went over to the back of the cave, lighting his way with a twig from the fire. He raised the torch up to a life-size portrait of Elisha, alone, crouching down with her chin in her hands. He pierced one of her painted eyes and inserted the Stone in place of the pupil. The little flame went out.

Toby turned toward the real Elisha. She was standing in front of the fire.

"Don't give yourself up to Joe Mitch," she said. "I'll help you."

22
Educating Young Girls

Wielding a stick that weighed more than she did, Bernie whacked the old man over the head.

"Now, let's go home!" called her father, who was watching her antics from a distance.

The little girl didn't bother to answer, but stood in front of the old man she'd just hit, then put her hand on his bald head.

"It's growing," she said.

Sure enough, there was a nice big bump coming up. Bump number five. Definitely time to go home.

Gus Alzan had two concerns. The first was being in charge of a thousand prisoners. He could handle that. His methods didn't necessarily follow the rules, but they satisfied the Friendly Neighbor. Gus lived with his daughter at the heart of the mistletoe ball at Tumble, in the central knot. All the tendrils in the ball led out from this point, so he had total control.

Gus's other concern, his real one, was his daughter, Bernie. For a while now, he'd been worried about how she was growing up. Of course, he knew she was only ten years old, so Bernie was bound to change. She would mature, turn into a nice young lady. People had said to him, "It's perfectly normal, at that age; there's so much going on inside them." And so, at first, he'd looked on rather fondly as Bernie smashed the furniture or strangled her governesses. "My, she is growing up!" he told himself. "She's the spitting image of her godfather." Bernie's godfather was Joe Mitch.

So Gus pandered to his daughter's whims. He even loaned her a few prisoners who were on their last legs anyway, to satisfy her appetite for bumps.

But after a while, Gus Alzan began to worry. It had dawned on him that one day he would have to marry off his daughter. Clearly he was worrying ahead of time, but he figured that the more challenging the path ahead, the earlier you had to set out. In Bernie's case, that path looked particularly challenging. In fact, it wasn't so much a path as a primordial jungle.

At ten, Bernie already had a few undesirable habits for a young girl from a respectable family. Gus overlooked the prisoners who were battered to death, because perhaps they'd asked for it anyway. And the strangled governesses, because maybe their teaching methods were to blame. No, the first serious act involved the cook at Tumble, when Bernie plunged his finger into boiling oil and made him eat his own flesh while it was still on the bone, like spareribs.

Gus fired the cook, who was no longer any use to him, and he punished Bernie by making her go without any dessert.

From that day on, he decided something had to be done.

Which is how Gus came to hear about a remarkable man who was an expert in manners and social etiquette. He was just a simple cook's assistant who had arrived at Tumble that winter, but his reputation had spread rapidly, and he soon got on people's nerves. He smiled all the time, spoke in flowery language, and insisted on being called Clot.

Clot showed up one Saturday morning at the Alzan home.

"My most respectful greetings," he said to Gus.

"Same to you," the governor answered him clumsily.

"I have been informed that you were requiring to see me. It is most enduring of you. To what, may I ask, do I own the leisure?"

"I . . . It's my daughter."

"Your daughter," repeated Clot, with a high-pitched giggle that was rather inappropriate, given the subject matter.

"Well, yes. My daughter, Bernie."

"Bernie!" exclaimed Clot, laughing now with a squeaky titter that grated on the ears.

Gus Alzan took Clot's whole face in his hands, squashed it a bit, and then pinned him against the office door.

"What's so funny, Clot?"

"I . . . er . . . nothing, it's just my way of relaxing."

"Good. Now, I want my daughter to become a young lady."

Clot set to work right away. He had lived with Joe Mitch's most formidable guerrillas, but the three days he spent with Bernie Alzan were the worst of his life. The following Tuesday morning, he entered Gus's office. It was the last week or so of April, and a fine spring day.

"Well?" inquired Gus hopefully.

A black ring encircled each of Clot's eyes. He had

so many bumps on his head it looked like a spiked helmet.

"I've come tho hand in my notith, Mither Althan."

Every other tooth was missing. He spoke with great difficulty and didn't laugh at all. Discouraged, Gus Alzan granted him one day's special leave.

"Spethial leave?"

Clot didn't know about this system of granting leave. Working at Tumble was like working for Joe Mitch; people never took vacations. Can vacations exist in hell?

Gus felt thoroughly despondent after this failed attempt. What would become of his Bernie, whom he used to bring along, as a little girl, to tickle the prisoners on death row before they went to the gallows? What could she have missed out on growing up in this prison? To console himself, he threw two prisoners to the birds.

Birds are partial to mistletoe. They love its juicy white berries, which are to be avoided at all costs during the winter if you don't want to be eaten by a sparrow or a thrush. When he needed to relax, the governor of Tumble would sit a prisoner on a large berry and wait for the birds. Since it was the end of April, there were only a few berries left, and they were so ripe that the birds wasted no time.

Gus had a dreadful night. He dreamed about Bernie bearing down on him with giant wings. She ate him raw, and he ended up stuck inside bird poo.

First thing next morning, there was a knock at his door.

"Ith me."

Gus recognized Clot's annoying voice. He opened up.

"If you own me the leithure to discuth with you a thecond time—"

Gus nearly tackled him. No one just knocked on Gus Alzan's door as if they were dropping by for a bit of "converthation."

If you came to his door, you were expected to be a jittering bundle of nerves, and you had to tremble and beg to be forgiven without even knowing what you'd done wrong.

Clot managed to avoid being reduced to a pulp by adding, "Ith about Bernie . . ."

Clot didn't have any more teeth than the day before, but he had his smile back. Curious, Gus let him in.

For once, cook's assistant Clot was very clear.

He'd spent his "leave" in a neighboring branch, taking the opportunity to reflect on Bernie's situation. He was convinced that the little girl had a problem with authority.

"Is that all?" asked Gus.

Clot's revelation was nothing new. But he went on to say that because of this, Bernie's particular problem could never be dealt with by a father or a teacher.

"A what?"

"A teather . . ."

"Is that all?" Gus repeated, his hands itching for action. He was getting ready to send Clot flying.

But Clot went on.

"What thee needth ith a fwend."

"A what?" Gus interrogated him.

"A fwend."

Gus Alzan had heard this word before. *Friend*. But he only had a very fuzzy idea of what that meant. The kind of person who isn't the boss, but who isn't anyone's slave either. A hazy concept that had been fashionable a long time ago.

As far as the governor of Tumble was concerned, you were either above or below him. Commander or commanded. Joe Mitch above. Everyone else below—with the possible exception of his daughter, because although she should have been below, she often climbed above.

After thinking it over, he reached the conclusion that, personally, he didn't have any friends.

"The only perthon Bernie can rethpect ith a fwend," Clot insisted.

Gus was still perplexed.

"Where can we buy one?"

Clot became all mysterious and explained that, with Mr. Alzan's permission, he would bring a friend with him the following day. Gus nearly choked. If Bernie's future friend was neither above nor below her, it meant she would be like Bernie. Which doubled the size of the problem. If there were two Bernies in Tumble, the prison would explode!

Clot immediately tried to reassure him. The young person in question was a shining example of somebody who was firm but polite. The perfect friend for Bernie. She was thirteen years old. Clot had met this friend last year. She had taught him everything. By an extra-ordinary coincidence, he had just met her again at the gates to Tumble.

Gus refused point-blank. No surprises there. It was unthinkable to let a stranger inside the prison. And espe-cially not now.

If something happened, Joe Mitch would squash him. And when Joe Mitch squashed somebody, there was nothing left, except a bit of blood around the edges.

"Well, I'll leave you, then, Mither Governor," Clot said sadly.

He shook the dust from his hat and left the room. He was already through the door when Gus grabbed hold of him. The governor kept Clot in suspense while

he thought back to some of Bernie's worst exploits. He
had changed his mind.

"If your little girl doesn't do the trick, I'll throw you
to the birds."

Clot left again with a strange kind of feeling. The
fact was that it wasn't his idea. He had run into that girl
from the Low Branches again and had ended up confid-
ing in her about the situation with Bernie. She had
offered her services. Clot trusted her, but he couldn't
help thinking about the threat of the birds.

His life was in the hands of . . . what was she called?
Bubble. Yes, that was it.

Bubble.

Bubble entered the prison at midday on April 24. She
was searched sixteen times before being led by nine
guards with crossbows. Bubble was a little girl who
looked straight ahead, wore black clothing, and had two
braids that formed question marks at the back of her
head. Her face was strange and rather flat.

She was ushered into Bernie's playroom, where the
doors closed behind her. The guards were positioned all
around the Alzan household.

That evening, at seven o'clock, Bubble was brought
out. The guards were expecting to find her sliced up or
reduced to mincemeat.

But not a hair was out of place.

Gus met with Bubble in his office. He felt extremely
intimidated by this girl with piercing eyes.

"I . . . Good . . . Well . . . So . . ." he said.

"I won't come tomorrow," explained Bubble. "I'll be here the day after."

"Good . . . Well . . . I . . . All right. . . ."

She walked over to the office door before turning back to face Gus again.

"I should stress one very important point. While I'm away, Bernie must not hit any one. Not a single bump. Or it will all be over."

Before leaving by the narrow exit at the top of the mistletoe ball, Bubble was searched eleven times. The only thing they found on her was a little wooden figure the size of a thumb. They let her keep it.

Bernie spent all the next day in bed crying despondently, her tears forming a puddle around her. Gus went to console her, splashing through her tears in his boots. She didn't ask for any prisoners to knock unconscious; she just asked for her friend. At seven o'clock that evening, she threw a tantrum. She ripped up her mattress and swallowed the foam inside it, but she still didn't hit anybody. Five men were sent out to find Bubble, but with no success.

The following day, Gus Alzan got up before dawn to wait for Bubble. At midday, she showed up at the gates to Tumble. She was searched sixteen times again. In her pocket, there was still the little figurine roughly carved from a splinter of wood. Nine guards escorted her through the prison. She didn't even glance at the hundreds of prisoners who were groaning behind the bars of their tiny cells. This girl was as tough as seasoned wood.

"You . . . I . . . You didn't come yesterday. . . ." ventured Gus.

"Isn't that how I said it would be?"

"I . . . Yes, yes . . . but—"

"If you'd rather," Bubble threatened in a cold voice, "I can leave."

Gus humbly apologized for the first time in his life (with the exception of Bernie's naming ceremony, when he had accidentally trodden on Joe Mitch's cigarette stub).

Bubble stayed with Bernie until seven o'clock and then left. Gus wanted to have a few words with her, but she said she didn't have time.

"I won't come tomorrow. I'll be here the day after."

Gus didn't dare comment.

When she was searched at the exit, nobody noticed that the little wooden figure was no longer in her pocket.

Two days later, the whole process was repeated, except that on her way out in the evening, Bubble summoned Gus.

She stared at him long enough for him to lower his gaze, and then she said, "You know what I'm going to say to you."

"Yes. I mean . . . you won't be coming tomorrow, but you'll come the day after."

"No. Not tomorrow, or the day after, or ever again."

Gus didn't bat an eyelid. If you'd gotten right up close to him, you might have been able to see his lip quivering ever so slightly and in the white of his eye the reflection of a tear. The last hope he was clinging to had just disappeared.

He would never see Bernie break free from her ghastly chrysalis to become a princess in a pale dress who would run toward him on an isolated branch, calling out, "Dad! Dad! It's me, Bernie!" He would never gaze at her beneath her bridal veil, with a young man in her arms, waltzing on a starry floor. Angry Bernie is who she would remain, barbaric Bernie, who would marry a bald old man, if she was lucky, just so she could make bumps on his head. A Bernie who would eat her bridesmaids and pageboys and suffocate her mother-in-law by crushing her in the wedding cake.

"You know why," said Bubble.

"No," groaned Gus Alzan, "you can't just let me down like this. Bernie is already getting better."

"Molmess."

"What?"

"Molmess or Molness. Does that mean anything to you?"

Gus looked up, terrified.

"No . . ."

"Bernie has admitted that yesterday while I was away she hit somebody called Molness."

Gus stared at Bubble.

"That's impossible. She didn't leave her bedroom."

"But there is somebody called Molness?"

"No . . ."

The way Bubble stared at him made Gus's head hurt, so he revised his answer. "Maybe a name like that . . . but it's impossible."

"I don't think you fully understand. . . ." Bubble said.

"She can't know him. She doesn't know the names of any of the prisoners."

Bubble got up out of her chair, dark-eyed.

"You're telling me I'm lying."

"No. Never . . ."

"So you're saying that your daughter is lying."

"No . . ."

His answer was a bit less certain.

"Come with me," ordered Bubble.

She took him into Bernie's bedroom.

"Bernie-wernie," called Gus as he went over to the bed. "Bernie-wernie, my little petal . . ."

Bernie was on her bed, surrounded by a cloud of foam that she had pulled out of her new mattress. Gus tried to catch her eye.

"Your friend tells me you gave somebody a few bumpy-wumpies yesterday?"

She didn't answer.

Gus persisted, "Did my little Bernie-wernie give somebody a bumpy-wumpy or two?"

The answer rose up from under the foam, "Lolness!"

Bubble and Gus looked at each other and walked out of the room. Gus had no idea what was going on. It was impossible. Totally and utterly impossible. Sniveling, he tried one last time to convince Bubble. But she wouldn't budge. She had laid down the rules from day one.

"And what if —" he started.

He cut himself short. Bubble pretended she hadn't heard him.

"Good-bye," she said.

Gus shook her hand. She went over to the door. He followed her. He seemed to be wavering.

"And what if there aren't any bumps on the prisoners' heads?"

"Which prisoners?"

"The Lolnesses."

"I thought that name didn't mean anything to you," said a surprised Bubble, still walking.

"There's a couple with that name in the high-security zone."

Bubble immediately came to a halt.

"If there's no bump on these Molmess people's heads," she said, "then that changes everything."

She turned around slowly. The governor detected a glimmer of hope.

"I'll go and find out! And then I'll let you know."

And off he trotted. Bubble called him back.

"I'll only believe you when I've checked the Losnells's heads for myself."

"Lolness . . ."

"What?"

"It's out of the question."

"Fine. Good-bye."

She set off again. Gus couldn't bear it anymore.

"Wait!"

"Too late. I don't want to check anyone's head now. It doesn't make any difference to me."

"Wait!"

"No. Too bad. Good luck with your daughter."

"Pleeeease. You can see for yourself. I'll take you to the Lolnesses' dungeon."

An hour later, night had fallen. After being searched several more times, Gus and Bubble entered the high-security zone. It was at the bottom of the mistletoe ball and was a much quieter area.

After various crossroads, they arrived in front of cell number 001.

"Here we are," said Gus.

The governor couldn't find his key, so a guard loaned him his. The name Lolness was written on a small sign. Gus entered the tiny room, looking very pale.

Bubble walked in behind him. She surprised him with an encouraging little pat on the back. She knew she was prohibited from saying a single word.

Gus Alzan was fully alert. These two prisoners were more precious than all the rest of the nine hundred and ninety-eight prisoners put together. Gus had learned not to trust anybody once he entered a cell. So he never took his eyes off Bubble.

He would have done better to have been on his guard earlier. If he had, Bubble wouldn't have the key in her pocket to cell number 001 that she'd just stolen from him.

But instead, he had taken the time to warn her that no communication whatsoever was possible with the two prisoners. He was adamant—she was to check their two heads in silence and then leave.

Which is exactly what she did.

A couple was sitting on the bench. Bubble went over to them, never looking away from their terrified gaze. She placed her small hands on their heads, and stroked them very slowly. She shook her head at Gus Alzan. His expression lit up—no bumps. He made Bubble walk in front of him and turned his back on the prisoners.

On the governor's back, and in spite of the gloom, the captive couple could make out a fine silk banner, with the words *Cheer up. Your son will help you.* When she'd entered the cell, Bubble had hung the banner from the only place Gus couldn't keep an eye on—his own back. She removed it discreetly as soon as they were through the door.

"Good," she said, patting his back. "I feel reassured. We'll be able to move on to the next stage now. The picnic."

Gus looked satisfied. He had no idea what a picnic was. He assumed it was some kind of modern teaching technique. Bubble explained to him.

"I won't come tomorrow. I'll be here the day after. And I'll take Bernie on a picnic."

23
The Mummy

When Bubble explained what a picnic was, Gus panicked. On the one hand, he didn't see how he could give his daughter permission to leave the confines of the prison. On the other, he didn't want to interfere with Bubble's approach, which had proved effective so far.

"I'll find you a nice empty cell. You'll be able to have your picnic where it's warm."

"No," said Bubble. "I'm taking Bernie outdoors. Normal friends have picnics outdoors."

It was out of the question. Gus couldn't let Bernie go off with a thirteen-year-old girl he had met only a week ago. The picnic was due to take place in two days' time — one day before the execution of Sim and Maya Lolness, which Joe Mitch would be attending. Gus couldn't take that kind of risk at such a crucial moment.

Gus suddenly wondered how he had come to place so much trust in this little girl. What did he know about Bubble? Nothing. Absolutely nothing. There was still time to put a stop to everything.

Bubble gave nothing away as she waited for his answer. She didn't take her eyes off the governor. She could read him like an open book. She could tell he doubted her. She could even see that doubt spreading.

Bubble realized she was on the verge of being fired. She had to act quickly. So she had an abominable idea.

There was a prisoner waxing the parquet floor of the governor's office. Exhausted and down on all fours, he was polishing near to where Bubble was standing. His knees were chafed raw from dragging himself across the floor. He was a sad-looking man—yet another prisoner who never understood how he had ended up there. They all had the same story; they were just going around minding their own business and then suddenly, with no notice, they would be taken away and thrown into a cell. If the prisoners dared to ask what they had done wrong, the only answer they got was "State secret."

Bubble made a show of backing away from Gus, but she was actually edging toward the prisoner. Gus was keeping an eye on her. Yes, this girl unnerved him. What was she up to?

With a violent stamp of her heel, Bubble crushed the prisoner's hand as he was waxing the parquet. This simple act of cruelty warmed the governor's heart. So Bubble was

on their side after all. A girl who behaved like that couldn't be all bad. He roared with approving laughter and sent the prisoner whimpering back to his cell.

Bubble didn't move. There was just a faint red rim around her eyes. The prisoner's pain had ripped her apart, deep inside. Bubble thought she was going to faint.

"All right," said Gus.

Bubble tried to stop her voice from betraying her as she asked for the picnic basket to be prepared. She specified the contents: butterfly pâté, honey éclairs, and, of course, a red-and-white checked tablecloth to cover the basket.

"If anything's missing, it won't be a real picnic," she threatened, as she walked out of the door for the last time.

Bubble arrived at ten o'clock in the morning, on April 30. Little Bernie was waiting for her in front of the entrance to Tumble, with her basket, her lace dress and her regulation straw hat. Behind her were nine bodyguards with exactly the same basket—even the same straw hat.

Bubble didn't get angry. She called Gus over and asked what all those strange men were doing there.

"They won't bother you. It's for security reasons."

After considerable negotiating, Bubble managed to get the team down to two guards. She was even allowed to choose which ones.

Bubble didn't go for the most alert candidates. One of them had hair that flopped over his eyes like a curtain. He was called Mince. The other, whose mouth was as stretchy as a tentacle or an insect's sucker, was called Pulp, and his eyes were all scrunched up like a fly's behind.

Gus Alzan watched all four of them leave. Bernie was holding her friend's hand. A few days ago, Bernie wouldn't have touched that hand without crushing it or extracting a few nails. Now, with her straw hat and parasol, the little girl looked as if she had stepped out of an old painting. Gus gazed fondly at his young princess disappearing into the distance.

But this idyllic scene wouldn't last long. At six o'clock that evening, he was informed that someone wanted to speak with him. Pulp had been sent on ahead. He was on his own, dead tired, and his big sucker of a mouth was all slack.

"There's been a bit of a problem. . . ."

"Bernie!" Gus cried.

"She's hurt herself a little bit. Just a bit."

Gus wanted to slam Pulp like a nail into the bark. But the blood drained out of him.

All he could say was, "Bernie! Bernie!"

"She's being put back together again," said Pulp.

Gus Alzan couldn't breathe.

"She's being . . . what?"

"Put back together again. She hurt herself a little bit."

"Where?"

"Everywhere."

Pulp couldn't have listed everything Bernie had broken if he'd tried.

"BUT WHERE IS SHE NOW?" Gus bellowed, shouting himself hoarse.

"Near a lake."

Pulp was wary of telling him what had happened, so he pretended to faint. Gus generously dished out slaps to bring him around, but Pulp just let himself be manhandled, his sucker-shaped mouth gaping left and right. He preferred these blows to what he would have been in for if the governor ever found out what he had just done to his daughter.

They had reached the lake at around one o'clock. Bernie had collapsed with exhaustion. Since she had never left Tumble, her very short legs were not used to walking. In three hours, her feet had puffed up like soufflés. Her toes looked like grub sausages bursting out of her shoes.

While Bernie slept on the beach, Bubble and the two guards devoured the picnic. Pulp and Mince had appetites like weevils. They were discovering the art of the picnic. For dessert, they munched on the wicker baskets as if they were pretzels, and once they'd blown their noses on the checked tablecloth, they started yawning.

Bubble suggested a nap. At first Pulp and Mince refused, but when they saw how soundly Bernie was asleep, they gave in. Bubble escorted them to a dark cave, which was pleasantly cool for a snooze. She promised them that nobody would hurt Bernie while they were asleep.

The two guards nodded off peacefully, with the skin on their bellies pulled taut. They were woken by blows. Blows in the darkness. Blows to their heads. Somebody was clubbing them to death with great big thwacks. An expert, who handled the bludgeon with cold-blooded efficiency, dividing the bumps evenly between the two guards' heads. A real artist.

But Pulp and Mince had no time to admire such talent. In seconds they were on their feet and giving the thrashing of the century to the club wielder. Oddly, for someone of this caliber, their attacker seemed surprised, as if he'd spent his whole life fighting lifeless dolls.

When the two bodyguards were satisfied that they would be leaving nothing behind but a small pile of bones in a bag of skin, they stopped. And it was at exactly this point that Bubble appeared, holding a torch.

"Why did you do that?" she asked.

"What d'you mean?" said Mince.

"Self-defense," Pulp piped up.

"What are we going to say to the governor?" asked Bubble.

"What d'you mean?" said Mince.

"Where's Bernie?" asked Pulp, who was getting worried now.

"She's there."

Bubble held her torch toward the floor, lighting up Bernie's remains. Pulp made a strange noise with his mouth, and Mince pulled back his hair to reveal his eyes for the first time, squinting monstrously.

"We've beaten her to death," he said.

Bubble looked very annoyed.

"I promised you that nobody would hurt her while you were asleep. . . . But it never occurred to me that it would be you who . . ."

Barely an hour after Pulp's return to the prison at Tumble, a strange-looking team turned up at the main gates. There was a stretcher made of twigs, with Mince carrying the front end and Bubble bringing up the rear. On the stretcher lay a strange object, like a reclining wax statue.

Gus Alzan rushed over to Bubble.

"Bernie! Where's Bernie?"

Bubble nodded toward the stretcher.

"There."

Gus leaned over the white shape. He turned very pale.

"WHAT? But what happened?"

Pulp had appeared behind Gus. He and Mince were both winking manically at Bubble to try to stop her from telling the truth. But since one of them had eyes the size of dots, and the other had a curtain for bangs, it was impossible to read their clumsy signals.

Bubble was very vague. "She fell. She disobeyed instructions, and she fell right down to the bottom of a hole."

Mince and Pulp relaxed.

"But where is she?" her poor father roared.

"In this wax shell, . . . It was the only way to put her back together again. She has to stay in the shell for thirty days. I found a worm beetle farmer-woman who was happy to cast Bernie in the wax. Her bones need to mend and her organs have to return to their proper places."

"You'll get a brand-new Bernie," Pulp added clumsily, immediately getting Gus's fist on his big rubbery mouth.

Feeling better for having hit somebody, Gus removed his hand from the sucker and went over to the wax shape. He could now see the place where the head must be, as well as the arms and the legs. It was like a white star.

"One month! How's she going to eat?"

"There are tubes in all the right places. It's specially designed. You have to put sapwood purée down that feeding tube there, three times a day."

Gus approached the end that presumably held the head. Very gently, he went tap-tap with his finger. When the only answer he got was a tiny movement inside the shell, he started to cry.

Wax-Bernie was allowed through the gates of Tumble, as were Mince and Pulp. But when Bubble tried to come through, Gus turned on her violently.

"Go away! And don't ever set foot here again."

Bubble was caught off guard. For the first time, she showed visible signs of distress. "But I have to look after her. . . ." she said.

"Out of my sight!"

Bubble seemed genuinely shaken. But she wouldn't give up. "Just give me one more night, because Bernie—"

Bubble knew she could win Gus over if she was given a chance to speak. But Gus Alzan was already roaring.

"Throw her out!"

Fifteen guards rushed over to keep Bubble from getting in. They drove her back beyond the main entrance. She wasn't shouting loud enough for Gus to be able to hear her anymore.

It was too late. In a flash, Bubble turned back into Elisha, and she trembled all over with fear. What she didn't know was that same evening, Mince and Pulp would be offered up to the birds on a mistletoe berry. So there were some fates that were even worse than her own. But when the stretcher disappeared into the heart of the prison at Tumble, she turned away, ashen-faced, heart pounding, and ran off.

If you've never spent even a minute inside a wax sarcophagus, then you have no idea how hot Toby was after several hours. He could barely hear the voices around him. Earlier he had been shaken around inside his shell, but nothing seemed to be moving now. He must be inside Bernie's room. A few more noises, the muffled sound of footsteps receding, then silence again.

He thought about Elisha, who would be right next to him, waiting for the perfect moment. She would warn him with five slow taps on the wax. That was their code. The two of them would split the wax shell open. And the great escape would start right there, in the heart of Tumble.

Time went by. The heat was suffocating. Suddenly,

there were heavy footsteps; the wax vibrated. Someone had entered the room. Toby heard a sort of sucking noise and then a warm substance was piped directly into his mouth. Sapwood purée. They were feeding him. He ate everything he was given. He had no choice. Anything he didn't swallow went inside his collar and, combined with the heat, turned the shell into a cesspit.

Luckily, the force-feeding stopped in time. New noises. Then silence again. Once more, Toby thought about Elisha, so close by. She had taken every risk, against all odds.

For a week now, Toby had let himself be led by Elisha's intuition. She had decided to spend some time going around the prison, looking for the right angle of attack. Her first stroke of luck had been meeting Clot on the first day, who had told her about the nightmarish Bernie. It hadn't taken Elisha long to hatch a plan.

At first, Toby categorically refused to let her take a job inside the prison. She couldn't face the danger by herself, to rescue parents who weren't even her own, especially since she'd never even met them before! Elisha vehemently defended her plan. This was too good an opportunity to miss.

Toby and Elisha operated very differently. Toby thought things over, looked at situations from every angle, made plans. He was prepared to take risks, but he always had several solutions as a lifeline. Elisha, on the other hand, seized opportunities without thinking about them too much. She jumped straight into the water, skinny-dipping as usual.

Faced with Bernie, she instinctively knew what to do. Without even glancing at her charge, Elisha made for the opposite corner, where she spent the first day fashioning a little figurine out of wood, a simple character the size of her thumb.

In no time, Bernie was driven to respond to this indifference. She picked up a club lying among her toys and went over.

Elisha didn't make any kind of gesture toward her but calmly said, "I know some heads that will never have a single bump on them."

Bernie was beside herself. She dropped the club on her toe and groaned.

"Where?"

"In my house," Elisha answered.

Bernie bellowed as she waved the club, ready to crush Elisha's head along with that of the wooden figurine.

Just in time, Elisha whispered, "I'll take you there, if you don't hit me."

Bernie stopped.

"If you don't batter anybody for six days, I'll show you the heads with no bumps."

The taming of Bernie had begun. A simple case of blackmail.

Two days later, on April 26, Elisha issued the same instructions, but that evening, on her way out, she left the little wooden figurine in the corner. When she came back two days later, Elisha found the figurine shattered into a thousand pieces.

"Did you hit the toy man?"

"Who?"

"The toy man!"

"What toy man?" Bernie asked again.

Elisha paused and was surprised at the name that escaped her own lips. "Lolness," she said. "He was called Lolness."

Why had she said that name? She had no idea. It just came out that way, words and gestures happening before thoughts, showing her the way.

"Lolness," Bernie repeated after her.

That evening, Elisha went to Gus Alzan to complain. Bernie had attacked someone called Lolness while she'd been away. Which was how she got to find out exactly where the Lolness parents were being held captive. She was even going to see them, after all these years of never meeting them.

Then came the idea for the picnic. In order to get the governor's permission, Elisha had been forced to carry out the worst act of her life. She had crushed the hand of an innocent person. Disgusted by the cruelty of her own actions, she made herself think of Toby's parents, of the lives she was trying to save. Yes, it really was a matter of life or death. But how far do you go in order to save somebody? During the nights that followed, this question often kept her awake when she was trying to sleep.

When Bernie set out from Tumble in her lace dress, she was looking forward to making a thousand bumps on new heads, as promised. It was this reward that got her through the walk.

After Bernie's nap, all Elisha had to do was lead her to the cave, offer her the guards' heads to bash in the darkness, and then take her battered charge to Isha Lee, who would finish off the job by casting her in wax. Shooing aside the guards out of respect for the girl's modesty, they slid Toby into the shell in place of Bernie. The plan was set.

Yes, too well set . . . Toby reflected ironically, finding it more and more difficult to breathe.

He thought of little Bernie waiting in another wax case, in the worm beetle's hut. Elisha's mother would be looking after her attentively. They were going to put her in a low-cut chrysalis that went only as far as her face—much more comfortable.

What was Elisha doing? Toby couldn't bear it anymore. Shut inside his wax casing, he was still waiting for the five taps. He couldn't hear any sounds around him now. Night must have fallen.

Suddenly, Toby felt very alone—abandoned. But there wasn't a moment to lose. His parents were due to be executed at dawn the next day.

Elisha! Why was there no signal from her?

Toby had run out of patience. He started wriggling around inside the wax to make it crack. He would have to risk making an exit. But his first movement made him realize just how trapped he was. No matter how much he tried to convince himself otherwise, the wax armor wasn't budging. Toby had been trapped in the cave by the lake, but this coffin was far worse. He couldn't even turn around. At this rate, he would be stuck here, helpless, while his parents mounted the scaffold. He would die of grief, slowly, over a whole month, showered in tepid purée, drowning in his own tears. Young Toby baked alive in a wax pie.

Perhaps it was midnight. Sim and Maya Lolness would be crouching in their cell, just a few centimeters away, counting down the hours to death. And in a month's time, when they pried him out of his stinking shell, Toby would join them, victim of the same punishment.

"Elisha . . . Elisha!"

Toby was shouting now from the depths of his casing. He would have given anything to bang with his fists, but he couldn't, because his hands had been sealed in an open position in the wax. His thoughts were becoming increasingly jumbled. His heart was racing.

Questions were pounding in his head, like in a nightmare.

Why do I have to die? Why? I want to get out of here! Leave the Tree! Find another world! Go wherever sticks go when they're thrown off the end of a branch! I want to get my fists back again, and my strength! My fists! Where do my fists go when my fingers are outstretched? Elisha! Whose side are you on? You've deserted me! And so has Leo! Why don't friends last for life?

Nothing could stop his descent into this infernal spiral.

Nothing?

He heard the first tiny tap, and then the second. Someone was knocking very gently on his coffin.

24
Flown Away

Elisha was crying, close to the fire.

Isha Lee had seen how upset her daughter was when she came back home. Elisha no longer looked like the valiant little soldier Isha used to watch setting out every morning. She looked like a thirteen-year-old girl who had seen all the hopes she had slowly built up come crashing down around her.

Isha wrapped a gray blanket around Elisha's shoulders. Not even the flames could bring the color back to this shadow of her former self.

Nobody has ever seen swallows at rest, but if they were suddenly unable to fly, they might look a bit like Elisha: stopped in action, disoriented, their crestfallen faces looking for a way out.

Elisha hadn't been able to pass through the gates to Tumble with Toby, and that was all it took for their whole project to crumble. Their plans relied on the two of them being inside the prison. Once the wax shell had been split open, Elisha was supposed to attract the guards' attention by shouting out that Bernie had disappeared. Toby would use the chaos as a cover to go with the key to the high-security zone. After that, Toby had a secret plan.

All Elisha knew was that the following day, after the scandal of the Lolness family escaping, the real Bernie would be discovered in front of the prison gates. No one would be surprised by this final twist involving the little pest. They certainly wouldn't link it to Sim and Maya's escape, so Elisha wouldn't even come under suspicion. She would take a break after a few days of good and loyal service.

This had been their plan. But none of it would work without her.

The thick layer of wax couldn't be broken by one person alone. And that was only the first problem. She felt horribly guilty for deserting Toby, even though she hadn't made a single mistake.

And now here she was, watching the flames in her own home. It was the only thing she could do. She had watched them so many times before, with her shoulder against Toby's. When they were out camping in the wild, at the far edges of the Low Branches or in the cave by the lake—watching the fire always sparked the same sense of wonder. Where did the force come from to lift those golden curtains? What invisible breath, what arm stirred all those flaming banners? Fire was a mystery that troubled Elisha.

Isha served a bowl of herbal tea to her daughter, who was wrapped in her swallow-gray blanket. She had put the bowl on a tray with a candle. More fire, thought Elisha. She stared at the candle. Her eyes suddenly opened wide. She looked hypnotized.

"Is something wrong, Elisha?" asked her mother.

Elisha couldn't take her eyes off the candle. Isha took her hand.

"Is something wrong?"

"Look," Elisha said flatly. "The candle. It's melting."

Isha looked at her poor daughter. Something had snapped inside her. But when Elisha slowly turned away from the candle, it was with a much calmer expression that she faced her mother. All was not lost. Toby would escape after all.

Because Bernie was scared of the dark, her bedroom always had to be lit by torches. Late that evening, once the wax chrysalis had been put down in the girl's bedroom, her father had lit all the torches as usual. There were even torches at each corner of the bed, which gave the wax mummy a funereal air.

The shell's feeding tube rose up almost as high as the flames. The gentle taps Toby heard weren't made by anybody. They came from the drops of melted wax that, after some hours exposed to the heat of the room, were falling, one by one, onto the shell. Toby had been expecting five taps, but he heard a lot more than that. His whole shell was melting in the overheated atmosphere of the bedroom, and the thin trickle of wax was dripping onto the bedsheet.

Toby still had no idea what was going on, and the heat was making him increasingly uncomfortable. He felt sticky. He had no idea that in a minute the layer of wax would become thin enough for him to break it. He had no idea that in a few moments he would be free.

But things are never that simple. At the same time as the melting wax was slowly freeing Toby, it was also soaking into the sheet underneath him. What do you call a piece of material dipped in wax? A wick. A giant wick was being created under Toby's body, ready to catch fire.

It all happened at once. Toby burst through the last layer of wax at the very moment the bed caught fire. Like a piece of rebellious steak refusing to accept its fate and rising dramatically out of the flames, in one leap, Toby shot to the other side of the room. FIRE!

The door was open. Toby rushed outside. Following Elisha's directions, he ran straight toward cell number 001 to free his parents. The alarm still hadn't been raised. A crescent moon watched over him with an ideal light— not too strong but not too veiled either.

On the soles of Toby's feet, the blue line drawn by Elisha glowed like war paint.

Toby heard groaning at a crossroads, close to where he was. He pulled up short. It was the kind of groan that sickened you to the core, a desolate whine. As he drew near, Toby found a prisoner in a small cage.

The man's eyes were wet with tears. He was blowing gently on his hand as he moaned. On the back of his hand was an obvious wound; it looked as if someone had crushed it underfoot.

Elisha hadn't told Toby about the episode when she had stamped on the prisoner's foot. She knew that he would shoulder all the blame himself, so she had decided to keep quiet about it. When he saw Toby, the man cowered at the back of his cage. Toby thought about the fire. There were a thousand prisoners like this one in Tumble. Hundreds of innocent men and a few reckless small-time crooks. They were all going to be burned alive.

The mistletoe ball was at risk of turning into a fireball. Should a thousand prisoners be burned at the stake just so two can be saved?

Toby kicked the lock to the cell. It held firm. He shook the bars as much as he could, to the horror of the prisoner, who probably thought this was one of those

nighttime visits, when the guards slipped into the prisoners' cells to torture them. Toby hurled himself against
the door. Nothing.

Then he heard stampeding feet approaching. The
mistletoe branch was narrow. They were bound to catch
him.

He flattened himself, his back to the cell bars. A
group of five or six guards rushed past. They didn't even
see him. They were running toward the center of Tumble,
where the red glow from the fire lit up the night.

Toby started breathing again. His back was still up
against the cage. He hadn't been noticed. He could pause
for a moment to think things over.

Just then, a hand whipped out from behind Toby,
pinning him in a violent neck-lock. The prisoner had
slipped his arm between the bars and was strangling
him. His blood-streaked hand was going to kill Toby any
moment now.

"Fire!" said the prisoner. "I can smell fire. We're all going to die. I know about the Final Plan. But at least there'll be one guard who dies with us!"

Toby couldn't utter a word. With his throat being squeezed, all he could do was let out a barely audible groan. He had been mistaken for a guard. How could he let the prisoner know that he was on his side? He was going to die, strangled by an imprisoned ally. In a desperate gesture, Toby got the big key to cell 001 out of his pocket and threw it a little way off. The prisoner loosened his grip on his neck slightly, but Toby still couldn't make a sound.

By throwing the key, he had become indispensable to his attacker. It looked just like all the other keys in the prison, so it would surely open this cell too. If the prisoner wanted to get out, he needed Toby alive to bring him the key that was glinting in the moonlight three steps from the cage.

Now, the prisoner's grip loosened enough for Toby to take a big breath. After a few seconds, Toby was able to say, "I am on your side. I'm here to free some prisoners."

"I know the Final Plan," the man repeated. "I used to clean Alzan's house. I've heard everything. Don't try pulling a fast one on me."

This was the second time he had mentioned this "Final Plan." Toby did his best to speak calmly.

"I don't know anything about the Final Plan. I don't know what it is. I'm organizing my parents' escape."

The hand relaxed a bit more over Toby's throat.

"Your parents?"

"Sim and Maya Lolness."

The man let go and stepped back. Toby was free.

"You're the Lolness boy?"

"Yes," said Toby, turning around. "Do you know my parents?"

"I've heard about them. . . ."

There was a moment's silence. The man was looking down. Toby ran to fetch the key, then hurried to the door.

"I don't think this is the right key. All the locks are different. What is the Final Plan?"

Toby was frantically trying to turn the key in the lock.

"In the event of a fire," the man replied, "they'll abandon all the prisoners. They'll leave Tumble to burn. But there's something I should tell you, little one. . . ."

"What about the Tree? What if the fire spreads to the Tree?"

"It won't spread. Listen to me. . . ."

Toby took the key out of the lock.

It wasn't the right one. The door remained depressingly locked.

"I'm sorry," said Toby. "It doesn't fit. Why do you say the fire won't spread?"

A brief silence.

"If they can't stop the fire, the orders are to cut the

link with our mistletoe ball," the prisoner declared without faltering.

Toby had put the key back into his pocket. With the oxygen returning to his brain, his thinking was back up to speed.

"Is there a reservoir in the prison?"

"The prisoners only get to drink the rainwater that runs down the bark. But there's a cistern above Alzan's house."

Toby was already running toward the heart of Tumble, in the opposite direction from cell 001.

"Wait!" the man called out.

But Toby had disappeared.

The Alzan home was deserted. There wasn't a single guard left in the central knot. They'd even managed to take the director with them, half suffocated from three attempts to rescue his dreadful daughter. Gus Alzan was a thug and a torturer with all the makings of an assassin, but he was also a brave father who loved his daughter to distraction. The mystery of paternal love had revealed that the governor did have another side after all. He had returned empty-handed, coughing, sobbing, and blinded by the smoke.

It didn't take Toby long to find the cistern. It was enormous, intended to supply the entire prison, but Gus had decreed that prisoners could make do with the water streaming over the flooded floors of their cells.

With one kick, Toby managed to make the first plug pop out of the reservoir. Then he dealt with the rest. The water came gushing out in a torrent. Toby stayed perched on top of the cistern. When the deluge reached the first flames, there was a great hissing, followed by a dense cloud of smoke. The water vapor spread in foggy patches across the whole prison. The fire appeared to be dying down, but the racket was still deafening. The cries of prisoners still held captive added to the commotion.

Toby found his way back, picking up the path again that led directly to the high-security zone. Despite the smoke, he recognized the cell belonging to the prisoner with the wounded hand.

"The fire will be put out!" Toby called out. "There's nothing more I can do. I'm going to take care of my parents. Good-bye!"

"Wait! Ever since I learned who you were, I've been wanting to tell you something. Your parents . . ."

Toby couldn't catch the end of his sentence. The other prisoners were shouting from every direction.

"What?" asked Toby.

The man repeated what he'd said. This time, Toby heard him perfectly well, but he wouldn't let the words enter his head. Every pulse in his body was trying to slow its journey so it wouldn't reach Toby's heart. The man said them one last time, however, and they pierced Toby's gut like arrows.

"Your parents are already dead."

Those were the words the man had been repeating.

Toby went right up close to the prisoner.

The boy's arms hung down limply by his sides. He couldn't hear the crowd anymore. Just the broken voice of this man.

"Your parents were executed back in the winter. I heard Mitch and Alzan talking about it. They pretended they were at Tumble in order to draw you here, so they'd be able to capture you. Don't trust anybody. Get out. Right now. They want you. And only you."

Toby stepped back, astonished.

"They're hiring the worst vermin to get you," the prisoner added.

He held up his bleeding hand.

"There's a kid called Bubble . . . she trampled on my hand with her heel. She did it in cold blood, for no reason."

"Liar!" Toby shouted. "You're all liars! You're lying!"

And he ran off into the thick white smoke.

Elisha saw them, he kept telling himself over and over again. Elisha saw them. He was making headway through the fog, using the same tactics as he would in a lichen forest. Elisha told me she saw them. She touched them. He was counting down the cells in the high-security zone. 009 . . . 008 . . .

But that man's hand was crushed. How am I could he believe that Elisha had done that? She could not have done such a thing.

He was dripping with tears and sweat. His vision was blurred. 004 . . . 003 . . . 002 . . .

Toby stopped in front of cell 001. He took the key in his hands again. He went over to the lock. The sound of shouting in the distance was muffled by the water vapor. He put the key in the lock, but before he had turned it, the door swung half open. The cell hadn't been locked. He pushed the door with his shoulder.

Sitting on the bench, in the pale light of an oil lamp, was a couple with their backs to him. They were in chains. Alive! A lump formed in Toby's throat. He walked toward them.

Toby didn't notice someone step out of the shadows until he'd leaped on him, pinning him to the ground.

But nothing could stop Toby now that he was just a step away from his parents. He was seized by a violent frenzy. In a split second, he had turned the situation around. Drawing on all his thirteen-year-old strength, he held his adversary by the hair, just above the ground, ready to smash his head open.

"Toby . . ."

The man had called him by his name. Toby dragged the face toward the light.

"Lex."

It was Lex Olmech. The son of the millers from the Low Branches.

Nothing made sense to Toby anymore. But he tightened his grip.

"Are you working for this filth too? Like your parents?"

"No," answered Lex. "I'm not working for anybody. I know what my parents did to you. I'm ashamed of them. But I'm their son, and it's my duty to free them."

"Free them?"

"They've been prisoners for seven months now. Because of the business at the mill—they'll die for it. I've been planning their escape all this time. I'm almost there. Let me finish."

Toby realized it had taken him seven days to get to the same point. In this tiny cell, right at the bottom of the impenetrable fortress.

"Where are they? What are you doing in this cell?"

"There they are," said Lex.

The man and the woman on the bench turned their heads.

It was the Olmechs. Or what was left of them.

Two bony faces with translucent skin, ravaged by hunger, fear, and remorse.

Toby let go of Lex's head and slid down the length of the cell wall. There was a long silence.

"My parents? Where are my parents?" a faint voice asked.

Nobody dared answer.

"Sim and Maya Lolness," said Toby, spelling it out. "My parents. My father is pretty tall; when he laughs, it's like sparks flying. . . . My whole head fits in his hands. One night, he gave me a star. It's called Altair."

"We know who they are, Toby," said Mr. Olmech gently.

Toby didn't know what he was saying anymore.

"My mother is smaller. She smells of leaf bread rolled in pollen. My mother only sings when she's alone. So the best way to hear her is to say something like, 'I'm just going to step out!' but then stay, with your ear glued to the door. She sings . . ."

Great big tears were rolling down his cheeks.

"My parents. You'd recognize them from the way they look at each other. You'd recognize them in a crowd of a thousand people. . . ."

Mrs. Olmech whispered, "I'd better tell you. We were made to stand in for them right from the start. They put a sign with *Lolness* on it over the door. But I don't think, my little Toby . . . I don't think . . ."

Her voice sounded more compassionate now. Adversity had worn it down until all that was left was the taut thread of truth. She took a deep breath.

"I don't think you should look for your parents any-more."

Toby left the cell.

On his way out, he tossed the key to Lex. It was also the key to the chains that bound the Olmech parents. Lex had managed to break open the door with a stick, but the chains had resisted. He thanked Toby and rushed over to set his parents free.

Toby walked along a path that glistened with dew. The mist was thinning, revealing another dawn. A gentle light was breaking over the mistletoe leaves, in waves of orange and red.

People with sad hearts should be banned from seeing sunrises.

With each step, Toby told himself that the end of this mistletoe branch would be the end of his life.

He was inconsolable. His parents were dead. The only glimmer or scrap of life he might have had left was Elisha, but she had betrayed him at least twice. She had pretended his parents were still alive, and then she had abandoned him in the wax coffin. As for the cruelty of the trampled hand . . . There was too much evidence against her.

Toby was choking with sadness. Elisha—his last link with life had just snapped.

That was when he heard the bird.

If he hadn't heard the squawking above him, this might be a very different story. He continued on to the edge of the mistletoe ball and came out by a large translucent fruit, big as a moon and made pink by the dawn. The bird drew near. Toby watched it swooping in the air. It was a sparrow, his father's favorite bird.

Toby had always been frightened of birds. The only book he could never bring himself to open was his father's volume on the brown-capped sparrow, a slim tome, full of terrifying pictures.

But at this dawn, Toby was no longer frightened. He continued to stand in front of the ripe fruit, then, like a worm, he did a full-body dive through the soft, fleshy white window. With both arms, he managed to cling on to the seed that he found in the middle. He stayed there, huddled in the belly of the berry. And it was there that he said farewell to the world.

A moment later, without even stopping to land, the sparrow grabbed the milky fruit.

25
Somewhere Else

When Professor Lolness was a child, there was an old and abandoned mistletoe ball called Saipur in the Far Northern Branches, the region where he lived. A small inn had been built there many years earlier. People from the neighboring branches would visit for short vacations, because the air in Saipur was said to be purer.

But a sudden incident forced the tourists out. It was a tragedy that made headline news. A sparrow had swallowed a whole family: the Astona parents and their two children.

The inn at Saipur was closed down, and many tears were shed. A few days later, however, the entire Astona family was discovered safe and sound at the other end of the Tree. Nobody ever found out what had happened to them. The family members themselves couldn't remember a thing.

Eventually, people forgot about Saipur.

Young Sim Lolness wasn't too fond of adventures, and neither was his friend Zef Clarac. But there was a third friend—El Blue, Leo's father. El Blue was barely nine years old, but he seized every chance to risk his life, which was why he dragged Zef and Sim into the mazes of Saipur, and it became their kingdom.

The three young boys spent all their free time in the mistletoe ball. Their parents thought they were visiting an old professor who helped them with their homework. In the evenings, when they went home, all three of them showed off their exercise books covered in expert handwriting.

Their homework had been done to perfection. Professor Bickfort was clearly a wonderful teacher. Young Zef talked to his parents at length about old Bickfort, who stroked his mustache and called them by their sunames: Clarac, Blue, and Lolness. Now that Bickfort was retired, what he liked doing best—according to Zef—was helping children get a head start. He had only one rule: he didn't want to hear his students talking about their parents. Zef imitated Bickfort's gruff voice: "Parents, huh, I've seen too many of them in my life! If I ever see one again, I'll turn them into grasshopper pâté." Zef's parents trembled when they heard these words. He already knew how to impress his audience.

Plenty of parents wanted their children to attend these study days with Bickfort. But the three boys explained that unfortunately the old man wasn't taking on any new students.

On their days off, Zef and El Blue would arrive at Saipur by nine o'clock and give their exercise books to Sim, who took barely an hour to do the homework for all three of them.

There had never been anyone called Professor Bickfort living in the Tree.

By ten o'clock, the homework was done and the day belonged to them. Clarac daydreamed, Blue played with his boomerang, and Sim observed the world, making painstaking progress with the files he was beginning to put together.

Sometimes, El Blue led his two friends to watch gigantic birds gobbling the mistletoe berries. Sim and Zef kept their distance. But it was on one such occasion that Sim discovered the brown-capped sparrow, which is a bird with a stain on its head that looks like a beret.

In the course of those Bickfort Days, Sim, age nine and a half, wrote an illustrated essay called "The Sparrow with a Beret." He kept that first essay, and from then on he always wore a beret.

The sparrows, which were much smaller than robins, never ate the fruit right away; they carried it off in their beaks and disappeared. All of Sim's work was concerned with what the sparrows did with the fruit they carried off. By doing so, perhaps he would come to an understanding of what had happened to the Astona family. . . .

It was several weeks before he dared to go up to one of the big white fruity spheres and measure it. After lots of calculations, one thing was clear — the sparrow was incapable of eating the fruit whole. Its beak was too small to swallow the hard part of the fruit, that long seed in the middle wrapped in soft flesh. This conclusion gave the budding researcher plenty of food for thought.

Sim was already obsessed with finding out whether life existed beyond the Tree. In order to nibble away skillfully at the fruit without swallowing the seed, surely the sparrow would have to land somewhere. And since Sim had never seen sparrows perched in the Tree, then where did they land?

Sim developed his theory of the perch during those Bickfort Days. He didn't dare suggest the idea that there might be other Trees at this stage in his career, so he talked about "perches" instead. In the conclusion to his book on the brown-capped sparrow, he stated that somewhere in the universe, beyond the Tree, other perches did exist.

Who knows what they look like? They are distant countries, where sparrows land, scrape the fruit off the mistletoe berries and leave the seeds behind. . . .

Two years later, in deepest winter, the mistletoe ball at Saipur dropped off. It was midnight on the last day of December. A decision was reached to cut off all the other mistletoe balls in the Tree, given the danger they posed. Only Tumble would remain to be fitted out as a prison.

The following week, when El Blue, Zef Clarac, and Sim Lolness found out that their magic world had vanished, they cried all the way home, telling everybody that Professor Bickfort was dead.

Toby had never read his father's study "The Sparrow with a Beret," so he believed he was going to his death as he was carried off in the bird's beak, still clinging to the seed in the middle of the berry. And it was a relief.

Mistletoe has white berries. But they are like picture windows, with the light flooding in on all sides. The aerial spectacle Toby was experiencing was like the precursor to Heaven. It was an extreme experience, a vision of a new world. All of a sudden, from his vantage point at the center of his picture window, he could see life from on high. Everything looked bigger and brighter.

Above him was a sky of pure purple, with midnight-blue clouds scudding across it. Below was a horizontal world without end, Toby's only memory of which would be a dream in green and brown.

It was as if the Tree had been placed on top of another Tree, infinitely taller.

Toby hugged the seed with both arms. The landscape was turning to the beat of the sparrow's flapping wings. Toby was slipping away, becoming less and less aware of his body. How long did the flight last? It could have been an eternity. It ended with a few twirling loops, and Toby losing all notion of anything.

A song.

A short song with no words.

Five or six repeated notes, sung by a woman.

And then the heat. A hot humid bath.

Toby opened his eyes.

A few steps away, a woman was busy darning a shirt. Toby recognized it as his own shirt. He was bare-chested and in the mud. He tried to find something to grip so he could pull himself up, but his wrists were tied together. His ankles too.

He called out.

The woman stopped her song and turned toward him. Her face made Toby shiver. The features were both strange and familiar. She smiled serenely. Then, lowering her gaze, she continued singing the same refrain. Toby let the notes wash away his fear.

He looked around. The landscape didn't resemble anything he had ever seen before. A green forest, higher

than all the forests in the Tree. It wasn't a moss grove, but a forest a hundred times taller, where each blade of tapering grass seemed to stretch all the way to the sky. Light flickered in this jungle, and its peaks swayed in the wind.

What was he doing here?

He tried to arrange his last recollections in order. The Tree, the bird, the sky . . . It was like a dream. And now, on the one hand, this gentle voice, and on the other, his hands all tied up.

You think your life is over once and for all, but it always turns out to be more complicated than that.

"Who are you?" he asked.

The woman looked at him. She went on with her song. After the final short note, she said, "They'll be back. The sun is soft. They'll be back when the sun is hard. I'm guarding you. I'm sewing your bag."

Toby's eyes bulged.

"That's not my bag. It's my shirt."

"Shirt." The woman smiled, then started singing again.

The woman's own clothing was odd. The only thing she was wearing was a short piece of bright red material around her body. She looked pretty young, but Toby couldn't guess her actual age even within ten years. She could be twenty. She could be double that. Her eyes slanted toward her temples. A long stretch of eye like a light under the door.

The song had changed now. It was a heartbreaking melody. Still no words. But Toby understood every note. They were telling him he hadn't left the world yet. Such a sense of nostalgia could only exist in the real world.

The whole of his life came crashing down on him, heavy as an old dresser, bitter as crushed bugs. The death of his parents, Elisha's betrayal . . . He found his grief just as he had left it. Even his tears tasted the same.

"So, I'm alive, then?" he asked.

The woman didn't hear him. He went back to sleep.

When he woke up, it was still daytime. A chorus of a hundred people seemed to be whispering all around him. He opened his eyes, and a hush fell.

Men, women, and children were staring at him in silence. They were all dressed in bright colors. Some of the clothes were bigger than others, some more worn,

but they were as bright as if they'd been freshly lifted
from the basins of dye. A little boy wearing a yellow belt
had hoisted himself above the group by climbing a blade
of grass.

"They send out their soldiers with so little linen,"
said an old man in a blue cape that came right down to
his ankles.

Every face radiated sympathy. They all looked at
Toby the way you would a sick child or a prisoner on
death row.

"We must keep a hard heart. The grass is fragile. It is
flattened by the wind. It burns under the snow."

These words were gobbledegook to Toby. All he
knew, from the looks on the faces leaning over him, was
that they wouldn't hurt him. The world he had landed in
didn't seem hostile. The woman who had been darning

his shirt kept humming her gentle refrain. With so many eyes directed at Toby, it was almost enough to lift him off the ground.

"We must keep a hard heart," some of them repeated.

But they kept looking on sympathetically, and their gestures were peaceful. The child on the blade of grass slid gently down to the ground.

Silence again, then the old man in blue said to Toby, "You will go back there, Little Tree."

Toby felt his eyes spinning and his tongue stick to the back of his mouth. He found the strength to speak.

"Go back?"

Why was there never any break from his cruel fate?

"Yes, Little Tree. The grass is fragile, and you must leave. Your people took away nine of our people last night. And twelve more at the last snow. As well as one woman, three nights ago. Your people killed a woman who was gathering a bit of wood on the bark of the Tree, at the Border. . . ."

Toby tensed.

The man went on. "If all your people know is the language of death, then we will have to learn that sad language too."

Toby managed to raise his head to shout. "My people! My people hunt me down; my people killed my mother and father; my people tore my friends away from me; my people HATE me! And now I've got to pay for their offenses?"

He was writhing around in all directions, rolling on

the loamy earth he'd not felt against his skin before. Finally, he fell back down, exhausted. His voice was just a whisper now.

"Kill me. Otherwise they'll capture me, just like you have. I come from nowhere. I have nobody. I want to stop right here and now. Kill me!"

"You have the glimmer in your eye, Little Tree—I know you have suffered," said the man in the blue cape, with a lump in his throat.

A cloud of sadness descended on all their faces. The glimmer in the eye, a tiny speck in the pupil, was the sign of those who had lost their parents. These people knew how to detect that scar of grief.

Instantly, they disappeared into the green surroundings.

Toby was all alone. He didn't move. He was covered in earth. In the Tree, earth was a rare powder brought by the wind. People collected it in hollows in the bark. You made small gardens out of it, or dyes. But here . . . Where could he be, then, with so much earth around him?

Toby heard a low whistle, and a rustling to the side. The little boy dressed in a belt of yellow cloth appeared between two stems. He came up to Toby.

"Where are we? What part of the Tree are we in?" Toby asked with his eyes half closed. "Why were they talking about a glimmer in my eye?"

The little boy didn't answer. He leaned over him. With his finger, he removed the mud from around Toby's eyes. He must have been about seven years old. He had a moon-shaped face under his bushy hair. A layer of earth formed a makeshift pair of socks, and his whole body was colored light brown.

"You want to know where your Tree is? Well, look . . ."

Moon Boy clapped his hands. An enormous shadow cast itself over them. Toby felt as if they were under a spell. The little boy started laughing.

"What is it?" asked Toby.

"It's your Tree."

The child laughed again in front of an astonished Toby, then tried to reassure him.

"It's the Tree's shadow. I know when it's about to reach the grass in the evening. Just before, I can feel a cold sigh behind my ears."

"The Tree's shadow?"

In this world where the bird had dropped him off, the Tree was just a shadow on the grass before nightfall. Just a faraway planet that eclipsed the sun toward sunset. And if you got too close, to pick up firewood or to chase away the ants, you ran the risk of being carried off.

The Tree was a forbidden planet to these people in the grass. They lived peacefully in the harsh world of the prairie and slept where they could, in makeshift shelters that would inevitably get destroyed at the first appearance of bad weather. Yes, the grass was fragile; it got flattened by storms, burned by the snow, flooded by the rains.

These were nomadic people, barely tolerated by the grass forest that made them lead a hard life. If the people from the Tree started killing them, that would be the end of this delicately balanced life.

Looking at his small companion, whose brown skin was covered in a fine layer of cracked mud, Toby understood why, in the Tree, these folk, whose existence was as fragile as a blade of grass, were referred to as the Grass people.

26
The Last Walk

Toby bore no hard feelings when they came at sunset to take him away.

The young moonfaced boy had never left him. The two of them had just stayed there, lying side by side. Moon Boy sang a refrain similar to the Grass woman's, but his mouth was closed. He was rubbing two grass shoots together to make the plaintive sounds, and tapping his feet on the ground.

Toby was trying to work out if there was anything still linking him to life.

His parents, his beloved Low Branches, Elisha, Leo Blue, and Nils Amen had all abandoned him. Nobody alive cared about him anymore. Toby had no expectations of anyone or anything.

The man who approached him didn't look particularly strong. He was young and slim, with calm eyes. He watched Toby lying in the dust. But then he bent down, hoisted Toby up, and tossed him like a haunch of cricket into a cloth hood he was carrying on his back.

Now Toby understood why the woman had mistaken his shirt for a bag. The Grass people had never seen shirts before, but they were equipped with a sort of knapsack with long sleeves that spread the weight over their shoulders and arms.

The man waved good-bye to Moon Boy and started walking. Toby knew he was setting off on his final journey.

They marched like that for a long time, going through the darkening forest. The porter walked with a steady rhythm, and his breathing made no sound. Doubled up inside the bag, Toby didn't move. Through a small rip in the cloth, he had noticed the moonfaced boy following discreetly a few steps behind.

Sometimes, the porter would turn back around and call out to the child, "Go back to your own ear of wheat, Strand of Linen! Make sure you don't get eaten by frogs!"

Ear of wheat. Frog. This strange language. Perhaps the boy didn't understand it any more than Toby did, because each time, after a few minutes, he showed up again behind them, between two creepers, on the bend of a grass thicket.

"Leave us alone, Strand of Linen! Go and find your sister. She'll make you some pancakes. . . ."

Toby gave a start in his bag. *Pancakes.* He couldn't help thinking about Elisha. He wiped his eyes on the coarse material. The memory of melted honey made his mouth water. No, he would never taste happiness again.

The ground sloped gently downward. Toby noticed shallow water flowing everywhere. The man had lit a lantern. The forest was reflected in the flooded ground. The grass seemed to go on forever. Toby was surrounded by the mystery of this new world.

His father had been right. The Tree wasn't man's only horizon. This flat, jungle-covered planet also existed. And maybe other worlds did too, somewhere else, even in the stars.

Toby would die with this secret. From now on, he wouldn't bother defending himself anymore. He didn't want to fight back. He let himself be carried in a bag, tossed around like a doll dressed in mud. He wasn't resisting anymore. He had already taken his leave. He had overstepped all the boundaries of his own life.

Sometimes, he couldn't help letting a memory wash over him. His mother's voice, the cracking sound that buds make in spring, the faces of the Asseldor sisters, his father's hands on the nape of his neck . . .

His last day with Elisha.

It was the day before Bernie Alzan's picnic. A clear, warm spring day. The two of them were on top of the cliff above the lake. Up there, the moss grew right to the edge. Toby and Elisha had climbed up through the green foliage to perch there.

That morning, the mirror of the lake was disturbed by two water bugs, who looked as if they were dancing a love duet. One of them was pouting. The other was slowly sneaking up behind in a roundabout way, making big loops on the water's surface. Sometimes it dived, then reappeared farther off, snorting. The first one finally answered by moving its legs, which looked like batting eyelashes. And then the charming dance started all over again.

Propped up on their moss thicket, Toby and Elisha smiled as they looked on.

"I'll miss all this," said Toby.

Elisha started. She fixed her eyes on Toby.

"When?"

Toby realized he shouldn't have opened his mouth.

"When will you miss all this?" she asked again.

"If . . . if I manage to get my parents out," he said, "we might have to go very far away for a while. . . ."

"For a while!" Elisha groaned. "So that's what I'm getting up for every morning, to prepare your departure! Thanks, Toby."

Abruptly, she looked away. Toby wanted to explain.

"Try to understand it from my point of view. I can't stay in a cave with my parents for ten years! Life's for living!"

"So go away, then, if you've got to be so far away to start living again. Off you go! Nobody's stopping you."

She hid half her face in her collar. Her eyes were fixed on an imaginary horizon. She looked the same as she had during those sad days, when she wore the mask of wild Elisha. Toby remained silent, and an unbridgeable gulf opened up between them.

"If I do have to leave, I'll be back. I swear to you. I'll be back, and—"

He stopped.

"And?" Elisha asked indifferently.

"And I'll find you again."

"Why?" she challenged him.

Silence again. Toby felt a knot in his belly.

"Why? Do you really want to know?"

But he couldn't say any more. The ball was stuck in his throat. Elisha realized how far she'd provoked him, but she was hurting too much to relent. She wanted to say she was sorry, tell him how sad she was. But instead she heard herself blurting out, "You know what? I haven't had many friends. Just one, counting you. . . ."

And then she deliberately slid all the way down the moss. Toby followed her.

Watching her bumping ahead of him, as he had done so many times before all over the Tree, Toby felt there was something new happening between them. An unfamiliar bond, which quickened his breath and made his heart race.

She dashed off across the bark, never once looking back, running over crevices. Behind her, Toby was tearing through the air, which had a different quality to it now. Both of them hurled themselves at the slope, without holding back or braking. The lake was getting bigger before their eyes. Their bare feet made the lichen powder fly behind them.

They reached the beach, panting, gasping for air. Bending over, hands on knees as they tried to catch their breath—they couldn't take their eyes off each other. They didn't say anything. They just let the precious thread they had suddenly discovered between them grow taut. Their heads were spinning. The air seemed too rich, like the steam from a soup. They were now back-to-back, leaning against each other to balance. Their swinging arms touched.

Just then, on the other side of the lake, they noticed Isha waving and calling out to them. But they lingered for a few more seconds, back-to-back.

"Me too," said Toby.

This wasn't in answer to anything; Elisha hadn't said

a word. But those two words did not surprise her. They were the seal of a silent pact.

"Me too," Elisha said in turn.

She was the first to run off.

Down at the bottom of his sack, Toby wiped a new tear on the linen.

The forest they had arrived at was less dense. Each step the porter took prompted a splash accompanied by a little wave, which came crashing over the bases of the reeds. Toby was peering into the half-light through the slit in the knapsack. He felt as if he kept catching people's eyes in the dark. But the little grass boy was no longer following them.

Moon Boy was just another person Toby would never see again. This was the law of his life; anyone he liked vanished, and all he was left with was a golden dust that made his eyes sting.

Night had taken hold of the forest. It was different from a night in the Tree; it was teeming with mysterious noises and reflections, and warm too. Toby had no idea how long they continued to forge ahead like this. The water was getting deeper. It was up to the porter's waist now. He was pushing a small raft ahead of him, with his lantern swaying on it.

"Aaaaaaaaaahhhh!"

An enormous lump dropped out of the sky in front of them, causing a spectacular wave.

Crying out in terror, the porter threw the bag with Toby in it a few steps away and managed to cling to a blade of grass. Toby floated. The waves washed to and fro, but he stayed on the surface. A final surge of water wedged him between two grass roots.

His hands and feet were still tied up, but Toby managed to poke his nose through the rip in the bag. As if in a dream, he discovered what had fallen out of the sky.

It was a living lump of something — a sort of monster tucked into itself with two big fat legs broken in two. The monster's skin was shiny and grainy. It was about fifty times the size of a beetle or a slug and cast an enormous shadow over the forest. Toby could now see the animal's impenetrable eyes staring at the porter, who bravely refused to flee.

The horror lasted only a moment. The monster shot out its enormous tongue and snatched up the poor porter. Toby heard just one cry, and the grass man disappeared, arms and legs flailing, into a mouth as wide as any tunnel. Toby caught the man's burning stare for the last time. Down at the bottom of his bag, Toby swore he would never wish for his own death again.

The creature, unlike any he had seen before, made a small leap in Toby's direction and gave the pocket of soaked cloth a long hard stare. Its bulging eyes almost touched the bag. Toby didn't move a muscle. He could see a tip of slimy tongue peeping through its green mouth now and then. When the animal cleared its throat, the

sound was like thunder. Toby shuddered, and the effect of this tiny movement combined with the wave's wake was enough to flood the bag and make it slowly sink.

Regretfully abandoning his prey, the terrifying creature uttered its war cry once again, then took off.

Toby had vanished beneath the surface of the water.

It was perhaps the fiftieth time that Toby thought he was going to die, but this time he was convinced it was true.

A person left to drift in water, deep in the heart of a forest, with his feet and hands bound, imprisoned in a sack, and with his sole companion eaten by a frog, doesn't stand much chance of making it out alive.

Totally submerged and in the pitch black, unable to breathe, Toby still counted each second as if anything could happen.

He didn't want to die anymore. Just when it was too late. Why is it always like that?

Toby was surprised when he felt his bag being dragged for a few seconds, then lifted up and emptied like a wineskin. He swallowed a great gulp of pure air, filling his lungs.

He saw a small hand search the sack and felt it tickle his chin.

"It's me. . . ."

Toby recognized the voice. The bag opened. What he saw made his eyes well up with tenderness. It was Moon Boy. The tiny Grass boy with his yellow belt had followed them every step of the way.

No other face could have reassured Toby as much as this one. A child. The most innocent thing left under the sky.

"That was a naughty frog," said the moonfaced boy. "She ate Vidof."

Toby thought of his poor porter. So his name was Vidof.

"Did he have a family?" Toby asked.

"No. He wanted to marry Ilaya."

Once again Toby noted how fragile life was here in the grass. You couldn't rely on anything. The lot of the Grass people was as hazardous as that of pollen grains. Moon Boy went over to the lamp, which miraculously hadn't gone out on its raft.

"Ilaya's going to cry," he stated.

There was no answer to that.

The boy's skin was glowing because all the mud had been washed off in the water. His white shoulders were clearly visible. He undid Toby's bindings so that he could stretch out now that he'd been released from the bag.

Toby stood with his chest above the water.

"You're free to go," the little boy said to him. "Wait for the morning. Your Tree is that way."

"What about you?"

"I'm going back to comfort Ilaya."

"Aren't you frightened? How old are you?"

Moon Boy gave a broad grin.

"If I get caught by a lizard or a frog, Ilaya will cry even more. So I'd better watch out."

"Who is Ilaya?" asked Toby.

"My big sister."

The water came up to Toby's hips. But on the little boy it was at least as high as his shoulders. It was a miracle he had gotten this far.

"Why did you follow us?" asked Toby.

"Don't know. Didn't think about it."

And he walked away, saying, "Farewell, Little Tree."

Toby took a step in the direction the boy had pointed. He pushed the lamp in front of him, but no sooner had he done so than it spluttered and went out. The night was black.

Once again, Toby thought he saw eyes blinking in the darkness. He'd never felt so lonely in his life.

A long time passed.

Dampened noises slid over the grass forest.

"I'm frightened."

The voice came from right next to Toby. It was the

little boy, and his natural fear made Toby's own worries fly away. He drew strength from the little cold hand that curled up inside his own.

Toby had never been a big brother to anyone. But at that moment, he became one, of sorts. He felt responsible for this child. He wouldn't let go of his hand until it was clasped around the neck of his sister or mother.

This simple responsibility gave a sense of direction to Toby Lolness's life again. He was no longer a tiny piece of flotsam floating in black bark juice, being given a rough ride by life.

"Don't be frightened. I'll take you back home."

He helped the little boy climb up onto his shoulders, and together they forged their way into the marsh.

27
Another Life

The arrow struck the lizard, hitting exactly the pale area in the neck where the body armor is at its softest. A ten-year-old boy appeared, without waiting for the animal's final death throes. He was brandishing a long blowpipe.

He watched the lizard's final collapse. It was a tiny beast, but there was enough meat on it to feed the boy's family for the whole winter.

The child gazed proudly at the animal. After making a capture like that, he would be able to choose his own name. He wouldn't be known as Strand of Linen anymore.

The size of cloth worn by the Grass people was granted according to age. Small children went around stark naked, then a little linen band was placed round their waist and they were called Strand of Linen. Every year they added a few new rows. You would say of a young girl, "She wears little linen," or of an old man, "He wears a field of white linen." At fifteen, the garment stretched from the thighs to the chest. At the end of a life, a final row of cloth would transform the garment into a shroud.

Shortly after they were ten, and once they had performed an act of bravery, the children could choose their own names.

The young hunter already knew what name he would take on. He wanted to be called Moon Boy.

He started running between the yellow grass. The earth was giving off a real August heat. At any moment, a vole might appear and snatch the lizard. Moon Boy needed to call in reinforcements in order to cut the creature up and put the delicious red meat in storage for the winter.

After running for ten minutes, he reached a stem and scaled it easily. At the top was the wheat ear where he and his sister had made their summer home. A grain had been rolled out and pushed overboard to create a round room that smelled of delicious bread.

"Ilaya! I got one!"

Ilaya opened an eye. It was afternoon nap time. She was sleeping on the floor in the yellow light, with just a straw pillow. Her long hair formed dark bundles around her, sprinkled with a golden powder.

"What's the matter, Strand of Linen?"

The little boy pulled up short.

"Don't call me that ever again."

She smiled as she stretched.

"What's going on?"

"I caught a lizard."

She smiled again. Moon Boy loved this smile, which had only reappeared on his sister's lips a few months ago. Ilaya had experienced terrible grief two years earlier. She had been engaged to a young man called Vidof. He had died in tragic circumstances. For months—in fact, for two whole years—she had been inconsolable. But just recently, she had begun to lead a normal life again.

"I'm going to ask for help," said Moon Boy as he climbed to the top of the ear.

He could hear Ilaya calling out, "What are you going to be called? Hey, Strand of Linen! Which name?"

He reached the top of the ear.

"My name is Moooooooon Boooooy!"

He was level with the tops of the other wheat ears, and the vast golden field spread out on every side, mingling, in the distance, with the heavy shadow of the Tree. It was a dazzling view. The tall stems were swaying gently, making ripples across the prairie. Summer was the only enjoyable season out of the whole year. Only the clouds could spoil this blessed period and transform it into a nightmare.

"What's going on?"

The question came from a neighboring wheat ear, where someone had heard his wild cry.

"Ah! Is that you, Strand of Linen?"

"My name's Moon Boy! I need some help over by the thistle. I've caught a lizard."

The other person, on his wheat ear, shouted out in the opposite direction. And so the news was passed from ear to ear. Soon, a crowd had gathered around the remains of the lizard, each of them cutting off his share of the fresh meat.

It was rare to hunt lizards. Even though the meat from the dangerous reptile was a delicacy, the advantage of lizards was that they protected the Grass people from mosquitoes, which they wiped out by the dozen. Mosquitoes posed a nastier threat than lizards. The expression "not a lizard in the grass" actually meant "if there's no lizard, that means there aren't any mosquitoes either, so life is sweet." As a result, the lizard was only hunted four days a year.

"Nice catch, Strand of Linen. Well done!"

"I'm not called Strand of Linen anymore. My name's Moon Boy."

Moon Boy walked around his trophy. He was looking for somebody.

"Who are you looking for, Strand of Linen?"

"My name is Moon Boy! Get that into your head!"

Moon Boy couldn't find the person he was looking for, which was a shame, because he wanted to share this joy with him. He went over to an older boy.

"Aro, take my share of the meat up to the wheat ear and give it to my sister, Ilaya. There's something I must do urgently."

Aro tried not to laugh, but he was touched by Strand of Linen's sudden change of tone. The previous evening, he'd been a little boy. Now he was giving him orders and acting as if he was on important business.

"Whatever you say, Strand of Linen."

Moon Boy sighed.

"I'm not called Strand of Linen. . . ."

He disappeared behind the thistle, grunting.

It didn't take him long to reach a clump of dried reeds—long leaves that curled inside themselves. From late summer onward, they were bathed in water and attracted mosquitoes, but now, in the middle of the hot season, the reed bundles looked like tall towers that framed a green palace. And someone had chosen this palace as his home, the same person who—

An arrow brushed against Moon Boy, piercing the small linen ribbon that hung down from his cloth. The arrowhead ended its flight in the reeds, where it stuck nicely. Moon Boy was pinned to a big post. He tried to detach himself from the arrow, but couldn't manage it. The linen was woven so it would last a lifetime.

Where had this arrow come from? Moon Boy realized that his only chance of escape was to abandon his clothing and run away, naked. But that was out of the question. He wasn't a Strand of Linen anymore!

He strained his ears.

The noise was coming from a little pile of dried grass, a bit farther off.

A deep croaking. Terrified, Moon Boy spun around and around, unwinding himself from his yellow cloth, and ran off in the opposite direction.

Just then he heard laughter. Turning back, he saw a boy who was at least fifteen years old, not particularly tall, but with strong legs and solid shoulders. He was holding a blowgun that was taller than he was.

Moon Boy dived into the straw for cover.

"Did you do that, Little Tree?"

Toby hadn't really changed. But two years with the Grass people had naturally left their mark.

He was wilder looking.

When Toby had returned with Strand of Linen on his shoulders, everybody had been touched by this act of bravery from a boy who was prepared to confront those who had condemned him. He had told them about Vidof's death, and in so doing he triggered Ilaya's harrowing pain. She had thrown fistfuls of mud at him before trying to eat the mud herself.

"You killed him! You killed him!"

She shoved her blackened fists into her mouth. It took four of them to hold her down.

Moon Boy had explained to his sister that it wasn't Toby's fault. But nobody could contain the young girl's grief and bitterness. She wore a mask of hatred.

Toby's bravery and his concern for Ilaya were proof that he wasn't an enemy like the rest of his people, but once again the Grass people decided to take him back to the Tree. Too many misfortunes had descended from that brown and green planet. Everything that came from the Tree had to go back there. Toby couldn't believe his ears when he heard the new verdict.

The expedition set out the next day. This time Toby was escorted by two men. They carried him rolled up in a hammock, hanging from a pole propped on their shoulders. On the third morning, the two grass men realized that they were carrying a piece of cloth containing a clay doll.

Toby had given them the slip once again.

They turned back for home, ready to give the news that Little Tree had escaped. But they found him sitting next to Moon Boy, in front of a perplexed gathering. Toby had arrived before them.

How were they going to get rid of this will-o'-the-wisp?

"You must go back home."

"Then you'll have to kill me. I don't have a home."

An approving murmur rose up from the crowd of Grass people every time Toby answered. This little boy spoke like one of them. It was as if he had been born in the grass.

For the third time, volunteers were found to escort him as far as the Border.

Before dawn on the day of their departure, a fine rain began to fall over the prairie. From high up on a grass spindle, Toby watched the Grass people come out of the shelters to expose their bodies to the pure water in the moonless night.

He watched the mud run down their skin.

Suspended in midair, Toby also threw his head back to catch the raindrops. A drop bigger than the rest fell on him and instantly washed his skin.

Just then, all the Grass people nearby turned toward him. Toby could see a blue reflection in their staring eyes. The children were the first to draw near, under the beating rain. Then everybody gathered below him.

They were staring at the soles of his feet.

Toby realized that the blue color came from the slivers of light on the soles of his feet, the lines Elisha had drawn with caterpillar ink just before he had left. Washed in rainwater, these lines glowed in the night, just as they did on the soles of Elisha's feet.

Toby was untied from his grass stem. He had no idea what was going on.

"Stay. Do whatever you like. You have the sign."

These were their words before they left him alone, free, under the rain. The crowd dispersed in a bluish halo. The same lines of luminous ink also shone under their rain-washed feet.

That morning, hardly able to believe his luck, Toby had crawled as far as the little clump of reeds. He spent the first few months there, with no visitors apart from Moon Boy, who came without his sister's knowledge.

"She doesn't want me to have anything to do with you. She's too sad."

"Do what she says. Don't come and see me anymore."

But Moon Boy, whom everybody still called Strand of Linen, went to visit Toby every day. Slowly and secretly, the young boy taught him how to live in the grass. And gradually, Toby found out about a harsh new life.

He was excluded to begin with. The community was afraid of the boy who had appeared out of nowhere but who wore their sign.

That first summer, Toby had no reason to worry about what a lifetime spent in the grass might mean. The weather was mild and dry—ideal conditions. By Moon Boy's side, he learned to hunt with a blowgun. He always had enough to eat, and he furnished his shelter in the reeds. He rediscovered the joy of being free. It was the only joy he had left.

But the first storms at the end of August brought him back to reality. The whole prairie was flooded. From that day on, for the next six months, he didn't see Strand of Linen once.

By the time autumn came, he had already moved three times to flee the water, mud and wind. But the worst was still to come. The first frosts were merciless. Then came the snow.

Winter was one long battle. Abused by the sky, bogged down by the earth, Toby stopped thinking or even suffering. All he did was survive. Luckily, before the snow came, he had procured a tiny bit of potato that provided him with sustenance. He became a wild child, a tiny animal all huddled up, who faces the winter with a single instinct: survival.

On the first day of spring, when a group of Grass hunters discovered a small being with disheveled hair and a look in its eyes as hard as ice, they no longer recognized Toby.

"It's me, Little Tree."

The hunters all pulled back. The will-o'-the-wisp had survived the torment.

From then on, the Grass people looked at Little Tree differently. Gradually, they included him in community life. And so Toby came to find out about the secrets of survival gathered by these people over generations.

Twice he met Ilaya, who refused to catch his eye. Twice she reminded him of Elisha in her obstinacy. He chased away this memory as if he were being choked by smoke.

Toby wouldn't let his mind bring up the past again. He was building a new life for himself without suspecting that the foundations would crumble and crack, revealing the rotten wood of his former life beneath.

One day, in the cave by the lake, Toby had told Elisha that he was dreaming of a new life.

"You only have one life, Toby. And it will always find you," she had replied.

Toby was trying to prove that law wrong.

The second winter was less cruel. Toby discovered the extraordinary power in coming together. These people were bound by all the links they knew how to forge.

During the summer, they tied together the stems of the tall grasses that were most firmly planted in the earth. This created a stiff clump like a fortress where everyone gathered at the first cold weather. Neither wind nor snow nor torrents of mud could make this straw castle collapse.

Toby was granted permission to live in one of the ears of wheat.

Little by little over that winter, he managed to tame Ilaya.

And Moon Boy noticed his sister's cheeks finding their natural bloom again, and her eyes becoming less hostile. She still wasn't talking to Toby, but she was prepared to listen to him with her eyes lowered.

Toby didn't realize he was planting the seeds of something much deeper in the heart of the young Grass girl.

There's a grass proverb that goes: *What you plant in a wound before it's healed over, grows to be a captive flower that never dies.*

Ilaya was falling in love. She was shifting gently from an impassioned hatred to another kind of passion.

It would be reasonable to imagine that these two hearts, sweeping their pasts aside once and for all, would find each other and piece together a new kind of happiness. But Toby's heart was a prisoner in the dark caves of his memory. Until an extraordinary turn of events rescued him from his memory and thrust Toby back into the adventure of his real life.

You only have one life, Toby.

28
The Tyrant's Fiancée

An old man turned up among the Grass people at the beginning of autumn. He pushed his bark boat between the grasses without saying a word. He came from the Tree and looked exhausted.

The Grass people wanted to interrogate this Old Tree, but he remained silent.

There was no ill-treatment, but he was placed under the guard of two men. The Grass people were still suffering numerous losses from their ranks, victims taken away by militia from the Tree. Toby had lost two good friends, Mika and Liev, who had disappeared in the Border regions by the Trunk, at the end of spring.

So the Grass people distrusted this Old Tree, who had appeared as if by magic in a climate of war.

Toby was away on that particular day. He had set out with Moon Boy and two other hunters. A vole had carried off two strands of linen and their mother into its hole. The rodent had snatched up an ear of wheat that had fallen to the ground, with the family working inside it. The father, who was left behind, had collapsed. Toby quickly spotted the animal's footprints and decided to follow them.

When he had set off, Ilaya bid him a fond farewell, much as a hunter's wife would have done, but all Toby heard was a good-bye from a sister or a friend.

Only Moon Boy realized the truth of his sister's feelings for Little Tree. Toby didn't suspect anything, or else he would have tried to avoid a misunderstanding that could have tragic consequences.

When she found out about the man who had come down from the Tree, Ilaya was frightened. Anybody who came from up there could spell trouble for Little Tree and their future happiness together. She did all she could to make sure the visitor was driven out. But nobody echoed her desire. On the contrary, the Grass people hoped Toby might be able to make this silent Old Tree speak.

Five days went by, and Ilaya was anxiously on the lookout for the return of the expedition.

Toby and Moon Boy returned with the little family, whom they had managed to extricate from the vole's claws. There was joyous celebrating.

Whenever somebody would try to talk to Toby about the man who had appeared, Ilaya tugged on Toby's arm to keep him from listening.

That night, Toby slept soundly in his wheat ear. A hand woke him up halfway through the following day.

"Is that you, Strand of Linen?"

"I'm called Moon Boy! Couldn't you, of all people, call me by my name?"

"Did you sleep?"

"Yes. But something happened while we were away. A man has turned up. He carries a great load of linen on his back."

Toby liked this expression for talking about old age.

"Where does he come from?"

"They think he comes from the Tree."

Toby had a sinking feeling. He closed his eyes again.

"They want you to talk to him," Moon Boy went on. "He won't open his mouth."

"Why me?" asked Toby.

"Guess."

"I don't know what you're talking about."

"You're known as Little Tree here. You can't forget everything."

"I want to forget everything."

"Come with me. All you have to do is ask him a few questions. They'll leave you in peace in your ear of wheat after that."

Toby kept his eyes closed. He didn't want to open them again. Moon Boy pried open his eyelids.

"Come on!"

"I don't want to. Tell him to go away."

This time, Moon Boy gave him a gentle kick that made him roll over.

"Leave me alone!" shouted Toby. "I've done everything I can to be like the rest of you! I've wallowed in mud, I've braved snowstorms, I've tied my ear of wheat to all of yours to survive! And now I've got to become a son of the Tree again, just to suit you?"

Moon Boy sat in a corner. The room was golden with the rays of autumn sunshine. He folded his arms, his hair flopping over his eyes. He stayed for a moment or two, then left.

Toby opened his eyes. He let the warmth of one ofthe last days of good weather calm him. He thought back to how relieved the children had been when he'd gotten them out of the vole's hole. But most of all, he could see the faces of all his grass friends who had disappeared because of the Tree people.

He stood up.

He would talk with the stranger.

Toby would be able to tell right away if he was a spy. The vermin from the Tree had made him suffer enough. He couldn't let them spread across the prairie. Toby knew how fragile the grass was.

Coming out of his wheat ear, he found Ilaya on the threshold.

"Little Tree."

"Ilaya, what are you doing here?"

"There's something I want to tell you."

"You can tell me anything you like, my sister."

She hated when he called her that.

"But first," Toby went on, "there's someone I have to see. Wait here for me."

"I want to talk to you right away."

"Yes, right away. I'll be back before you know it, and then I'll listen to what you've got to say," Toby said gently.

"Are you going to question the man who came in the boat?"

"Yes. Did you want to talk to me about him?"

"No, it's about someone else. Someone who came here longer ago than him."

"I'll be right back. Stay here. I enjoy talking with you. I'm very fond of you, Ilaya."

"Enjoy." "Fond." Ilaya couldn't bear these words of friendship. She wanted "I love you." Nothing else.

She called after him.

"Wait! I want to tell you something important. Listen to me."

He turned around. She looked panic-stricken, and her eyes were too shiny.

"What's the matter, Ilaya?"

Little Tree was staring at her. He was there, ready to listen to her. At last. She would tell him that she loved him.

Overcome, Ilaya waited a second too long before speaking, a second she wanted to savor, when important words should be sent out in one breath like arrows from pipes. Moon Boy appeared, out of breath. Ilaya lowered her gaze. It was too late.

"They've taken two more of our men!" her brother shouted. "This time, Little Tree, you don't have a choice. Come and see the stranger!"

Toby crossed the threshold.

"I'll be back, Ilaya. And then you can tell me what's so important. All right? You can tell me. . . ."

Ilaya heard their voices disappearing down the stem.

She crumpled. Happiness had brushed so close, she had felt its warm breath on the back of her neck, beneath her hair. Now she was taken over by another feeling, and it chilled her.

The man was being held in an abandoned snail-shell. Two guards had been posted at the entrance. They let Moon Boy and Toby through. The old snail-shell was pocked with small holes that let the daylight into the spiral corridor.

Once they had passed through the first loop, every-thing got much darker. It took a while for them to get used to the gloom. Then they saw a shadow sitting by the wall. Toby stepped forward, signaling to Moon Boy to stay back.

He couldn't see the man's features clearly. White curls, like tangled corkscrews, framed two eyes that shone in the half-light.

Toby recognized those eyes. He went a bit closer.

"Pol Colleen!"

The old man started. His eyes flickered in the gloom. It was clear that he had been living in fear for a long time, and even Toby's gentle voice made his blood run cold. He still didn't say anything. The light in his eyes faded, like two burning embers thrown into a pond.

Toby crouched down next to him.

Pol Colleen. The man who wrote.

Toby touched his hands. He hadn't seen him for years. He had aged a lot.

Pol Collen started in fright again. His eyes flickered, recognized Toby, and started a reddish dance.

"Who is he?" asked Moon Boy.

"You have nothing to fear from him. He's a friend. This man doesn't speak. He writes."

"He's right?"

"No. He writes."

There was no such thing as writing in the prairie. Moon Boy looked puzzled. Toby tried to explain it to his friend.

"When you can't speak, you tell the story with symbols instead. Writing is made up of lots of little symbols that you draw."

Moon Boy was crouched down next to them now.

"Do you know how to do that, Little Tree?"

Toby didn't answer. He realized he hadn't forgotten anything at all. Just seeing Colleen's face had been enough to wake up great chunks of memory.

"Toby Lolness," Colleen said.

Toby let go of Colleen's hands. He could speak!

"What did he say to you?" asked Moon Boy.

And Colleen spoke again.

"Toby Lolness."

"Is that another language?" wondered Moon Boy.

"Yes," whispered Toby, moved by the sound of his own name.

Pol Colleen had a deep, cultured voice. He pronounced each word as if for the first time.

"I recognize you. You're Toby Lolness."

Moon Boy turned toward Little Tree.

"They think you're dead, up there."

"I am dead," said Toby.

"You've turned into one of the Grass people."

"What's that?" asked Moon Boy.

"Grass people . . . That's what they call your people, up in the Tree."

Toby felt as if a door were opening between his two lives. He was cold. There was a blast of icy air blowing in. He wanted to close the door again and send the old man back in his boat, but what Colleen said next tore the ground from under his feet.

"Why did you desert your parents, Toby Lolness?"

Toby felt himself being flung backward. His lips were moving, but no sound came out.

"Why did you desert your parents?" the man repeated.

Toby's voice came back, strong as thunder.

"Me! Desert my parents? I nearly died ten times over trying to save them! Don't ever say that again, Pol Colleen. You insult the dead."

"Dead? Who?"

"Sim and Maya Lolness, my parents!"

Colleen ran his hand through his white curls. He bent his head for a moment and then suddenly looked up at Toby again.

"Words have meanings, Toby Lolness. You've just told me you're dead, when here you are talking to me. And now you're saying your parents are dead, when—"

"They really are dead," Toby interrupted him.

"Why do you say that? It's cruel to say that."

Toby clenched his fists.

"My life is cruel, Pol Colleen! Do you understand that? Life isn't like in one of your poems. Life is extremely cruel."

"I don't write poems."

Moon Boy was listening to this conversation but having problems understanding it.

Toby didn't move. He'd never asked himself what Colleen actually wrote.

"I am writing the history of the Tree. Your own history, Toby Lolness." And he added, in an unwavering voice, "Your parents are alive."

This time Toby shouted as he threw himself at the old man. Moon Boy grabbed hold of Toby's feet and tugged hard. Toby slid to the side and hit his head against the wall of the snail-shell.

Pol Colleen caught his breath again. Toby lay there, out cold. Moon Boy slapped his cheeks to bring him around again.

"Sorry, Little Tree, did I hurt you?"

Pol Colleen put his hand on Moon Boy's shoulder.

"I think the little one really means what he says," said Colleen. "He doesn't know the truth about his parents."

Moon Boy looked at the old man.

"Why do you say that? You know his parents are dead—he's got the glimmer in his eye."

Pol Colleen knew about practically everything, so he knew what the glimmer meant to the Grass people. It was the mark left by the death of parents.

"Yes. He has the glimmer, I know."

He leaned over Toby, who was coming around.

"Sim and Maya Lolness are alive. I've been living near them for the last two years."

Toby had no strength left to fight. He was crying.

"I know you have the glimmer in your eyes," said Colleen. "I know that."

He paused.

"Sim and Maya didn't give life to you. They adopted you when you were a few days old. Yes, your parents from before them are dead. And that's why you were as good as born with the glimmer."

Toby closed his eyes.

"But as for Sim and Maya Lolness, they are alive. You were lied to."

Toby felt as if he were seeing the snail-shell from on high, poised between the grass blades. His gaze followed its spiral corridor. Toby's mind was in similar turmoil, spinning faster and faster. Then he blacked out.

He woke up in the same place. Night had fallen. Moon Boy had made a fire. And many people had joined them in the snail-shell.

Pol Colleen was warming himself by the flames.

Everybody was watching Toby, who lifted one eyelid and then the other.

Pol Colleen didn't so much as glance at Toby.

"If you want me to talk, then say so," he said in his deep voice. "Otherwise, I'll leave tomorrow morning."

Toby let the silence hover a while before saying, "Talk."

Voices were strangely distorted inside the shell. Even the noise from the fire seemed amplified.

"Sim and Maya Lolness have been locked up by Joe Mitch, along with all the other intellectuals in the Tree. I was with them. But I escaped. I'm the only one."

"Joe Mitch is in control of the whole Tree?" Toby was staggered.

Colleen shook his head.

"Joe Mitch is a dangerous madman. He doesn't really control the Tree anymore. He just imprisons the people with the most powerful brains. He makes them dig in his crater, together with a few Grass people, instead of the weevils."

Toby's eyes were open wide now.

"The weevils were wiped out in an epidemic," explained Colleen. "Which is a stroke of luck for the Tree, but now Mitch wants Balina's secret more than ever."

"He won't get it," whispered Toby through clenched teeth.

"Oh, yes, he will."

"Never."

"Your father will end up giving in. He'll hand over Balina's secret. There isn't any other way."

"My father will never give in."

"Unless—"

"Never!"

Pol Colleen hesitated before going on. Did he have to spell out the whole truth to the boy? For a long time, Colleen had wondered why Mitch insisted on Sim Lolness keeping his wife close to him. She was no use in the crater.

On the day when Pol Colleen finally understood, he had felt totally sickened.

"Maya, your mother . . . Joe Mitch has told Sim that if he doesn't give in . . . then Joe will make your mother his business."

Toby choked. He thought of Mitch's oily hands on Maya's skin. His heart raced at the idea of such monstrous blackmail. Toby took a big gulp of air, which emptied his head.

"Once he's got the secret," Colleen added, "Joe Mitch will destroy the Tree for good."

Confused, the Grass people in the shell listened to the fire crackling. None of this violence meant anything to them. It was like listening to a foreign language.

Toby broke the silence in a sepulchral voice: "Who controls the rest of the Tree?"

"The rest of the Tree is as uninhabitable as the crater. I can't say more than that. It's awful."

"Who is in charge?"

"Someone just as dangerous. His law is the rule. And that law is fear. Fear of . . ."

Colleen hesitated again, as he looked around him.

"Fear of the Grass people. He wants to annihilate them. When there's not a single one left, then and only then, he says, will the Tree live again."

Not one of the spectators recognized themselves in the description "Grass people." Only Moon Boy shuddered.

"This new boss is about your age, Toby Lolness. Perhaps it's him I'm most worried about. He is the son of a great man I once knew, El Blue. The boy's name is Leo Blue."

Toby didn't flinch. So that's how it was. Leo, the new master of the Tree.

"Leo Blue is getting married," Colleen went on. "He's very young, but he's crazy about a girl from our region, in the Low Branches. A girl from the farm at Seldor."

Lila and Lola! All of a sudden, Toby could see the two Asseldor daughters in his mind's eye. An Asseldor daughter marrying a tyrant called Leo Blue. . . . Not even Toby's imagination could stretch that far.

"The girl refuses to go through with it."

For the first time Toby gave a hint of a smile. So the Asseldor daughters hadn't changed. He could almost hear their voices, their laughter and boldness.

"The wedding has already been called off once. The girl had shaved her head. Leo Blue didn't dare appear with her in public. But soon, she'll be his. Nothing will be denied him in the end."

Toby was listening to each word. Which of the two Asseldor daughters could have done something so extreme? Shaving her head . . . They had changed a bit, after all. Toby admired this show of strength.

A long silence filled the snail-shell. Toby finally dared to dive into the shifting sands of his memory.

"I would like to ask you something. Isha Lee and her daughter—"

When Toby uttered this name, there was a great stirring among the crowd. A whisper circulated among the Grass people. *Isha, Isha* . . . Eyes lit up. Toby broke off.

A woman finally spoke.

"You mentioned Isha?"

"Isha is a daughter of the grasses," a man continued. "She disappeared fifteen years ago, when she was expecting."

Toby's jaw dropped; his vision blurred. He was almost smiling. He'd had an inkling about this for a while now. Isha Lee was a Grass woman. Toby's eyes came to rest on the woman who had spoken.

These faces had always felt familiar. Now he understood why.

"Is Isha still alive?" asked the woman.

Toby turned to Pol Colleen. He was the one with the answer.

"Yes, Isha and her daughter are alive," he said.

Toby didn't take his eyes off the old writer.

"The Lees moved into Seldor when their worm beetles were massacred, two years ago. It's the Lee daughter I've just been talking about."

Toby's eyes closed.

Pol Colleen said again, "Leo Blue is going to marry Elisha Lee."

Elisha.

Toby stood up in the middle of the gathering. With a long hard stare in which the flames were reflected, he gazed at the faces surrounding him, one by one.

Outside, a slender figure was walking between the grass blades. Ilaya could make out the light seeping from the snail-shell. She drew near. She had seen everybody leave the clump of reeds at nightfall. In the silence of this first autumn night, Ilaya sensed that something was wrong.

Ilaya was about to enter the corridor of the snail-shell when Toby appeared.

"Little Tree!"

"Yes, Ilaya."

Immediately, she saw that his face had changed.

"Are you leaving?" she asked.

Toby took his time before answering.

"Yes."

"You're going back to the Tree."

It wasn't even a question. Toby was somewhere else. He kissed her forehead and walked away.

Ilaya stayed there, alone. Her heart froze, becoming

as hard as ice. All the tenderness she'd found again after so many months was swept away by this glacial wind. But this time she didn't fall. Far from it. Her lips traced a cold smile.

Little Tree wouldn't get away from her. Vidof had died because of him. If Little Tree refused to replace him in her heart, then he would have to come to an end like Vidof's.

Ilaya owed it to the memory of her fiancé.

Perched in his wheat ear, suspended above the grass, Toby saw the moon rising behind the Tree. It was huge and soon engulfed that other planet, making the maze of branches a bluish ball.

Suddenly, that faraway world seemed extraordinarily fragile and beautiful to Toby. The shadow of the Trunk rose up toward the huge planet, which trembled in the evening breeze.

The autumn leaves rustled almost imperceptibly, but Toby imagined the murmurings of life up there.

Sunday evenings in the Heights, or picnics beside the great lake in the Low Branches, or an afternoon snooze on hot bark . . . all of these memories vibrated in the Tree and in Toby's head.

How had he strayed so far from the thread of his life?

He looked up at a lone shining star above him. Altair . . . The star his father had given him.

Toby couldn't even hear the farewell song of the Grass people, which rose from the glittering shell. And he didn't feel the furtive presence of someone approaching from behind. Ilaya's bare feet on the floor of the ear of wheat. Her eyes ablaze and an arrowhead in her hand.

Little Tree filled his lungs with the white airiness of the night, as if he were going to fly.

The voice of his parents. Elisha's eyes. These were reasons enough to set out on another adventure. Reasons to be Toby Lolness again.

Toby's childhood friend has become his worst enemy. . . .

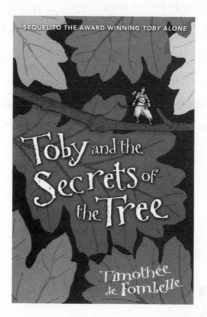

Toby and the Secrets of the Tree
by Timothée de Fombelle

The world of the great oak Tree is on the brink of
devastation under the control of power-crazed Leo
Blue. Once inseparable from Toby, Leo is now
capturing anyone who gets in his way, including
Toby's closest companion, Elisha Lee. Toby must find
the courage to save the great oak Tree, but will he be
able to defeat the boy who was once his best friend?

Turn the page for an excerpt. . . .

www.candlewick.com

1
Broken Wings

The Major was as light as a grain of pollen, but the weight of his stupidity should have snapped the branch he was sitting on, feet dangling in midair, firing arrows at a black shape writhing around below.

Major Krolo put a lot of effort into being this stupid. He wasn't just an expert in stupidity; he was a stupidity genius.

It was nighttime in the Tree, a night of thick mist and freezing wind. But it had been dark all day long: a black apocalyptic sky had shrouded the Treetop since the previous day, and the damp was causing a heavy smell like spiced bread to rise from the branches.

"Two hundred and forty-five, two hundred and forty-six . . ."

How many arrows would the Major have to fire to finish off the huge creature stuck in the sap? Wrapped in a stiff fur coat, he kept on counting.

an excerpt from Toby and the Secrets of the Tree

Krolo slipped his thumbs under his coat and made his suspenders go *ping*.

"Two hundred and fifty-eight . . ."

He felt a satisfied tingle and buttoned up his coat again.

The Major had a long-standing reputation as a bully. Following a few "personal issues," he had changed his name and made a new life for himself. He even tried to disguise himself by wearing suspenders instead of a belt. He had also awarded himself the rank of major, and to be on the safe side, these days he tortured only animals. He did this on the sly, at night and out of sight, like a grown man smoking in secret from his mother.

Below him the poor creature lifted its head toward its executioner for the last time. It was a butterfly. A butterfly with broken wings. . . . The job had been botched, thanks to a poorly sharpened ax. All the butterfly had left on its back were two ridiculous stumps that flapped emptily. This was the work of a thug.

"Two hundred and fifty-nine," counted Krolo, hitting the butterfly on the right flank.

A shadow suddenly passed by, in the thick fog behind the Major.

A silent apparition. The nimble shadow had come from above, brushing against the bark before disappearing into the night. Yes, somebody was watching this scene. But the Major hadn't noticed a thing, because being stupid was his full-time job.

Krolo's last arrow sank deep into the flesh of the

an excerpt from *Toby and the Secrets of the Tree*

butterfly. The wounded animal reared up but didn't groan.

The shadow passed by again, twirling with extra-ordinary agility. Half-dancer, half-acrobat, it was surveying the scene. This time, there was a reflection in the butterfly's eye.

Krolo turned around, suddenly uneasy.

"Soldier? Is that you?"

He scratched his head nervously, through his hat. He

an excerpt from Toby and the Secrets of the Tree

had a low-set forehead and wore a woollen cap with a few greasy curls peeking out from under it.

Now, Major Krolo may have had a small head with limited neurons, but he still knew that the shadow hadn't been cast by any of his soldiers. Everybody was talking about it: a mysterious shadow that moved around the Treetop in the evenings. Nobody knew who this furtive person was, but it was as if he or she was on guard duty.

In public, Krolo refused to believe this story. Instead, he made himself look even sillier than usual with pathetic remarks such as, "What? A shadow? At night? Ha-ha!"

But, given his problems in the past, the Major was scared of everything. One morning in bed, he had tried to squash one of his own toes, mistaking it for an insect sticking out from under the sheets.

"Soldier!" he shouted, trying to convince himself. "I know it's you! If you move again, I'll impale you to the branch. . . ."

A cloud of fog rolled over the Major, and in the freezing dark, he felt a hand on his shoulder.

"Eeeeeeeeek!"

an excerpt from *Toby and the Secrets of the Tree*